# THE MISCHIEVOUS LETTERS OF THE MARQUISE DE Q

## FELICIA DAVIN

ISBN-13: 978-0-9989957-8-6

# PRAISE FOR FELICIA DAVIN

Davin's book feels genuinely, shockingly rebellious in its insistence on the beauty of transformation. If overhyped books are plastic necklaces, [*The Scandalous Letters of V and J*] is a string of natural pearls, each a luminous gem on its own but even more exquisite in sequence.

— THE NEW YORK TIMES

But bodies and identity are never a space for trauma in [*The Scandalous Letters of V and J*]—only for joy, attraction, experimentation, and play. Within their sexual and romantic relationship, Victor and Julien are perpetually trying on different roles, different acts, even different bodily configurations, unfettered by the constraints of what's allowable to a person of this or that gender.

— TOR.COM

# CONTENTS

CONTENT GUIDANCE

This series takes place in a violent, unjust world, and there are some abominable villains in it. I wanted to write fantasy that wasn't about armies or the fate of nations, but with more individual stakes. In practice, that means the villains deal in intimate violence. There is rape and abuse in this book. There is also violent vengeance against the abusers. I can't promise that I've written things in a way that won't hurt you, but I hope this note helps you make the right choices for yourself.

Here is a more specific list of what you will find in this book. If you don't need to be forewarned and would rather avoid spoilers, skip it.

- A main character is in an abusive marriage. It ends fairly early in the book, but is referred to throughout.
- A main character has a pregnancy and gives birth to a child. The birth is not described and the pregnancy is only briefly mentioned.

- Characters have suffered various kinds of magical coercion.
- There are some incidents of sexual harassment and assault (unwanted comments, groping).
- Characters have been raped. There is a description of rape in the second "Ari Lazare to Ari Lazare" letter.
- A character has been abducted and imprisoned and suffers some symptoms of post-traumatic stress afterward.
- Characters have strained or estranged relationships with their families.
- There is physical violence, including murder. There are also some brief references to suicide.
- There is explicitly described consensual sex in this book.

*Pourquoi le beau sexe ne prendrait-il pas de temps en temps une revanche ?*

Why shouldn't the fair sex, from time to time, take revenge?

— HONORÉ DE BALZAC, *LES SECRETS DE LA PRINCESSE DE CADIGNAN*, 1839

# I
# A MARRIAGE
## 1822-1825

# ARI LAZARE TO DELPHINE DE MONTFLEURY, AUGUST 9, 1822

## UNSIGNED, LEFT BEHIND A LOOSE STONE IN A CHURCHYARD WALL

My darling,

I need to get lost, but I want you to find me. I have left you the means to do so, hidden under the floorboards of a top-story room in the Maison Laval, the one where the garret window faces the Rue de la Montagne-Sainte-Geneviève. The current resident is called Forestier. He's unaware of what I have put in his room, and has a generally unpleasant air, but I'm reasonably certain he won't stop you from retrieving the package. I trust your skills; you've charmed sterner men.

When you do, you will find my compass—your compass, really, as you were the one who divined its unusual function—and a linen kerchief shoved into one of my old stockings. Don't touch the kerchief with your bare hands. I've used it to forget something I can't know right now. Keep it hidden for me. I'll remember some day when it's safe.

I don't know where my journey will take me, but the compass will tell you.

Avoid Maximilien Taillefer at all costs.

# DELPHINE DE MONTFLEURY
## TO ARI LAZARE, AUGUST
### 12, 1822
#### UNSIGNED, WRITTEN IN DUPLICATE,
#### ONE COPY LEFT IN THE CHURCHYARD
#### AND THE OTHER HIDDEN

My darling,

What do you mean by this alarming letter? You make me fear you will never read this, but I write in hope. I know I once complimented your alluring air of mystery, but I meant your serious, dark eyes and tendency to gaze into the distance while lost in thought. Leaving me bizarre instructions and then disappearing is not at all the sort of mystery I enjoy.

I wish I thought you were joking, but I'm the funny one. To be clear, since I know you are not well-versed in humor, in case you <u>were</u> attempting a joke: this is not funny, and I would never do it to you, and I would like you to come back now.

I did do as you asked. It took me two days to plan my attack, hence the delay in my response. You know it's not easy for a girl of my status to stroll into a shabby boarding house on a whim. (To think that you lived in such a place and refused all my offers to pay for somewhere better! You do know that the purpose of a roof is to keep water outside? A man with your scientific education ought to know that.) My mother has become fanatical about marrying me to that ogre and won't let me out of her sight, so I had to make use of all my cunning wiles and enlist a lot of help. Fortunately for me, I am rich in wiles and friends.

It's also not easy for a girl of my status to get her hands on a crowbar to pry up floorboards—I did not even know the word "crowbar" before I embarked on your quest—but I did that, too. F*** was as gruff as you said. I regret that your trust in me was misplaced, but he was unmoved by my pretty face, my ample bosom, my social graces, my fluttering lashes, and my many other wonderful qualities, except he did smile a little when I slid the world's shortest, daintiest crowbar out of my skirt pocket. I interrogated him about your comings and goings prior to your disappearance, but he knew nothing useful. Thankfully, he asked no questions about why you'd buried something for me under the floorboards of his room. He doesn't know what it is, as he pointedly averted his gaze. He must think all this was something disreputable related to our love affair, which is, I suppose, not false. I made him promise to contact me if he learns anything. He was surprisingly amenable to that, offering me one full, silent nod of his head.

I have your compass in hand, and whenever I think of you, the needle points south and slightly east. Every so often it wobbles, but it always aims south and east again in the end. What am I meant to do with this information, you handsome riddle? Where are you? You know I cannot wander Paris until this device leads me to you, as it once led you to me. I remind you: girl, status, mother, marriage, ogre.

Regarding that impending marriage, there is something

I need to tell you, but I think it best not to record it in writing. The spot where we exchange letters remains undiscovered, and my name isn't attached to this paper, so it isn't entirely secrecy that stops me. There are some things that ought to be shared face to face and hand in hand.

As for M*** T*** and your warning, the idea that <u>you</u> would need to tell <u>me</u> which men are vile and untrust-worthy lechers is laughable, though I wouldn't characterize it as funny. I will continue to avoid him as I always have. Why do you think I've spent so many years honing my wiles? It isn't to ensnare men—until you vanished, I had the only man I wanted—but to repel them.

Ah, but you, you I would track down and ensnare and keep forever if only I knew how.

# DELPHINE DE MONTFLEURY TO ARI LAZARE, SEPTEMBER 7, 1822

## UNSIGNED, WRITTEN IN DUPLICATE, ONE COPY LEFT IN THE CHURCHYARD AND THE OTHER HIDDEN

My darling,

I have sent A*** to check for a response every day since my last letter. Sometimes twice a day. She humors me because she's very kind and she can see how your absence haunts me.

I have also sent L***—he works in the stables and always smiles at me, and I gave him a silver bracelet for his troubles—to search for you on several occasions. Teaching L*** to use the compass required telling him who you were, not merely in name but in character. It took quite a few stories before he could reliably make the compass needle point toward you as I can. He knows now how much I love you, but I deemed the search worth that risk.

Every time L*** has followed the compass, he's gone southeast until he's surrounded by pastures, and still the needle urges him on. You are not in the city. I don't have enough silver bracelets to send him on an unknown journey outside Paris.

No letters and no movement. Your compass needle has not so much as quivered in seven full days. I sleep with it under my pillow. Every morning and every evening I hold its brass case until the metal is hot and clammy from my desperate grip. South-southeast. South-southeast. South-southeast.

Either you're dead or you abandoned me in my condition—in which case you're not my darling. I know you didn't know because I never had a chance to tell you, so it's not your fault, but still there is a little ember of anger lodged in the ache of missing you. From a great distance—a cosmically great distance—our collision of catastrophes is almost funny. How dare you get in trouble when I was already in trouble. One of us ought to have waited their turn.

In either case, dead or gone, I shouldn't be writing to you, but this letter is the least of my futile grasping. I am so very alone.

I know, I know, I've just mentioned A*** and L***, so I do have people who can help, but there isn't any help for these circumstances. A*** is in my confidence and she offered to find someone who could "solve the problem," but even if it wouldn't kill me, which it might, I don't want that. I might possess the last trace of your life. It's not you, but what if it's the closest I can ever come? I have failed you in everything else. I would do anything to preserve this remnant of us. Sometimes envisioning our child is the only thing that gives me hope.

In a matter of days I will marry.

I dream of you climbing through my window in the darkness to whisk me away from my dire fate, but if you're going to do that, you need to do it now. Admittedly my novelesque imagination fails me after the scene where you slip in and lift me from my bed—in addition to scaling the walls of my family's townhouse in the dead of night, you can also carry me effortlessly in this fantasy, your soft, intellectual physique and my rather more generous one notwithstanding—and I am not sure where we would go, or how we would find shelter or food for ourselves, let alone keep alive (nurture? educate?) the other consequence of our actions, but I know in my heart that if you were here, we could find a way.

I'm the one who needs to climb in through your window to rescue <u>you</u>. But I don't know how. Too much of the world is south and east, and in any case, I am not free to explore.

Please don't be dead.

# DELPHINE DE TOUSSERAT, MARQUISE DE QUENNETIÈRE TO ARI LAZARE, FEBRUARY 15, 1823, UNSIGNED

## UNSIGNED, WRITTEN IN DUPLICATE, ONE COPY LEFT IN THE CHURCHYARD AND THE OTHER HIDDEN

My darling,

It's been months since I've written, but I suppose in the absence of any response, it doesn't matter. I'm a mother now. He's named after a Roman emperor, and I had no more choice in that than I did in his family name.

But I love him. I wanted to tell you that.

# DELPHINE TO ARI, OCTOBER 2, 1823
## UNSENT, HIDDEN

My darling,

You know I've never overflowed with spiritual feeling, but the scent of fresh bread <u>is</u> heavenly. I missed you so much that I sent Amélie to a bakery in the Marais to bring me some of the challah you once described. It was delicious. A little less so after being splashed with tears, but it didn't go to waste.

I wish you to think of me beautifully overcome with sadness like a woman in a painting, draped over a bed with tears shining in my lashes, perhaps robed in folds of cloth that artfully cover my nudity, rather than splotch-cheeked and sniffling into a loaf of bread. But I suppose you don't think of me at all, or read these letters, so it doesn't matter.

In February, I asked Amélie to put a letter in the churchyard wall, and when she did, she found the previous one I'd asked her to deposit. The paper was spotted with mold and the words were illegible. She brought them both home. I will not bother to leave a copy of this letter.

Thinking of you is the sweetest of bittersweet things. I

would have gone back to that bakery myself every week if only my husband didn't forbid me to leave the house. (That isn't the bitterest of all bitter things, but it's tongue-shriveling enough.)

You and I used to talk so endlessly about what an unacceptable match we made—myself wealthy and Christian, beautiful and uneducated except in manners, and you, poor and Jewish and educated in all things except manners, and beautiful, Ari, <u>beautiful</u>. I must write it twice. Since you never write back, I can at last say that to you without argument. I miss your rough dark stubble and soft lips. I miss the way your formidable brows used to draw together when you were giving solemn consideration to whatever idly curious question I posed about how to make Thénard's cobalt or how steam locomotion works. No one else ever takes me seriously, you know. The frills and the giggles put them off, but not you. It is my favorite of your many wonderful qualities, though I also love your less wonderful qualities—an excess of spleen, for instance, and a strong inclination toward distraction and forgetfulness, and a sort of simmering anger about the world that never causes you to raise your voice, but manifests instead as fatigue and disgust. I miss all these things. I even miss how you stoop your shoulders out of habit because the ceiling in your room slopes so low. I know I'd be happier shivering in your leaky garret than I am being titled marquise and married to a villain.

I didn't do it for the money, Ari. I'd wither if you thought so. You're the one who made me think about where all this money comes from, and how wrong it is for a few to have so much while most have so little.

I did it for Octave. We'd have starved otherwise. Yes, I know that's a question of money; what I meant is that I didn't do it for the riches. I do need food and shelter, and more importantly, so does Octave. My happiness is a trifle, but I would carve out my own heart before I would see him suffer. So I married the villain and did my best to scramble my tracks on the question of when Octave was conceived. No need for jealousy. Drowning that particular fish was ghastly work, but necessary.

Fortunately, my husband is a dullard, lacking both curiosity and perception. It is his best quality. Well, that, and the fact that he ignores our child. He probably thinks he'll have ten, but I use a sponge and drink an eye-watering brew that Amélie makes every month. I gag every time and I would drink it morning, noon, and night. This secret refusal is the only power I have.

You see how unsuitable I am for my well-matched marriage? Duplicitous and adulterous. I'll have to burn this letter, but it feels good to write freely.

Amélie, by the way, has no need of her own brew at this time. She is solely devoted to Marthe, Octave's nurse-maid. I discovered their love by accident. Marthe had taken Octave into the garden to give me a rest—I spend more hours a day with my child than is proper, according to my husband—but I was taken by a sudden whim to hold him again. When I entered the garden, Marthe and Amélie were kissing. It was quick and discreet and seemed to me the greeting kiss of long-time lovers. They broke apart when they noticed me.

I could think of no way to make Marthe trust that I wouldn't tell except to give her a secret of my own—Amélie, of course, already possesses my most valuable secret—so I said I wanted sponges and anything else they knew of that could prevent children. They proved enor-mously resourceful. Marthe even knew of a shop that sold unusual artifacts and found two different wedding rings there with contraceptive properties, but if I wore a new ring to bed, it would raise suspicion. A sponge, at least, can be inserted unseen.

We have also had several illuminating conversations on the appeal of women kissing other women. Marthe and Amélie have been in love for some time, though Marthe is married to a man named Eugène who works in the stables. She reports that he is decent, both a good friend to her and a good father to their daughter Caroline, a sweet girl of the same age as Octave. Imagine that! To be friends with one's husband! He is not troubled by Marthe's liaison with Amélie because he has a male lover of his own. It is a situation of some complexity, but everyone involved seems happy.

These conversations with Marthe and Amélie have made me reconsider some moments of my youth—I know, I know, I'm only twenty-three, but marriage has aged me. Anyway, reflecting on all that made me think of you, because everything does. (I still check your compass every day.) Do you remember how flustered you were when Hassan flirted with you, and then again when I asked if you'd tell me what you liked about men? You did it, though. You always did what I asked.

Since I will throw these pages on the hearth, or lock them away and bury them, or devise one of your strange magical objects that will make these words illegible to anyone but us, I can first tell you about Octave, who makes life in this wretched house almost bearable. He can crawl on his belly now. Five hundred times a day, he grabs my skirts in his little fists and pulls himself to standing. Every time he sees me anew, he smiles with his whole face and flaps his arms. He makes the sweetest cooing sounds when he's fascinated, which is most of the time since he's so avidly curious. He has your big brown eyes and your unfairly lush fringe of lashes. His face is mostly cheeks and he doesn't have much hair yet, but something in the brows and the shape of the lips reminds me of you.

Oh, damn it. These pages won't burn if I soak them with tears. I wanted to tell you something happy. Every happiness in my life is like watered wine now. The flavor is familiar, but it used to taste better.

If you come back, I'll be drunk so fast that my face will redden and I'll trip into your arms. Entirely unsuitable, but I never wanted to be suitable for anyone but you.

My darling,

Even though I will not send this letter, the urge to beg your forgiveness for not writing is almost overpowering. It's been a year. I suppose I've resigned myself to your absence—except that I'm writing.

My husband is as hateful as ever, but I've become adept at wheedling my way out of the house, or sneaking if he forbids it, and going to a few parties and salons has made me feel almost myself again. That's not why I'm writing, though.

I'm writing because <u>I met Camille Dupin</u>.

I had to buy myself a new copy of her novel <u>Virginie</u> to replace the one we read together, you know. After I carried that poor, beloved book in my skirt pockets for all those months, it was quite worn. You must remember the thrill of reading it. There was always the slimmest chance we'd encounter each other at some gathering and be able to hide ourselves away in a corner and read a few pages together—among other things. I've never read such a good novel so slowly, but I couldn't stand the thought of turning the page without you. We sustained the pleasure of reading far beyond the end of the book, too, discussing it constantly and then cataloguing every bit of gossip we could find about its mysterious, androgynous author.

She—Camille is a she, though she wears trousers (seeing a woman in trousers is a revelation, in case you haven't been so lucky, and it made me question what kind of world we live in that would frown on such a wonderful thing, though in a strange way it was the forbidden nature of the sight that thrilled me—well, that, and her bottom, to be perfectly frank, though I tried my best to exercise subtlety in looking)—oh I've tangled my sentence and will have to start over. This is how it goes with my embroidery, too. I should spend less time thinking about Camille's bottom, but I won't. I don't want to.

In her suit, Camille was very handsome. She's only a bit taller than me, but managed to appear far more imposing through means unknown to me, and I think her handsomeness is the same way. It has little to do with her features—brown hair, brown eyes, an unremarkable mouth, a long, narrow nose in a long, narrow face—and everything to do with her presence. You know how dearly I appreciate a well-dressed person, so it's her clothes, certainly, but also her postures and expressions. She has an air of such strength and confidence that it almost crosses the line into haughtiness and disdain, but I overheard her speaking voice before we were introduced and it was low and warm like a banked fire.

Can you blame me for wanting to stoke it?

Camille was preceded by her reputation of having many lovers, and on seeing her, I understood it immediately and wished to add my name to the list. I will, but the game itself is a joy. To give up before we'd even played would be such a disappointment. From the way she smiled at me and said her name, she was clearly accustomed to an easy victory.

It pleased me to refrain from falling at her feet. "And what do you do?"

"I'm... a novelist?" Camille said.

"Oh?"

"I wrote, um, <u>Virginie</u>, that's what it's called."

Ari, the thrill of flustering my favorite novelist nearly sent me floating to heaven. I could have beamed, I could have giggled, I could have grabbed her by the shoulders and hauled her into an embrace. Instead I tilted my head and offered a sliver of a smile to encourage her to continue.

"It's, uh, about a girl. But also how the institution of marriage crushes women. She falls in love anyway, though. There's a dog in it."

She blinked and drew her brows together, adorably stunned and mortified. I swear I am recording exactly what she said, Ari. You know I love to dismantle men, but until then I'd never had the pleasure of discomposing anyone else. The only thought in my head was <u>Camille Dupin finds me attractive</u>. I was soaring so high I think I heard angels.

I laid a hand and my most wicked grin on her, closing my fingers around her arm as I leaned in to whisper, "I know. I wept all through the ending. It was brilliant."

The realization that I'd been teasing her caused Camille's jaw to snap shut. I don't usually bother to soothe anyone else afterward, but I wanted her to like me, so I did more or less fall at her feet then. She was still too frazzled to do anything about it, but I am determined to see her again. It will be a bit like after you met me and followed me all over the city for days, except I won't use your compass for anyone but you, so I'll have to devise some other means of finding her.

I wish you'd been there. Your presence wouldn't have prevented any coquetry on my part—indeed, the opposite —but you would have found it amusing, having such common ground with Camille Dupin, and you do love her novel so very much.

DELPHINE, MARQUISE DE Q
TO CAMILLE DUPIN,
OCTOBER 12, 1824

SENT BY PRIVATE COURIER

Dear Mlle Dupin,

Do you go by Mademoiselle? I wanted to write to express that it was my honor to make your acquaintance last night, but now that I compose this letter, I think perhaps I <u>haven't</u> made your acquaintance, as I don't even know how you prefer to be addressed.

I do know the address of your home, though, as I interrogated every single friend and enemy I have in this city until I found the answer. If you will be so kind as to reacquaint us and correct my salutation, I will write you another, better letter.


You might not believe me, but I entreat you to accept my profound respect,

Delphine, Marquise de Q

# CAMILLE DUPIN TO DELPHINE, MARQUISE DE Q.
## OCTOBER 13, 1824
### POSTMARKED PARIS

Madame la Marquise,

I am, on occasion, addressed as Mademoiselle Dupin, though I confess it doesn't suit me. I am unmarried and have no wish to be Madame. I might like to be Monsieur Dupin, except for the barriers it would erect to our intimate friendship. Could you be persuaded to call me Camille? I would be delighted to make your acquaintance under such terms.

Your profound respect is no more difficult to accept than the notion that a person of your considerable charms might have enemies in this or any city. Though I must say, whoever they are, I fear for them. You will surely find out where they live.


Your new friend,
Camille

Dear Camille, my newest friend,

How quickly I have risen through the ranks from stranger to acquaintance to friend! Please call me Delphine. My title is a burden to write, and I only wanted to make sure you would not mistake me for any other Delphine. I am desperately greedy for every word you address to me to come directly to my hands and eyes.

Indeed, many times a day I ask my maid to check for letters, that no one in this house but she and I might know of them. I read yours in the privacy of my bedroom. I carry it tucked into my dress.

I ought not to sign this one at all, I think. You should not be so surprised that I have enemies, Camille. They are small in number, but they loom large in my life. I know quite well where they live.

I must sign, though. It is a risk worth taking. I want us to call each other the right names. To protect me and prevent anyone from finding this letter, perhaps you could fold it tightly and hide it in one of the pockets of your elegant suits? You could burn it, I suppose, but I prefer to imagine this page warmed by the heat of your body.

I must be judicious with my pages, you understand. I prefer to see my friends in the Luxembourg, or at tea salons, or on rare occasions, at their homes.

If you ever wear dresses, and might need to order one or a dozen, I do recommend the dressmaker whose address is enclosed. If you never wear dresses, my recommendation remains the same. I visit her shop <u>frequently</u>.


Your friend,
    Delphine

# DELPHINE TO ARI, JANUARY 16, 1825

## UNSENT, HIDDEN

My darling,

I have spent every possible instant with Camille. It's hard work, coaxing my husband to let me go to the modiste or the park or the museum or the tea shop or some other harmless place, and of course in the evening I have to wait until he's at his club before I can slip away.

He goes there nightly to drink and argue with his friends, or rivals, I suppose. A dozen or so men all obsessed with collecting the sort of objects you know about, like your compass and your kerchief. These men are all unbearable, most of them unrepentant lechers. The worst offender used to be Horace Faucheux, whose leer made me feel filthy, but he seems—well, not reformed, as he's still devoting his time and wealth to the pursuit of what I can only assume is evil, but in the past year or so, he's left me alone. I don't know what changed and am afraid to inquire.

Maximilien Taillefer is among these men. I have never forgotten your warning. I think he's the only one you know, as the others don't frequent salons. Once when he was here to dine, he cornered me to ask about you. I pretended to need a reminder of who you were. Taillefer would have been cruel otherwise; I could tell he wanted to. My husband saw Taillefer speaking to me alone and interrupted, and it was the only time I have ever been grateful to him. Obviously I have pretended ignorance on the subject of unusual artifacts in front of my husband, which is no difficulty as he thinks me a fool to begin with.

I hate to think of these terrible men amassing such items, but I confess I never try to stop the Marquis from leaving the house in the evenings. I need that time for myself—and Camille.

She is worth every effort. Her liberated, alluring presence has made me realize how small my life has shrunk. With Camille, I can draw a full breath. Thanks to her (and secretly, thanks to you), I've started hosting a salon when my husband is out of town. I've managed it twice so far, and the one last night was marvelous. Discussion has tended more toward the arts than the sciences, which I know you'd find slightly disappointing, but without you I don't have as many connections in that world. I haven't seen your lovely naturalist friend Hassan, but if I had, I would have invited him. Everything is still shadowed by your absence. I don't cry over you as often as I did—the wound still aches, but it doesn't sting like it did when it was bleeding—though I think of you all the time.

Octave will be two next month, and that does make me want to cry.

Oh, but I wanted to tell you about Camille. She makes me happy. And it's only fair that I should tell you about her, since I've made sure to tell her about you. It puzzles her, I think, my endless fount of Ari stories, but she tolerates it. The stories are the only way I can have all three of us together at the same time.

Now that I know Camille, I'm even more pleased with myself for flustering her at our first meeting. Her usual demeanor is calm and assured, and if you're lucky, flirtatious. In this one way, I have the best of luck. I can't even tell you exactly what it is she's said to me because there are hardly any words involved. It's all glances. Easy to deny if anyone ever catches her at it, but I feel them like a hand on the small of my back or a finger to my lips.

Her sartorial elegance is almost as refined as her intellect. Just like you, she's always answering my questions, except instead of asking her how electricity works, I ask her what makes people trust each other, or forgive each other, or fall into or out of love. She always claims not to know, but then she says things like, "Don't you think the heart is a palimpsest?" I had to ask her what a palimpsest was, and she said it's a page with traces of faded writing that remain visible under a new layer of words. She doesn't know I compose these unsent letters to you, Ari, because I'd feel silly telling anyone, except I think maybe she does know. Maybe she has one of your curious objects, like a loupe or a pair of spectacles that let her see right into my head.

As for the rest, she walks too fast, scrawls all her letters illegibly, carries an entire library in her head, takes a shocking number of lovers of all kinds, gets misty-eyed after two glasses of wine, listens so intently I feel we're alone even when we're surrounded, holds a radical but logical set of beliefs about the world that you would agree with, adores music but stumbles through the simplest of compositions, gestures uselessly but beautifully when she talks, and lets Octave ride around on her shoulders whenever she sees him, though he always irretrievably ruins her coiffure.

Our meetings are constrained by too little time and too many witnesses. That never stopped me with you, but I've become more cautious. Every time we find a moment of privacy and I think she might kiss me, we are interrupted. I will perish of it.

# DELPHINE DE TOUSSERAT, MARQUISE DOUAIRIÈRE DE QUENNETIÈRE TO ARI LAZARE, JANUARY 29, 1825

## UNSENT, HIDDEN

My darling,

I'm writing from Camille's country house at Verneuil.

My husband did something terrible to me. He's dead now. Camille saved my life, I think. She and her friend Julien rescued me from that house. I want to explain the last few weeks to you—and to myself—but I can't find the words. My hand is trembling and I've splattered ink everywhere.

I wish you were here.

# II
# AN AFFAIR

1825

# DELPHINE DE TOUSSERAT, MARQUISE DOUAIRIÈRE DE QUENNETIÈRE TO JULIEN MORÈRE, JANUARY 31, 1825

## POSTMARKED VERNEUIL

Dear Julien,

Please accept, once again, my profound gratitude for everything you did to save me. My son and I are quite happy here in the countryside. It is generous of Camille to host us, though she's been locked in her study writing most of the days we've been here. I do hope she's well.

My late husband's sudden and unspeakably tragic collapse has given me quite a shock. Never did I dream of such an event. I am corresponding with the family lawyer; he assures me I will find a way to continue. I think he may be right.


Your friend,
    Delphine

My dear Julie,

Have you ever seen a dog chase after something much larger, like a carriage or a horse? Pure joy of the chase drives the dog forward and it spends not one instant contemplating what might happen if it catches its quarry.

Delphine is not a quarry, but I feel a bit like a dog. For months I have wanted nothing but time alone with her, and now I have it, but she's trapped here with me and her life is in turmoil. I can't possibly pursue her. What kind of reprehensible rake takes in a stranded, wounded woman and then seduces her? She deserves better than that.

I know you can't write about what you've been doing, but I hope you are safe and that you found what you've been seeking.

Your friend who's mired in self-doubt,
    Camille

# JULIE MORÈRE TO CAMILLE DUPIN, FEBRUARY 3, 1825
## POSTMARKED PARIS

Dear Camille,
  I am safe and I did find Victor.
  Talk to Delphine.


Your friend,
  Julie

My dear Julie,

Such amusing advice you offer. Can you hear me laughing in Paris? I talk to Delphine every day. She and her child now live in my home, with me, I remind you.

Do you know what an astounding amount of work goes into entertaining a small child? I didn't. It's my horror of pregnancy and marriage that kept me from parenthood, not a horror of children. Octave is a sweet creature. It is very rewarding to make him laugh. Still, the sum of his care is exhausting. All day we feed him and chase him around. Well, Delphine does, and I try my best to help now that I have given up enclosing myself in my study to write. She says it is easier at home, where he has many more people to care for him, including his nursemaid and her child, who is a beloved playmate. We arrived here in such haste that my staff are mostly still living in Paris, except for the groom and groundskeeper who always live here. I have been employing some people from the village to cook and clean. I think some of the villagers have children of a suitable age (Octave will shortly be turning two) and until then, he is delighted by horses and loves riding around with me.

Delphine also asked to ride with me, and when I explained that it is tiring for a horse to carry two adults, she asked me to teach her to ride astride. You know the company we keep, Julie, and such a request—the <u>tone</u>—wouldn't have shocked me coming from an actor or one of the women of the demimonde, but Delphine is a marquise. A dowager marquise. She was holding Octave on her hip while she said it, but his presence didn't deter or distract her from meeting my eyes. I had to pretend the saddles needed cinching again.

I'm not accustomed to feeling like a prude, Julie, and I don't like it. In different circumstances, I could have offered her all the depth and finesse of my expertise.

God, I wanted to. You know what she looks like, but you've never seen her as she was right then, standing by some happy accident or undetectable cunning in the single ray of light through the stable rafters, a dusty halo around the amber glow of her hair and all the clarity of a short February day coloring her pink cheeks, like the sun broke through the thatch just to touch her. Delphine and Octave fled Paris with nothing, so I bought them both clothing. Simple, sturdy stuff, since there wasn't time for embroidery or lace. In plain brown wool, with one of my old cloaks covering her from shoulder to ankle, the hem decorated with clumps of snow and broken straw, <u>still</u> she looks like a tempting confection I can't afford.

But I must protect myself somehow, and if prudery is my only escape, then so be it. I have resolved not to sleep with her, not while she's trapped here. She is apparently determined to make that difficult for me.

. . .

Your friend,
   Camille

Dear Camille,

If a grown woman wants to ride astride, why shouldn't she? She asked you to teach her; you have the skills. I don't see the problem.

You once told me you wouldn't give up your roguish bachelor's life for anyone, certainly not me. I still have the letter if you need reminding. An interlude in the country-side with a willing widow sounds exactly right for a roguish bachelor.

The small child is an unexpected addition, but you sound very taken with him. You sound very taken with his mother as well. The only one making things difficult is you.


Your friend,
Julie

My dear Julie,

Let us return to discussing literature and art, topics where you display great insight and where your passion, curiosity, and strong opinions are welcome.

My notes for a possible illustrated edition of <u>Virginie</u> are enclosed, including a list of suggested scenes, but on this matter—and <u>only</u> this matter—I defer to your judgment.


[*a scribble*]


I have left this page blank for hours in a futile attempt to report nothing more. But I can't do it, Julie. I need to tell someone about last night, and I want to tell <u>you</u>, not because I want your opinion, but because I trust you. I know quite well what you will say; you are released from the burden of saying it.

In the evenings, after Delphine puts Octave to bed, she

and I sit together. Shoulder to shoulder, or her reclining with her feet in my lap. Sometimes I read to her, or vice versa.

When we first started this practice, I asked her what she wanted to read, hoping she'd share my taste for lurid Gothic novels. My work is less sensational, but she does like it, so I thought we'd enjoy some fiction together. Instead she inquired as to whether I owned any philosophical texts. Or any new writings about physics or chemistry or biology. Or any volumes of the Encyclopédie.

I knew Delphine was a fount of intellectual curiosity; it shouldn't have shocked me. And you know I believe fiction to be as worthy a pursuit as any other. Still, I confess a certain feeling of inadequacy in the face of her genuine desire to educate herself about the functioning of the natural world or the human mind while lying on the sofa after a long day of keeping her child alive. I wanted to read about heartbreak and villainy. It turns out she is fond of poetry as well, which also shook my confidence, as I have always preferred the lesser art of prose. We compromised and I have been reading her some of the medieval stories I'm studying for my current novel. They are written in verse, but still contain plenty of betrayals and noble deeds. Hearing them aloud interspersed with Delphine's commentary is a pleasure. She's a lively reader.

Certainly both of us are better at reading than we are at making music, though we do plunk out a few notes on occasion. The house is quiet this winter. As tired as I am from helping Delphine care for Octave, and as much as I love her company, I miss hosting a crowd. Can you imagine Delphine here among all the poets and composers instead in a Paris ballroom full of bankers and gentry? She would wear her hair down and make the filthiest of jokes. Everyone would love her.

Delphine retires first. I spend an hour or two writing, by which I mean stare balefully at my manuscript while I waste lamp oil and smoke a cigar. I was writing in this fashion when she interrupted me last night.

You know my study at Verneuil. With its single chair and the desk pushed against the wall, it's meant only for me—and my books and the hideous piles of paper that pop up like mushrooms over the dark red rug. It is a small space. Delphine made it seem both smaller and larger at once with her arrival, as though a storm had blown it apart. This morning I was surprised to find my drafts still in their stacks, unscattered by the wind. That is the force she has. She walks in the door and her presence alters everything.

Last night it was not because of her arresting beauty, though she does possess a certain allure even in the most wretched conditions. Wrapped in a baggy old greatcoat that dragged behind her, with her amber hair piled in a sort of lopsided bird's nest, she had the look of someone who'd just emerged from years in a cell. I imagine vision-struck prophets in a similar, trembling grip. A terrifying zeal lit her eyes.

I stopped smoking and put out my cigar.

I'd never seen Delphine in such a state. Not directly after I rescued her from her husband and not in the days since his death and our escape. She has not screamed or sobbed. She has taken care of Octave, and made cheerful conversation with me, and treated this whole excursion as a grand adventure. Nothing in her behavior has hinted at distress over the past or the future. Nothing until last night.

"I'm going for a walk," she said.

As mildly as possible, I said, "It's nine o'clock."

"So?"

"It's also February."

"So?" she repeated. "There is no one to stop me."

"I suppose not, but it's black as pitch outside, and there's snow and ice on the ground, and we're the only people around, so if we slip and break our legs, we're in trouble—and so is Octave when he wakes up tomorrow."

"You'd come with me? But we can't leave Octave alone."

"So you wish to fracture your bones in the dark by yourself? Delphine."

She made a loud, uncouth sound of frustration and threw up her hands. "Camille, I feel—" She clutched at her chest as though something was stuck there, and let out such a rough exhalation that I thought she might sob.

Gently—thinking of you and your tearful stay here last summer, Julie, and more selfishly, imagining that I might offer a chaste, comforting touch—I said, "You've suffered a great deal. I would think no less of you if you needed to cry."

"Cry!" she shouted, and then slapped a hand to her mouth, remembering Octave sleeping upstairs. More quietly, but with the same ferocity, she said, "Camille, I have spent two-and-a-half years crying. I was trapped in that house and trapped in myself and now I am here and I want—I want—" She lunged for my cigar and waved it at me. "I want to go outside and scream. I want to spit and hiss and howl. I want to shoot a gun. I want a cigar. I want wine, or brandy, or laudanum, or absinthe. I want to <u>smash</u> something—my skull against the wall, perhaps."

Craving destruction, in voluminous robes and with a

frizzy halo, she might have been a vengeful angel. But it's the mortal woman I'm weak for, the Delphine who's pasty and red-eyed and vibrating with barely suppressed emotion. You know my appreciation for the Delphine of ballrooms and dining tables, exquisitely dressed and coiffed, devilishly clever and flirtatious. But what a rare pleasure to see her façade crack, to glimpse the animal underneath. What an honor to be entrusted with something hidden.

I said, "For now, I can offer you a cigar or wine or brandy. Tomorrow, in the daylight, I'd be happy to teach you to shoot—perhaps when Octave is napping. When he's awake, we can walk as far as you like, or ride. My only condition is that your skull remain unsmashed."

"What is the point of being an eccentric writer if you don't have anything stronger than brandy?" she demanded with a touch of affected petulance that was more like her usual self.

I shook my head fondly. "Come with me."

She accepted my hand and I led her to the kitchen, where she stood in puzzlement as I began to pack a basket. "I'm not hungry, Camille. Not for anything that requires a plate, at least."

"I know," I said.

With my gathered supplies balanced on one hip, I exited through the scullery. A few flagstones are laid into the earth there, the beginning of a path to the refuse heap. We didn't venture farther than the protection of the eaves. The ground was clear of snow. The sky was cobwebbed with clouds. I lit the wall sconce outside the door, and the flame yellowed the dim moonlight.

From the basket, I grabbed the uncorked bottle of wine and an old saucer. I handed the latter to Delphine.

Amused, she said, "Wine is usually served in glasses. Unless you expect me to lick it up like a cat?"

There was no response to <u>that</u> but to drink directly from the bottle. Afterward, I wiped my hand across my mouth. "You said you wanted to smash something."

She hurled the saucer against the stone. It snapped with a clean, high sound. Delphine jumped back and shards ricocheted off my boots. We stared at the wreckage, then at each other, and she laughed. A loud, free sound that broke the silence of the night.

The saucer pieces glinted white as I bent to retrieve another dish.

It was gone from my hand and shattered on the ground almost as soon as she touched it.

The next one, she got for herself. As she threw it, she shouted "Ha!" Not a laugh, but a forceful exclamation.

She fired plate after plate into the flagstones. Little bits of pottery flew everywhere. I took a few steps back and leaned against the cold wall of the house while she worked. The tinkling and clattering of the pottery was occasionally punctuated by a huff or a grunt, but after that first shout, she lapsed into silence, though we were on the opposite side of the house from Octave's room and she'd told me she wanted to scream. The exertion of throwing the dishes seemed to satisfy her. Her breath curled into the icy air, as hot as her fury.

She might have kept methodically destroying things if I'd brought her a second basket. When she reached the end, she strode to me, wrapped her fingers around the neck of the wine bottle and slid it from my slack grip.

One deep gulp later, she passed it back to me, and I saw that her eyes glittered with tears.

"Oh, Camille, your dishes," she said in a thin approximation of her usual bright tone. "Let me sweep up the mess I made."

"They're only dishes. Leave them. We'll clean up tomorrow."

"You've been so good to us," she said. "People only like me because I'm pretty and amusing, and I haven't been either for you. Octave and I have disrupted your writing. We spend all day with him, and then when he's asleep, I— I become strange and—and angry."

That last word was almost a whisper.

"Do you think I am not also strange and angry?" I asked.

She knew I was, though I have, I think, less reason than she does. We've had many conversations about our families and the way they have judged us insufficient as women. It shocks me that anyone could accuse Delphine of performing womanhood incorrectly, but her mother's narrow definition excludes spirit, opinion, inquiry, and— apparently—the world's most beautiful figure, with perfect, soft abundance in the breasts, belly, and hips. I am viciously glad Delphine's mother is not much in her life these days.

Meanwhile I have never been able to hide what a poor facsimile of a woman I make, not even when I dressed in skirts daily. My own family does love me in their clumsy, conditional way. They tolerate my androgyny as long as my novels earn money and acclaim, as though I wear trousers to sell books. I've resigned myself to not being understood, and it's better than what Delphine has, but I'd be lying if I said I never yearned for more. You are so lucky in your family, Julie.

It was not the moment to get into all that. Delphine left my question unanswered.

"You should be angry," I said. "I like that you're angry."

"You do?"

"I don't only like you because you're pretty—beautiful —and amusing. 'Intriguing,' I think I'd say. Well-read and curious. You've been all of those things here; you can hardly disguise or discard your nature. But I also—" I had to pause to clear my throat. It surprised me, the difficulty of speaking the truth. I did it for her because she deserved it. "I also admire your bravery. And your devotion. To Octave."

God help me, Julie, but it was not Octave I was thinking of. Delphine is a devoted mother, and I do admire that, especially since she had no good example to follow. But it was her love for Ari on my mind. I envy him. I hate him and I envy him and I want to steal his place in her heart, but I've arrived too late. And paradoxically, her refusal to abandon him—even though he disappeared—is part of what I admire.

I want to be loved like that. Unreasonably.

You know things are grim when I'm writing "God help me." That is not the sort of God I believe in, but a desperate prayer to an entity who cannot answer is, I think, an apt representation of my situation.

"I haven't been brave," Delphine said. "I've been a coward. If I'd been brave, I would've left the Marquis, or... I think if he'd ever hurt Octave, I would've clawed his eyes out. But he didn't. He hurt me instead."

I can hardly bear to think of it, the way Delphine's late husband rendered her docile with that vile necklace. You've lived with the knowledge of magic all your life, Julie. I am still grappling with the existence of such horrors.

Delphine's marriage was a horror before her husband

wielded magic against her. A more mundane one, but nevertheless an injustice.

Octave will not remember his first two years. He may never know that his pretty, smiling mother possesses such iron courage. Such violent devotion to him. But I know.

We were standing quite close by then, and I was shivering in my frock coat, not having bothered to dress in something warmer. Delphine took the bottle of wine from me and drank again.

"You were brave," I repeated. "You were alone and you were brave. To survive in that house, in that marriage, as you did, subjugating yourself and placating that monster in order to keep your child fed and sheltered—it is a terrible, unthinkable thing. You should not have had to suffer so, but it cannot be undone. It can only be reckoned with."

"I might need to smash a lot more crockery," she said with a shaky laugh.

"I'll buy some."

Another uncertain laugh made a little puff of vapor in the night air. "So few people ever look past my surface, Camille. I think it's only you and—"

"I know," I said, not wanting to Ari to intrude on our moment, though he was already there. He is always already there. I took the wine from her and drank. Unwisely, I said, "It's a very good surface, Delphine, but what's underneath is better."

She made a broken sound between a laugh and a sob. We were past the point of words, expressing admiration or pity or anything else. She's not a tragic heroine; she's alive. I threw my arms around her. Pottery crunched under my boots. She smelled like sweat and the musty wool of her borrowed coat, a flawed and earthly creature, and I inhaled deeply and tightened my hold. Our cheeks brushed. Hers was hot against mine except for the wet drip of her tears.

She said, "I fear sometimes that I have grown into the shape of my cage and don't know how to live without it."

"You will," I said. "You will."

There you have it, Julie. I don't need you to tell me I'm fucked.


Your friend,
  Camille,

# JULIEN MORÈRE TO DELPHINE, FEBRUARY 12, 1825
## POSTMARKED PARIS

Dear Delphine,

I am glad to hear you and your son are well. I admit that I scolded Camille in private for her inhospitable behavior at the beginning of your stay. That is unlike her. I hope that she has now offered you everything you could possibly desire.

I've also been charged with conveying another message in this letter. An acquaintance named Isabelle de Tourzin would like to speak with you about your late husband. She may call on you when you return to Paris.


Your friend,
Julien

DELPHINE TO ARI, MARCH
1, 1825
UNSENT, HIDDEN

My darling,

Camille brought me back to Paris today, or I suppose it was yesterday, given the late hour at which I'm writing. I can feel fatigue dragging at my eyes, but my heart is hopping like a rabbit after what just happened, so I'm writing to calm myself.

I should have said Camille brought <u>us</u> back to Paris today (yesterday), as Octave was with us. I couldn't have left him here. I would have crumpled in his absence. Besides wanting his sweet little face within kissing distance, it was good to give Marthe a few weeks of rest after she and Amélie did so much while I was incapacitated. Octave loved the countryside. It snowed several times in February, deep drifts that made everything dreamlike. So Camille and Octave and I were blanketed in snow and then in actual blankets in front of the hearth.

She was so good to me. Our urgent departure from Paris meant Octave and I had nothing with us, not one extra stitch, and Camille bought us everything we needed in addition to housing and feeding us for the month. I told her I'd pay her once we'd returned and I'd reclaimed my husband's fortune. Technically, the fortune is now Octave's. How that makes me laugh and rage at the same time! As he turned two a mere two weeks ago, our son has little interest in bank accounts. Regardless, Camille continually insists that it makes her happy to take care of us and will not hear of being repaid in francs.

I'd like to repay her in kisses—she would object to hear it described as payment—but she spent every evening skillfully evading my offers. I know she enjoys my company (from our incessant flirtations) and appreciates my figure (from her lingering glances), so I can't understand why we haven't gone to bed yet. If jealousy seizes your heart at the thought, please take a breath and remember how long we've been apart. (Look at me, telling you to take a breath. I've always been absurd, Ari, but your absence has rendered me more so.) I still love you and always will, but I want to kiss Camille, too. "Kiss," ha. Why write to someone who can't reply if I don't intend to be honest? I want Camille to shove my skirts up and slide her fingers into my cunt.

(I also want to kiss her in the usual way, to feel that clever tongue touch my own. And I want to do all sorts of things to her, but as the purpose of writing this is to calm myself, I will stop there.)

If one <u>must</u> be rescued, rather than liberating oneself, a dashing and enigmatic personage such as Camille Dupin makes an excellent rescuer. She freed me from that prison and whisked me away to the country in my hour of need. It wasn't exactly like I once imagined that you might rescue me from my marriage, Ari, sneaking into my bedroom and sweeping me off my feet, but it was close. And, of course, it happened. That matters. I try not to resent your absence, Ari, as I cling to my belief that you had no more choice than I did in what transpired, but in certain moments my emotions overpower me.

(If you'd tired of me, you'd have said so to my face and probably offered me your evidence and reasoning for why we should separate. And you were, at our last, long-ago encounter, not in the least tired of me. On the contrary, you were in your usual condition—both energetic and thorough.)

I will find you. I fear it's too late for a rescue. Octave is too small for a journey into the unknown in any case, and I won't leave him, but I sent someone trustworthy to follow your compass. The path may end in a grave, but I need to know.

On the subject of rescues, my preference would be never to need one again. I don't mean to shut myself in safe, dull seclusion, though. I have come back to Paris to take what's mine and to destroy every last trace of my late husband's wealth and reputation. There was a towering pile of letters waiting for me today. I haven't read them yet, but I know their contents. How strangely thankful I am that my brother is a titled drunk with enough money that he has no interest in me, and my mother's deteriorating mind and body prevent her from writing or visiting. Otherwise I'm sure they'd be in touch, and I have no desire to speak to either of them.

Everyone else wants to wheedle their way in. When my late husband's family discovers that they will all get the same share of the fortune—nothing—they will never forgive me. I will sell this house and disperse every other property. His covetous cousins will be furious. The gossip will be vicious. I'll never be received in polite society again. I don't care. This is my way of rescuing myself. After what that man did to me, what do I have to fear from gossip?

Tonight I saw my first glimpse of how to begin dismantling his legacy. What happened this evening was both terrifying and exhilarating. After Marthe and I put Octave to bed, I wandered the darkened rooms of the house, touching a door here and the frame of a painting there, trying to understand that the man who'd controlled my life behind these walls was dead. For once, the silence didn't press close and grave. It felt open, alive, huge with possibility. Wax pooled in the bottom of my candlestick by the time I climbed the stairs.

When I entered my bedroom and found someone climbing in the window, I clutched the candle to my chest and nearly set my hair on fire.

In the half-dark room, a voice said, "Don't scream. My name is Isabelle de Tourzin."

I balked at being told not to scream when I hadn't, and that grain of spite helped me control myself. Though shock had rendered me insensible to both the night air and the heat from the hearth, I said, "Please shut the window, it's cold out."

I lit as many lamps as I could. As the light grew, so did my courage.

I knew the name Isabelle de Tourzin because Julien had written to me at Verneuil to say she might call on me. There was no indication in Julien's letter that this stranger would break in like a thief.

Madame de Tourzin furrowed her thick, dark brows in consternation, but she closed the window and drew the drapes as well. That was a tiny relief. She's a few centimeters taller than me, not quite as generously proportioned, but sturdily built and clearly strong enough to scale the exterior wall of the house and work open the window. I didn't think I could make her do anything she didn't want to do. Some silver in her black hair marked her as older than me, though the olive skin of her face carried only a slight wrinkle at the corners of her eyes and a few scoring her forehead.

She didn't come any closer. That was also a tiny relief. She was wearing trousers and all black, as Camille often does, but Camille radiates elegance and allure, not clandestine schemes. Camille has never once given me the impression of hiding knives all over her person; I suspect Madame de Tourzin would provoke that suspicion regardless of attire.

She stood stiffly and said, "We have suffered the same rare torture."

I hadn't even said my name, though I suppose a person who slithers through a window doesn't need to wait for introductions. The closed door of the bedroom pressed against my shoulders, a support and a reminder that I could flee and raise the alarm if I needed to. To my surprise, what I wanted was to hear her next words. So I said, "Were you also married to the Marquis de Quennetière, then?"

"The emerald necklace," Madame de Tourzin said, impatient with my attempt to skirt the topic. "I was its first prisoner. You were its last."

I hate to think of that vile thing. My late husband locked it around my neck. His legal and material power over my body was not enough to satisfy him; he required magical control of my mind as well. I rubbed my throat to make sure it was bare.

Camille rescued me from the necklace. Her friend Julien destroyed it through some magical means. And yet to meet someone else who had survived it... I needed to know everything about Madame de Tourzin. Still, some caution was required. I said, "The necklace is gone. Why are you here?"

"Your late husband collected cursed artifacts," she said. "My associate Victor and I can get rid of them for you."

Victor, I guessed from context, was Victor Beauchêne, Julien's lover. We don't know each other, but I trust Julien. Still wary, I asked, "Could we not have discussed this during the day? You and Victor could even have used the front door."

"Victor will enter through the front door tomorrow if you want that," she said. "Arranging for the disposal of your husband's collection is not the only reason I am here."

Nothing about her rigid posture or tone suggested that she intended to make a normal use of the bedroom, but my gaze strayed nervously to the bed. It had never seemed such a hulking, looming thing before.

Madame de Tourzin shook her head sharply and then said, "I want to teach you to snap a man's neck."

I made a small, choked sound. "I beg your pardon?"

In the silence of the room, she knew I'd heard her correctly the first time. She mulled over what to say next, and at last, offered an explanation. "So it doesn't happen again. The necklace."

"The necklace no longer exists," I reminded her. I remind myself every day, sometimes every hour. The topic and her sudden arrival had driven the breath from my lungs, and I was still struggling to get it back. Years of training kept my mask of polite composure in place.

She said, "I still want to teach you to protect yourself."

"Thus, necks."

"Perhaps I should have said 'killing blows.'" She lifted and dropped one shoulder. "I could teach you to slit throats or stab people, but then you'd have to carry a knife everywhere. Without the knife, it's a meaningless skill."

"I suppose that's why you aren't offering me some mysterious, magical artifact that can kill with a touch," I said. Her practical, nearly bored way of discussing slaughter made me feel a bit untethered, almost giddy, like nothing we were saying was real.

"Artifacts that cause death are common enough," she agreed. At last I'd found a subject that inspired her to talk. "But you don't need one. Magic isn't necessary for murder. For that we have knives and guns and poisons. Killing is easy. The hard part is covering it up."

"So if I do snap a man's neck, I'll still have to hide his body," I said. This woman had crawled in my window to teach me about murder. It was the most absurd conversation I had ever participated in. I think by that point I was smiling.

The truth is that I thought about murdering my husband for years, Ari. Every day he was a danger to me, a danger to Octave. Life would have been so much easier without him. I didn't do it. Not for lack of desire, but for lack of opportunity and means. I used to fantasize that I'd catch him standing at the top of the grand staircase, where I would take the world's daintiest, most perfectly timed and targeted stumble. Oops.

Those circumstances never materialized. I waited, doing nothing, and instead my husband did something to me. He used the necklace to imprison me in my body. For nine days—<u>hundreds</u> of hours, <u>thousands</u> of minutes—I could neither move nor speak a word he had not ordered. I suffered and seethed every second. Writing of it makes me shudder.

I should have killed him, Ari. I wish I had killed him.

But Madame de Tourzin was right. I didn't know the first thing about killing a man. Once she offered, it turned out I was glad to learn, even though the man in question was already dead. She demonstrated over and over again various techniques. I don't have a natural facility for neck-snapping, alas. She doesn't have a natural facility for teaching, either, but uncharacteristically, I held my tongue and did not tease her about it mid-lesson. I do have some sense of self-preservation.

Unaccustomed to exertion, I was breathing hard by the time she had given up trying to teach me to drive my thumb into an attacker's eye or grapple and wrestle and free myself from holds. You might think this sounds titillating. With you or Camille it might have been, but Isabelle is a touch too frightening for my tastes. I focused on the knowledge she was trying to impart, how to break a grip on my wrist or jab my elbow into someone's belly, that sort of thing. I was a poor student.

I slumped on the edge of the bed and rested my hands on my spread knees. We were far beyond ladylike behavior. Sweat dampened my hairline.

Isabelle leaned against one of the bed posts. With resignation, she said, "You may need my help."

"Oh, is this not help?" I replied, because we were no longer mid-lesson.

"I live on the Right Bank in Nouvelle-Athènes—nine, Rue Branoux," she said. "If you're in need. Come in person. I hate letters."

She straightened and made as if to exit by the window, but I said, "Wait. You said you were the necklace's first victim. Was it..." I didn't know how to finish. The question hung in the air between us. Caught between a profound regret for broaching the topic and an inexplicable yearning to know if her torture had resembled mine, I closed my mouth.

"Perhaps you're asking if the man who hurt me is still alive."

I gave a slow nod in response, though I had many more questions than that. It hadn't occurred to me that her tormenter might yet live. After the way I'd met Isabelle, it was hard to imagine anyone hurting her, let alone hurting her and living to see another day.

She let out a breath, and I knew. That monster was still out there. A sudden urge arose in me to return to our lessons, as if I could shape myself into someone deadly enough to help her. She said, "He cannot escape me forever."

I blinked. "You don't have a magical object that locates people?"

"No," she said. "Though that wouldn't solve the problem—Malbosc is very difficult to kill."

"Malbosc," I said. "That's the name of the man who murdered my husband."

I hadn't witnessed it. Julien and Camille had rushed me out of the city as soon as the necklace had slid free of my neck, and besides, neither of them had known Malbosc was lurking in the study with a knife. We'd learned of the murder afterward.

She nodded. "He wanted to reclaim the emerald necklace."

Enumerating on my fingers, I said, "He created it, and used it against you, and murdered my husband to take it from him, and he's still alive." Even with all the lamps lit, the bedroom took on a cavernous air. I shivered.

"The necklace is destroyed and Malbosc has no reason to concern himself with you," she said. If she aimed to reassure me, she failed. I don't think Isabelle de Tourzin knows what a comforting tone sounds like.

"He's concerned with you," I protested. "He hurt you once already. He must be hunting you."

"Without a doubt. More importantly, I am hunting him." She smiled grimly. "He has many associates—perhaps I should call them disciples. Most of them are wealthy collectors. Your late husband was among them until he took that necklace for himself. At least one of Malbosc's followers must be sheltering him. I know their names. I'll find him eventually."

"But sooner would be better, and knowing where he's hiding would help," I said.

"Well... yes."

Her expression of consternation seemed less formidable this time. You'd laugh, Ari, but I'd begun to like her. She'd already slipped from being Madame de Tourzin to being Isabelle. We were tied together by the suffering we'd both survived, and she knew it as well as I did. She'd sought me out to protect me. The notion warmed me. This frightening middle-of-the-night visit was an overture. A strange woman breaking into my home and offering me lessons in murder is a solid foundation for friendship, I think.

I put a fingertip to my chin. "So if you had, say, a compass that points the way to the person you're thinking of while you hold it, that would be useful, I imagine?"

Isabelle's gaze sharpened. "Delphine. Do you have such a compass?"

She'd used my given name. That was as good as an admission of friendship. "The terrible irony of it is that I lost the person who made it."

"He's dead?"

"I don't know. He vanished." I didn't want to try her patience, so I shortened the story. "He wanted me to search for him, but I never had the chance—until now. But I don't know how far away he is, only that he's somewhere south-southeast, and I'm afraid to take poor Octave on what might be a dangerous journey."

"If I find him for you, will you lend me the compass?"

She gets right to the heart of things, Isabelle. "Lend," I emphasized. "Not give. I'm sentimental about it."

"Tell me about him. And this compass."

She wanted the details after all. "I will tell you everything, and lend you the compass in exchange for finding Ari, on one other condition," I said. "When Victor comes tomorrow—through the main door—to rid this house of my husband's vile collection, there is a magical artifact in the house that he cannot take. It's a white linen kerchief, and it belongs to Ari. You can destroy everything else, but not that."

"Consider it done."

I neither know nor care what items I am consigning to oblivion. My late husband never discussed his collection with me, though I have some notion of how acquisitive he was. Whatever artifacts remain in this house might be priceless. Ancient. Powerful. One of a kind. I hope so. I feel lighter just imagining my late husband's most precious possessions gone. Imagine how good it will feel when I ruin everything else he loved.

# DELPHINE TO ISABELLE DE TOURZIN, MARCH 2, 1825

## SENT BY PRIVATE COURIER

Dear Isabelle,

I know you don't like letters, but going out in public poses some difficulty while I remain in mourning, so I hope you will forgive this one. I am haunted by our conversation.

The simplicity of your quest appeals to me. I wish it didn't. I wish I had faith in other, less violent solutions. I wish I believed in justice.

Does it trouble you that there might be some better, more righteous answer, one that you have missed? Do you ever worry that your vengeance might harm <u>you</u>—your heart and your mind and your ability to feel at peace—as much as it harms the man you seek?


Your friend,
    Delphine

# ISABELLE DE TOURZIN TO DELPHINE, MARCH 2, 1825

## WRITTEN AT THE BOTTOM OF THE PREVIOUS LETTER AND DELIVERED BY VICTOR BEAUCHÊNE

No.

My darling,

Victor Beauchêne entered through the front door, as promised. He's a blond whirl of excitement. I don't think he stopped moving or talking the entire time he was here. Isabelle didn't accompany him, though he did carry a note from her. (I had written to express some doubts that were plaguing me. I'm surprised she responded.)

Victor's lover Julien came with him. Camille was happy to see Julien, and I certainly did not pout to see her embrace someone other than me with such obvious warmth.

I like Julien, but sometimes a person being likable is an irritation. If Camille had already kissed me, perhaps it wouldn't rankle so much that her best friend is tall and handsome. He wears suits like her, though they're never starched and fitted quite so exquisitely, and his brown hair falls almost to his shoulders in a fashion that must be intentionally queer. I've never seen him keep it shorter or tie it back. Just as Camille doesn't fit neatly into the category of womanhood, Julien is not a man. When he told me that, I asked him if I ought to address him some other way, but he said no. I've heard Camille say "Julie" and "she," but since Julien didn't tell me to do that, I won't risk it. Camille and Julien are so close. They touch each other with as much ease and familiarity as they converse about the latest styles in art and literature. Rumor has it they were lovers once. If you mock me for keeping careful account of Camille's many lovers both rumored and real, I will take it poorly, Ari.

Camille and Julien stood aside and chatted while Victor interrogated me about where my late husband might have kept his cursed artifacts. I led Victor through the rooms of the house. He ran his hands over all the shelves and knocked on the walls and crouched down to the floor and climbed up on chairs and generally turned everything upside down. He has some sense of what might be imbued with magic. He mentioned the ability as though anyone could, but Julien quietly corrected that assertion. You would have been fascinated. I tried to put myself in mind of you and ask the questions you would have, but mostly the answers were "nobody knows." Julien always said it with a sort of apologetic sadness and Victor always grinned. He's short, about the same height as me, and not physically imposing, but he has such an excess of personality that one almost forgets his size. His little blond goatee and mustache exaggerate his impish effect.

We found nothing until we unlocked the study. Sequestered at the back of the house, it was the impenetrable private domain of my late husband. A servant had been allowed to dust once a week, but I had never crossed the threshold.

Clear winter light pierced the gloomy interior through a lone window. The view of the damp, brown garden outside was jarring to me, though I know the layout of the house well enough and could have guessed what I'd see once I entered. I suppose I was expecting a hidden, lush courtyard, some palatial other world only accessible through the study. The room itself didn't live up to its forbidden nature, either. Shelves lined the walls, filled with untouched books and well-read correspondence, built of the same dark wood as the desk that dominated the space.

I sat behind the desk because there was no one to stop me.

My late husband's papers were untouched. My staff had removed his corpse. A sweeter and gentler woman might have quailed to sit where her husband had died. If I ever was those things, I am no longer. Rifling through his letters, a splatter of tiny rust-colored stains caught my eye. With cold detachment, I thought, oh, he must have bled when Malbosc killed him.

While Victor examined the contents of the book-shelves and desk drawers, I read the private correspondence of the man who'd imprisoned me. How it burns me to know how ignorant and dull he was, Ari. If he'd been a genius, at least I could console myself that there was nothing I could have done to stop him. He was only a man. Alas, I am only a woman, and society ranks me far lower because of it.

One letter interrupted my regrets.

"Henri was in the middle of a letter to Malbosc," I said. Victor halted in his search, and Camille and Julien paused their low, intimate conversation from where they stood near the doorway.

"Unwise. Malbosc hates letters," Victor said.

"So does Isabelle," I said.

He stared at me for using her given name, and then

agreed, "She does. Neither of them like to leave traces. What did your late husband have to say?"

I told him the address, which he said was out of date already, and then I read him the obsequious contents of the letter—Henri desperately wanted to please and impress Malbosc, which was strange to read, because he never cared to please and impress me or anyone else I saw. As it turns out, the reason there were no magical artifacts in the house is that Henri sold his whole collection to a dealer named Aveux in order to obtain what he called "a power beyond price," which I can only assume meant the emerald necklace he used to torture me.

I'm glad he's dead.

Victor shut a desk drawer with the toe of his boot and sighed. "He didn't happen to list what he sold to Aveux, by chance?"

"As evidenced by his intimate association with his murderer, my late husband wasn't a cautious man," I said. "He didn't care for anything that resembled work, so no, he didn't make a list."

"I'll never get that information from Aveux," Victor said, dejected. "So whatever the Marquis sold is now circulating the city."

"You'll find it all eventually," Julien assured him.

"Probably, but Savigny will be insufferable about how indispensable he is. I wanted to find it all myself," Victor said. "If there's nothing else in those letters that might tell us where Malbosc is hiding, then my work here is finished."

I reread the letter and shook my head. "I'll tell you if I come across anything interesting. I plan to examine all these papers and the mail I've received from his friends thoroughly."

"His friends have written to you?" Victor asked with what seemed to me unnecessary urgency. "You haven't touched anything, right?"

"No. You think there is some danger in reading the letters?"

Victor and Julien exchanged a glance, and Camille frowned severely at both of them. I could tell she didn't like being left out of their conversation. Eventually, Victor said, "If you wouldn't mind, could we go through the correspondence with you?"

Most of it was exactly what I expected—demands, occasionally couched in polite concern for my wellbeing—and as far as Victor could tell, none of it was magic. But there was a letter from Maximilien Taillefer.

# MAXIMILIEN TAILLEFER TO DELPHINE DE TOUSSERAT, MARQUISE DOUAIRIÈRE DE QUENNETIÈRE, FEBRUARY 20, 1825

## POSTMARKED PARIS

Madame la Marquise,

I write to offer you my profound condolences on the loss of your husband, one of my dearest friends. You may know that I am grieving not only Henri but also my wife, who I lost a mere two weeks after Henri's passing. I know you must be as lonely as I am. Life is so full of sorrow.

Perhaps you might permit me to call on you. It would grant me a measure of solace to see Henri's cherished wife and home.

I will keep you in my prayers.


Please accept, Madame la Marquise, my most heartfelt sympathy,

Maximilien Taillefer

As you can imagine, Taillefer's letter caused an uproar among my companions. Victor swears with admirable vigor, and Julien and Camille talked over each other in their haste to warn me against responding.

"Don't be absurd," I said. "Of course I'll write back. Good manners demand it."

Both Julien and Camille know I like to provoke people, but they failed to see that I was teasing them. "That man is a viper," Camille said, while Julien, troubled and earnest, said, "I painted a portrait of Taillefer and his wife in November and she was in perfect health. I hate to say it, but I suspect..."

"Oh, he killed her," Victor said. "The letter's as good as a confession, though no authority would ever see it that way. He wants you instead, Delphine."

As if I needed to be told any of this. I cleared a space on the desk for a blank page, dipped a pen into the inkwell and began to write, narrating aloud, "Monsieur Taillefer, I offer you my condolences in return..."

Victor continued, "I'd wager he's hoping to gain access

to your husband's collection, too. Nobody knows what became of the emerald necklace except for us."

"I am heartsick to learn of your wife's sudden, unexpected passing," I wrote and read aloud. "You must be grieving deeply, as I am. I will be in mourning for many months yet. To honor my husband's memory, I pass my time in prayer and solemn contemplation. I regret that I cannot offer you the solace you seek, but I am not receiving visitors at this time. Please accept, monsieur, my most distinguished consideration, Delphine de Tousserat, Marquise Douairière de Quennetière."

I signed with a flourish while they stared at me. Very patiently, I explained, "I know I'm distractingly beautiful, but I've managed to think one or two thoughts in my life. Yes, Taillefer is a disgusting lecher who pinched my bottom every time he passed me at a salon, and yes, he wants to trap me into another marriage so he can own everything my husband owned, and yes, he probably murdered his poor wife. She hated me with every rigid, brittle bone in her body and the entirety of her cruel little heart, but she didn't deserve that." I gestured sharply at his letter. "This is brute force. I've seen oxen with more subtlety. You needn't worry that I will fall for it. But it's noticeable if I don't reply to his perfectly proper note. So I'm declining in a respectful, unremarkable way."

"Oh," said Victor.

"I should have known you'd have experience fending off men," Julien said apologetically.

Camille cleared her throat delicately. "I think it's that we recently saw you... as less than yourself, and we all have the urge to protect you. Because we failed so terribly before."

I shuddered at this reminder. I hate that Camille saw

me in such a state—and Julien, and Victor, who I hardly even know—but Camille most of all. I don't want to be the pitiful creature that she rescued. I just want to be a pretty girl who teases her until she can't stand it and has to kiss me.

However, in less piqued moments, I don't mind the idea that Camille wants to protect me. I don't mind it at all. But I think I might like to protect her, too, and I don't know if she'll let me.

"I think we've finished our business for the day," I said, bringing my hands together.

Victor said, "Julie and I will leave you two to your afternoon. Thank you for your help, Madame la Marquise."

"Please call me Delphine," I said, trying not to show my revulsion at the title my marriage had conferred upon me. It's good for signing letters to the likes of Taillefer, but I don't care for it in other contexts—except that every time I think about how much I hate it, I also think about you, and how you rearranged the whole order of the world for me. You made me question what worth these titles have. Why should we treat some people with more respect simply because of who their fathers were? What superiority does their birth confer? Why should some people have enough wealth to live in luxury while others starve? Once one has asked these questions, one sees that they have no good answers. I was taught never to think of these things. You taught me better. That, I like.

Besides, I want Victor to be my friend.

"Do tell me—or, I suppose, tell Isabelle if Taillefer doesn't accept your distinguished consideration," Victor said. "She's good with brute force."

"I know," I said, causing both Victor and Camille to lift

their eyebrows. I hadn't explained what had transpired in my bedroom last night.

Victor and Julien took their leave and then it was only Camille with me. We returned to the study under the flimsy pretense of sealing the letter I'd written, though we both knew we were going there for something else. I sat. She closed the door and surprised me by saying, "Why did you ask me to come here?"

"To the study?"

"To your home, today."

"Did you not want to see Julien?" I was slowing our arrival at my intended destination; Camille had been so curiously skittish at her country estate. If I leapt into her arms the way I wanted to, she might flee.

"I did, of course, but I can see Julien any time," Camille replied. "So I will ask again why you, Delphine, wanted me to attend this meeting."

"I grew accustomed to your presence during my stay at Verneuil," I said. She had already seen me powerless, and reminded me of it, and I did not wish to revisit my own vulnerability by telling the truth. That the prospect of going through all the possessions my dead husband prized more than me—perhaps to discover more artifacts he'd acquired specifically to crush me—was too much to bear without her.

Camille offered me a tepid half-smile and tilted her head. Her expertly twisted and pinned bun didn't move, but the pair of brown ringlets framing her face swung gently. "As one grows accustomed to a favorite chair?"

"If that's an offer to let me sit on you, I accept."

Camille didn't laugh. I've never seen her blush. Her expression twitched in a familiar, "Delphine has said something inappropriate" way. As usual, she refused to respond.

How I long to know what she is thinking at these moments. One of these days I'll provoke a better reaction.

I made a cautious approach, rounding the desk so there was no obstacle between us but the short distance between her body and mine. A devilish impulse made me hoist myself onto the edge of the desk, where I let my feet dangle under the hem of my skirts. I lifted one of her hands in mine and drew it into my lap. Dots of ink from my earlier letter-writing flecked my fingers. Camille's hand likely looked the same under her glove, which I began to peel off.

Studying our hands, I said, in a quiet and serious tone, "I know you like me."

She didn't withdraw from my grip, so I continued. "From your regards, and your touches, and your letters, and your stammering when we first met, and your constant visits to this moldering townhouse, and your daring rescue from my vile husband, and your hospitality at Verneuil for the entire month of February. And because on Octave's birthday you let him throw snowballs at you, and when it became evident that he couldn't hit you, you walked closer until he was essentially smashing a handful of snow into your thigh. You wouldn't have done that if you didn't like me. So that isn't the problem. And I know you take women as lovers—you take all kinds of people—and there isn't anyone right now, so that isn't the problem, either."

"As a clarification, I find Octave charming on his own merits, and I think it's only decent to help small children hit their mark," Camille said. "You're not wrong about the rest, though. But you were effectively stranded at my estate, Delphine. And you'd recently been through—"

"I am not stranded here," I interrupted before we could broach that topic again. "I own this house."

What I meant, what I wanted Camille to hear was "I own my body." I wanted to believe it. I wanted proof.

I could not bring myself to utter the words, unnecessary as they should have been. It is true in every breath, every hair, every little pore. I am the one who moves. I am the one who speaks. The one who thinks. The one who was born here, the one who will some day die here, and in between, the one who lives here, however I please. I am home. I inhabit myself fully. Freckles, toenails, navel, cunt, all of it is me.

Camille loosened my painfully tight grip on her bare hand, removed her other glove, pocketed it, and enveloped my hands in the warmth of her own. "And what do you want to do in your house, Delphine?"

I grabbed her by the lapels of her frock coat and pulled her into a kiss. It was quick. Barely there. An offer. A kiss for testing the waters.

She accepted it. Then she leaned forward, slanting her body over mine, and made a thorough counter-offer. Her tongue was velvet. Slow and deliberate, she shifted from warm and soft to hot and hard.

I clutched at her shoulders. I'd never thought to taste anything so sweet again, Ari. I thirsted for it as though I'd been poisoned and she was the antidote. Every time she retreated even a fraction, I chased the taste of her. I wanted to drink it all down. To swallow and swim in it, to let it course over and through me, to feel it inside, outside, everywhere. I wrapped both arms around her and tugged her closer, crushing us together.

Oh, Ari, you always came so willingly whenever I pulled. I shouldn't compare you two—and I would never compare you to determine who I like better, please understand, it's only that kissing you and kissing her are so similar, and yet so different.

Camille is well-muscled. She's passionate about the outdoors, riding especially, and there isn't much to spare on her. Her bosom is either small by nature or she binds it flat, and if her belly has any curve, it's hidden by her clothes. But her manner of dress reveals plenty. I knew from distant, devoted appreciation that it would be a pleasure to cup her bottom in my hands. I wandered there at my leisure, pausing at the hard line of her hip bones, noticeable under the silk hem of her waistcoat and the fine wool of her trousers, both black. Her thighs didn't dimple softly under my fingers as mine would have. My grip still might have left a mark.

Sweeping my tongue deep into the heat of her mouth tasted like joy. I'd been withering without it.

At last we broke apart to breathe and she laid her forehead against mine. With laughter under her words, she said, "Was that what you wanted? Are you satisfied?"

"Yes to the first, no to the second," I said.

She was already standing between my spread legs. I grabbed her hand and brought it to the apex of my thighs. Her slow perusal of me, from my flushed face to the high neckline of my black wool crepe dress, landed like a touch. She must have found whatever she was looking for, since she seized two handfuls of fabric and drew my skirt up. The movement was purposeful. In retrospect, she was probably giving me time to change my mind, to stop her, but that never occurred to me. As my hemline brushed my stockings and finally my bare thighs, I could only think that she was taunting me, making me wait for it. At last, cool air kissed my sex.

The room didn't matter to her. The study held no

ghosts for Camille. She hadn't walked in the door to claim ownership and cleanse herself, like I had. But she seemed to understand what I hadn't said—that this was a ritual. We'd come here to desecrate the past and sanctify the present.

I can write that sort of thing now, Ari, <u>after</u>. In the moment, my mouth went dry as Camille dragged that hot, dark gaze down to my breasts, my belly, my hips and the rumpled folds of skirt mounded between them, and without any words, I thought, <u>Camille is going to fuck me</u>.

<u>I want Camille to fuck me</u>.

Camille's warm hand pressed into the soft flesh of my thigh. The rucked-up mourning dress blocked my view, but I felt what she was doing. One long finger combed through the wiry hair between my thighs to tease the lips of my pussy. Already slippery and hot with desire, I welcomed her. I thrust my hips forward until I was barely perched on the desk and Camille was deep inside. We both let out a soft sound of satisfaction at the rightness of it. We grinned at each other.

"Delphine," Camille said, low and warm like it was an intimacy. She tipped her head forward until we were nose to nose. Her dark eyes, lit with amusement, blotted out everything else. Her eyelashes tickled mine. "You're perfect. Another?"

"Please." I wriggled and then arched my back when Camille slid two fingers in and out, hard. "Oh, yes. Like that."

"Mm," Camille said, her rhythm slowing and gentling. "No."

"What do you mean, no?"

"You didn't ask me in here to make you come quietly in two minutes," Camille said.

It was on the tip of my tongue to tell her what rank arrogance that was. How dare she refuse me. How dare she presume to know my desires. What came out was a wordless breath of pleasure. A needy, eager sound that proved just how right she was. Losing an argument has never felt so good.

Her touch was maddening, a languorous curling and uncurling of her fingers. When I moved my hips, restless and searching for more, Camille pressed forward, pinning me to the desk, forcing me to lean backward. She kissed the side of my neck in the same idle, masterful way, her tongue working in concert with her fingers. My breath caught at the sharp little drag of teeth. I grabbed handfuls of her suit to stay balanced, then traced one hand up her spine to rest between her shoulder blades and the other down to the firm curve of her backside.

Camille kissed my jaw, my earlobe, my neck again. I damned my mourning dress, sure that she would have kissed me below my collarbone, would have palmed and sucked my full and aching breasts, if only I were naked. But her hands were occupied, one holding my thigh down to keep me from squirming and the other buried deep in the silky, wet heat of my cunt, working.

Camille fingered me like there was nothing more important in the world. Her whole hand was probably slick; my thighs were. My petticoats and my skirt were soaked by the end, and I took a wicked delight in ruining the dress. All I could think was: is Camille this wet? Is she aching for my fingers? My tongue?

I pressed my hand between her clothed thighs to cup the warmth gathered between them. It lit me up inside to find it. I'd been too concerned with my own aims—banishing the past that haunted me in this house. With sudden desperation, I needed Camille to want this as much as I did. How selfish, to pull Camille into the study and not immediately slide to my knees in a puddle of skirts and offer her everything. I rubbed along the seam of Camille's trousers. If only we were naked, I thought, I'd dip my fingers inside and lick the sweetness from them. I'd learn what Camille sounded like when she lost control.

"Not yet," Camille said. "This is for you."

I kept my hand where it was. The radiant heat from Camille's body called to me. I couldn't bring myself to withdraw. Knowing that Camille wanted this, wanted to do this to me, was the best part.

It was almost too much. To be the sole focus of Camille's attention, to endure wave after undulating wave of this tide of sensation coming in, all of it overwhelmed me. I brimmed with it. Another kiss and I'd overflow. Another thrust and I'd spill. It was almost too much, and yet I wanted more.

Camille nipped at my mouth and brushed a thumb over my clit, unleashing a long, low moan of pleasure.

"Yes," Camille said, the words passing between our mouths, hardly touching the air. "That. I want to hear more of that."

I would have sung her an aria if she'd asked, and she didn't need to. The sounds came on their own. Every questing touch had its answer. At first they flowed soft and sinuous, curling from my lips like smoke, and stroke by stroke they became shrill and short. Camille's fingers were brilliant and relentless. I couldn't tell any longer if there were two or three. I was so wet that Camille might have slipped another in with ease. There was only the perfect, delicious fullness.

"When you come, I want you to scream like it could pierce the roof," Camille said.

I sucked in a breath. It wasn't preparation, but shock. At last, Camille fucked me as hard as I wanted. Her fingers thrust in and pulled out searingly fast, and I squeezed my eyes shut and shattered. Head to toe, I vibrated with a fierce rush of sound. Pleasure and release roared through me.

When they subsided, after a long, rolling ebb, I felt new again. Whole. Content. I peeked up and was surprised to see ceiling instead of sky.

Camille bit her lower lip in a poorly repressed smirk. I shoved ineffectually at her chest, then nearly fell backward to the desk. Two handfuls of Camille's fine wool frockcoat saved me from this indignity. It was a wonder that both Camille and I could still be fully dressed. I would have been less surprised to find our clothes in tatters, or disintegrated entirely.

Granted, my skirts were a mess.

"Thank you," I said to Camille, bizarrely shy.

"Of course." Camille slid her fingers out, the air cool where they'd been. I shivered as it touched me, and then again when Camille pressed her wet fingertips to her bottom lip for a taste.

"Camille," I said. It was the only word I could think of. My nipples couldn't possibly feel tight again already. I was still wrung out and boneless.

One corner of Camille's mouth quirked. She withdrew a neatly folded handkerchief, wiped her fingers dry, and then refolded it and put it back in her pocket. The calm precision with which she did it shouldn't have been erotic. My pulse, in repose since my little death, thumped to life again.

"Now it's your turn," I said. "You should get what you want."

"What makes you think I didn't?" Camille asked.

"I—" I found myself unable to continue. Speechlessness was a novelty. A warm flush rose in my face. I floundered and at last came up with, "Really?"

"Really," she said gravely.

I couldn't remember feeling so undone in years. Not since you, Ari, and I think you'd agree that I was usually more in control of myself. We always had to be so careful not to get caught. And with you I was always sure my devotion—my desperation—was equalled or surpassed.

Camille's fingers were cool against my cheek. I grasped her hand in both of mine, keeping it there, and said, "I want to do that to you."

"Render me speechless? You did that the first time we met."

"To fuck you," I clarified, the delicious, illicit word helping me find firmer footing. "Only next time let's be naked."

Camille drew my skirts over my sticky thighs. She smoothed the fabric as though my propriety could be salvaged with a bit of fussing, as though I hadn't been turned inside out and upside down. "I think that could be arranged—if Madame la Marquise is receiving visitors in her time of mourning."

"Nobody but you," I told her.

It's not quite true, of course. I'd receive you too, Ari, if only you were here.

# CAMILLE DUPIN TO JULIE MORÈRE, MARCH 2, 1825
## SENT BY PRIVATE COURIER

My dear Julie,

I've made a mistake. I'll be terrible company. I need some time to think and will not be coming to your studio today.


Your friend,
Camille

Camille knew the pounding knock at her front door was Julie. The household staff all knew her—some of them even knew her as Julie, rather than Julien. They would invite her inside unless Camille gave instructions otherwise, which was a touch too sulky even for her present mood. After a murmur of voices, the heavy front door swung home and boots tapped the stone floor of the foyer.

Camille didn't rise from her chair or exit her study. Her feet would have been steady enough, but her heart tottered and lurched like a wooden-mouthed drunk the morning after. Only a handful of hours had passed since Delphine had ruined her.

She'd been staring at the same illuminated page since she sat down at her desk, never progressing past the capital D glazed blue and edged with gold.

The page was the beginning of a medieval lai—a poem in eight-syllable verse—about a pair of lovers who were separated. The manuscript was a rare complete copy. Camille had acquired it for an astronomical price. Spending hours staring at a single letter was, in a way, getting her money's worth. Never mind that she had intended to read the whole poem.

Julie arrived in the doorway, divested of her coat and hat. Her shoulder-length dark hair was in disarray and her cheeks were slightly flushed with exertion. Under her arm was a large leather portfolio. She must have lugged it all the way from her studio in the neither-here-nor-there shabby outskirts of the city. The drafty space teetered at the top of a rundown building where every surface had an alarming slant. Camille should have met her there an hour ago.

Julie was her best friend. Camille loved her. Camille also categorically did not want to be seen, examined, understood, comforted, or advised, most of which Julie would do effortlessly, with teasing kindness, while nurturing a sweet, fragile little sprout of hope. Camille wanted to grind that hope under her heel and crush it back into the dirt where it belonged. Julie, having secured her own romantic happiness, now believed firmly in the possibility of love. Or rather, she believed specifically in the possibility of love between Camille and Delphine.

Camille was no longer—or did not want to be— governed by passions and sentiments. There was no need to discuss them. That only granted them more disruptive power. When her own interior state fell to turmoil, she simply turned to her work, as she had today. When fictional characters wanted impossible things, it was invigorating. She could grant their wishes.

A friend of hers, an intelligent man, though given to bloviating as novelists often were, had once told Camille, "I write the world as it is and you write the world as it should be."

She'd let their cigar smoke curl between them, evaluating the remark for insult, and then said, "Why the *fuck* would I want to write the world as it is?"

He'd laughed and clapped her on the shoulder and they'd gone back to their good-natured argument. She'd kept his words, though she still wasn't sure whether they were a talisman or a burr snarled in her hair. The world was not as it should be.

In a just world, Delphine would not have lost her true love, Ari Lazare.

"I knew you'd be brooding in here," Julie said, forgoing any other greeting. Like Camille, she preferred to dress in suits. Unlike Camille, she was long-legged enough to loom over anyone fool enough to remain seated while she stood. "I bet you've been staring at the same blank page all afternoon."

"You'd lose that bet," Camille retorted. "It's not blank."

The manuscript lay open on Camille's desk, each vellum page crowded tightly with black calligraphy, bordered with flowering vines, and bejeweled with brightly colored capitals. It was beautiful, and Julie gasped and stared appropriately, and then said, "How the hell do you read that writing? It looks like a lot of *n* and *m* all run together. Worse than my letters, even."

Camille sighed and admitted, "It's hard. I'm not very good at deciphering it."

"What is it?"

"A poem about separated lovers," Camille said. "I'm writing a historical novel. It's set in the twelfth century. I thought this manuscript would be good inspiration—and I wanted it."

"It's gorgeous," Julie said. "Beautiful, delicate, expensive, rare. A little bit mysterious. Survived things we'll never even know, but still intact. Strong, but vulnerable.

Requires a great deal of care. Exactly the sort of thing you like."

Camille narrowed her eyes.

"What?" Julie said with a cheerful shrug. "I'm talking about books."

"Hmph."

Julie set her portfolio on the floor and sat in the chair opposite the desk. "I bet you spent months pining for it, knowing nobody else would ever give it the love and attention that you could. And you're right. You should have the things you want, Camille."

"One begins to suspect that you are not, in fact, talking about books."

"Oh, I am, though. And you *welcome* my strong opinions about art and literature," Julie said. "What's your new novel about?"

"Separated lovers," Camille said, and then added, with an emphatic gesture toward the manuscript, "Like this poem."

"Like this poem," Julie repeated. She raised her eyebrows. Julie had handsome eyebrows, which she knew, because she'd edited her own face through some unknowable application of art and magic. Normally Camille found Julie's talent for self-portraiture intriguing and admirable. Today, like everything else in the world, it irritated her.

Camille couldn't look at Julie's beautifully androgynous and symmetrical features without scowling, so instead she cast her gaze down at the desk, where she found only the manuscript and its unreadable lai about a woman separated from her true love, a man who had inexplicably vanished.

It was possible that Camille had, perhaps, not been entirely honest with herself about the origins of her novel.

The writing had progressed quickly; there had not been time to reflect on entanglements with her own life. Camille never had time for such things.

The novel was narrated by an outsider, a man who was in love with the brokenhearted woman. He nobly chose to withdraw himself when her true love returned.

The story was, of course, a work of fiction. It had nothing to do with her. Still, Camille couldn't bring herself to recount the plot to Julie. Certainly she hadn't mentioned it to Delphine.

The draft remained nine-tenths finished because she didn't know what to do with it. She'd thought of publishing it under a pseudonym, or perhaps taking a long trip abroad after its release, or simply shoving her hundreds of meticulously composed pages into a drawer and writing a different book.

"You're a pest," Camille said to Julie, carefully closing the illuminated manuscript and setting it aside.

"I have it in writing from your own hand that I am your dearest and best friend in all the world," Julie corrected.

"My friend who is also a pest. I told you I wanted to be alone."

"When I was last suffering an episode of spleen, instead of leaving me alone to mope, *you* threatened to kidnap me if I didn't join you in the countryside," Julie said. "Whereas *I* brought you a portfolio of preliminary sketches for an illustrated edition of *Virginie*. Walked for half an hour in the cold wind—after waiting for you at my studio, that is. But if you don't want to see them, I'll leave."

The chill gloom of the study broke. Camille sat up straighter. At last, a distraction. "You did them already?"

"You think I would leave my dearest and best friend in all the world waiting?"

"Living with Victor has made you rude," Camille said. "I did tell you not to wait for me."

"Was that note meant to keep me away? It seemed like a cry for help," Julie said. "What kind of mistake could you possibly have made since this morning at Delphine's when she looked like she wanted to toss me out a window for standing so close to you—oh. Did you fight?"

"No." Camille's hands were both on the desk, and she was seized with a prickling urge to slide them out of sight, as though they were marked with the evidence of what she'd done. Restraining herself made her twitch.

"Camille," Julie said. "Did you kiss the Marquise de Quennetière? That doesn't sound like a mistake to me. That sounds like the thing you've wanted to do for months. Why would you be unhappy about it?"

Julie, who was prone to romantic yearning and had pined over Victor for ages, would never understand the problem. She'd told herself a certain story. Camille had to correct the account. "Yes, I was infatuated with Delphine, but it was a harmless, passing thing, you understand? A diversion. It suited me perfectly to be charmed by Delphine's wit and beauty when I thought we might provide each other with a few weeks of amusement. You know I like a friendly sort of affair."

"I recall you were extraordinarily dismayed to learn of her attachment to Ari," Julie said.

Camille ignored this interruption. She hadn't finished her explanation. "But then Delphine was in trouble, and we saved her, and she lived with me for a month, and it would have been rotten behavior to seduce her when she was so vulnerable and unable to leave, so I resisted."

"That never made any sense to me," Julie interrupted. "She wanted you then, she wants you now."

Camille gritted her teeth. She would have to state the problem directly. "I find that after so much time in her company, something altogether more serious has developed. Succumbing to her advances this morning was a mistake."

Julie's expression wrinkled in puzzlement. "So you *don't* want to kiss her again?"

"Of course I want to kiss her again, don't be dense," Camille snapped.

"You said *you* succumbed to *her* advances, so she wants to kiss you, too," Julie said, placid despite Camille's moody outburst. "I still don't see why any of this is cause for sulking."

"Because she's still in love with this godforsaken stranger named Ari! I'm only a dalliance to her."

"And you don't want to be," Julie concluded. Her cheer struck Camille as unseemly. "Have you ever seen this Ari? It's been months and he only seems to exist in Delphine's stories. Why haven't you asked what happened to him?"

"I have. She always evades me. The most she's ever said is that he 'went away.'"

"So he's not *here*," Julie said. "Did you tell her that you'd 'developed something altogether more serious'? I've heard women love it when you talk about your feelings like a disease you've contracted."

"No."

"So you didn't tell her your feelings and you've never clarified whether this Ari she talks about all the time is dead or alive," Julie said. "But you did kiss her."

"Among other things I shouldn't have," Camille muttered. She propped her elbows on the desk and put her face in her hands. "I'm a fool, Julie. She undoes me. I didn't even let her touch me and it didn't matter. I make plans and then—" Camille waved a hand in the air and returned to clutching her face "—Delphine."

"She's very pretty," Julie said with sympathy.

"*So* pretty." Camille drooped until the smooth wood of the desk pressed against her cheek. Another mistake—she couldn't think of desks now without Delphine flooding her senses. The sweetness of the memory was as dizzying as wine. Camille didn't lift her head. "The whole time she was at Verneuil, flirting with me mercilessly, I abstained. I held out for a month of that torment, Julie, and this morning she kissed me once and I lost all willpower."

"Camille. Are you *sure* her heart belongs to Ari?"

"I know it," Camille said sourly.

"It might be worth asking her how she feels about you."

"You can't *ask* someone if they love you, Julie." Camille had to sit up straight and look Julie in the eye for this part. "If they say yes, it's to please you. Delphine has already made it clear who she loves, and it's not me. She wanted a quick fuck in the study this morning, and in a moment of weakness, I obliged. That's all."

"And it's such a terrible mistake to sleep with your friends?"

Camille didn't return Julie's smile. "Certainly not—except when they cry afterward because they're in love with an unworthy scoundrel who faked his own death. You may have forgiven Victor, but I expect I'll always begrudge him those tears."

"Don't change the subject. We're discussing you and Delphine."

"We're discussing what a misfortune it is to fall in

love," Camille said. "Whether your beloved abandons you, or whether they simply never notice your devotion because they're enamored of someone else."

Julie pursed her lips and contemplated Camille for a long moment. Too long. "Does this have something to do with the men you lived with? Lucien and Félix."

"Félix never lived with us," Camille corrected absently, thinking of the blue bedroom upstairs, empty for years now, and never more than two-thirds full even when Lucien had lived there and she'd slept by his side. It had only ever been half-full to Lucien, she supposed. Camille had been counting all three of them as lovers, but in his heart, he'd only counted Félix. She hadn't mattered. Then she caught herself. "I wish I'd never told you any of that."

"Why? You've seen me at my lowest. Knowing that someone—or two people—once broke your heart doesn't make me think any less of you," Julie said. "It makes me think less of them. I didn't know Félix and Lucien, but I do know Delphine. You should tell her how you feel. At worst, she'll tell you that she loves Ari and only Ari, and you're nothing but 'a quick fuck' to her, and then you'll be exactly where you are now. At best, she'll confess that *she*—"

"No. No advice. I've had enough of discussing my mistakes," Camille interrupted. "I'd like to think about something I've done right. Would you show me your sketches?"

"She can't do the right thing unless you tell her the truth, Camille," Julie said, and then, at last, closed the matter and opened her portfolio.

Madame la Marquise,

I thank you for your response, brief as it was, since it lightened my heavy heart to receive a page from your hand. I understand completely your desire for prayer and solemn contemplation in this time of grief, and would, of course, leave you to your solitude, but I am bound by duty to protect you from the hidden dangers that might be in your home.

Your husband and I were both collectors of art objects. He would not have wanted to frighten you, and nor do I, but many of these objects have secret and possibly even deadly properties. Remaining in your home with them risks your life. As you have been kept safe from this knowledge, you will never recognize which ones might be perilous to touch or even to regard. You require my help.

I cannot in good conscience permit you to continue in such severe danger. I will call on you soon to begin identifying the threats. This project will not be concluded quickly. Your husband's collection was extensive and he may have kept much of it in secret places. I assure you I will not stop until I have found everything. Treat your late husband's possessions with great caution in the meantime. It is especially important that you not attempt to dismantle or crush any of them; such artifacts are often explosive in their destruction.

No harm will come to you while I am with you; we shall be inseparable.


Please accept, Madame la Marquise, my most profound sentiments,

Maximilien Taillefer

Monsieur Taillefer,

Your concern is touching, but unnecessary. The collection you speak of was sold to an antiques dealer named Aveux. I have included copies of the relevant correspondence.

You must respect my wish to reside in seclusion. My grief can only be soothed by pious solitude. Furthermore, it is not proper for me to have male company at this time. I know you were motivated only by the most selfless concern for my life, and that now that you are assured of my present and future health, you would never do anything to damage my reputation.

Please accept, Monsieur, my most distinguished consideration,

Delphine de Tousserat, Marquise Douairière de Quennetière

# MAXIMILIEN TAILLEFER TO DELPHINE DE TOUSSERAT, MARQUISE DOUAIRIÈRE DE QUENNETIÈRE, MARCH 5, 1825

## POSTMARKED PARIS

Madame la Marquise,

Of course I would not dream of damaging your reputation, though my heart does yearn for the solace of your society. I shall confine myself to letters while you are in mourning.

What a shame that your late husband rid the house of his treasures. He was a cherished friend—though not as dear to my heart as you are—and I would have liked to remember him by some of them.

If you cannot bear to receive company at home, perhaps we might chance to meet while strolling through the Luxembourg. You need not deign to speak to me while we are there; your reputation will remain untouched. It is only that I long to see your face.


Please accept, Madame la Marquise, my most profound sentiments,

Maximilien Taillefer

Camille, my favorite genius, gifted in literature and other arts,

I thought you would come to me after our adventure in the study, but you didn't even deign to send me a note. Heartless! Beastly! After more than a month of seeing your handsome face every day, in your absence I shrivel like a plant separated from the light of the sun.

Don't you want to continue what we started? I do. There are so many more rooms to explore in this house.

In utter seriousness, if I have hurt you or done something to make you stay away, only tell me what to say or do to make it right, and I will do it.

I spend my days answering piles of tedious correspondence in which everyone implores me to give them my money or my body or my dead husband's collection of cursed artifacts, or in Taillefer's case, all three. I write no after no after no.

You are the one person in the world I want to say yes to, and you haven't given me a chance. Write me a letter, Camille. Come to my door. Ask me for anything. I know you don't need my money or want my dead husband's collection, but I keep alight the hope that I still have something to offer you.

Please accept, sweet Camille, my most profound sentiments, both proper and improper,
     Delphine

# DELPHINE TO ARI, MARCH 7, 1825
## UNSENT

My darling,

Camille didn't come back for days after our tryst in the study. I thought I might scrape the paint from the walls in frustration. I was anxious that I might have done something wrong because of my inexperience—though she didn't let me do anything.

Instead she came back today, pale and frantic and making a demand that was not at all the one I'd hoped for. As soon as she saw me, she said, "Taillefer is still writing to you?"

"Yes," I said, which she already knew because I'd told her all about it, and also that I'd refused him again. "It's nothing to worry about."

"It seems to me exactly the sort of thing one should worry about."

"It's only letters," I said.

"For now."

The same worry had troubled me, but I was prepared. I slid my late husband's pistol out of my skirt pocket to show her. "A very handsome novelist recently welcomed me to her country home and taught me to shoot."

"We didn't practice with pistols. Besides, you told me you hated the idea of hunting," Camille said. "I don't mean to insult you, Delphine, but regardless of weapon, a couple of lessons wasn't enough to make you a good shot."

"I <u>do</u> hate the idea of hunting," I said.

I am, in fact, a much better shot than Camille thinks. When she taught me at Verneuil, I missed the tree trunk where she'd marked a target once by accident, which caused her to put her arms around me to demonstrate better technique. After that, all my shots were taken with the intention of getting Camille to stay where she was, her arms and hands covering mine, her lips near my ear, and her hips grazing my backside. I hit my chosen target perfectly.

I said, "If I use this on Taillefer, it will be because he's so close he's impossible to miss. But it's a last resort, I swear. I've recently made a terrifying friend who promised to help me if I was in trouble. I've missed you, Camille. I don't want to spend any more of our time together talking about that man."

"You have to tell me if he continues to write to you," Camille said. "Or if he bothers you in other ways. Please, Delphine."

"And what will you do about it that I cannot?" I asked.

"I don't know, but better two of us against him than one. I can't—I don't want you to get hurt."

I softened. I would never have kept anything from her, Ari. It's only that it rankles to be treated like I'm helpless. But what happened to me also made Camille feel helpless, I think, and now we're both trying to sort ourselves out. "I'll tell you," I promised. "And more importantly, I'll tell

Isabelle de Tourzin. Now can we continue what we started in the study?"

"Delphine, I—" Camille began.

I'd already mounted the first few steps, and Camille had halted at the bottom as though she wasn't going to follow me to my bedroom. "What is it?"

"I want to know what happened to Ari."

How strange it was to hear your name echoing in the grand, empty foyer of this house where I have kept our secret silent so many years. I opened my mouth and could not seem to close it. I clutched my skirt in one hand, squeezing and releasing the fabric. "Could we discuss that in private?" I said, or rather, squeaked.

There was no one in the foyer with us. My husband is dead. The only remaining staff are loyal, or at least they appreciate their recently increased wages and tolerate me as a better option than any of the covetous cousins. But I haven't spoken your name here in a long time, and I couldn't bring myself to do it carelessly.

I took the remaining stairs evenly, with great attention to my skirts and my posture, as though I were carrying something precious and was deathly afraid I might trip and crush it. My breathing stayed steady. It was not until I'd soundlessly closed the bedroom door to ensconce us in silence that I faltered. A blink, rapidly followed by another blink, left tears on my lashes.

Nothing escapes Camille. She took my hand and said, "I've upset you."

"I'm the one who should apologize," I said. "I told you to ask me for anything, and you did, you want to know something, of course you want to know, and I wish I could tell you—"

"Delphine." Camille could quiet a thunderstorm in that

tone. It certainly put a stop to the shower of words out of my mouth. Gently, she asked, "Do you... not know what happened to Ari?"

"I've spent two-and-a-half years refining my theories," I said, and I meant to smile, but I had to swallow half a pathetic, hiccuping sob in the middle, so it wasn't effective at all. "I'm sorry. It's just—it's not an easy thing to talk about him."

She tucked her chin and aimed a querying, authoritative look in my direction.

I must credit Camille; she elicited from me the smile that I couldn't call to my own lips. It was a weak and watery one, but I did it. After tolerating so very many stories about you, she's earned the right to prod me about it.

"Here," I clarified. "In this house. I only ever told you about him when we were elsewhere."

"I heard this house belonged to you now," Camille said.

Her reminder of our time in the study did nothing to ease the tightness in my chest. "I understand why you want to know," I told her.

"No," she said. "That was for my own reasons, and certainly not worth troubling you. Forget that I asked."

A tear spilled onto my cheek. I couldn't look at her. I've all but lost you, Ari, and Camille suddenly asking about you made me fear I might lose her, too. "I can't forget it. I want to know what happened to Ari, too. If he's alive or—well. If the answer is a condition of our liaison, then you should know that I have sent someone to look for him. We could wait until she returns."

She stroked her fingers over the hunch in my shoulders, and gradually the tension released. She pulled me into an embrace and kept me there until my breathing slowed.

Once a long, quiet moment had passed between us, she spoke. "Liaison?" she asked in her low, amused tone.

"What would you call it?" I asked. "I suppose it's friendship to you. The gossip does say you and Julien—"

"Julien is in love with Victor," she said—rather stiffly, I thought, though I've never had the impression that Camille is pining for Julien. She takes many lovers and doesn't seem the type to pine. In my place, she wouldn't be writing letters to you. "Though we did sleep together once. It didn't go well."

"That won't be a problem for us," I promised. It's rude of me to be so delighted that Camille and Julien aren't good in bed together, but I don't care. The notion dried my tears and brightened my mood. My hands had settled on her hips. I let them drift inward and then upward along the edges of her frock coat. With deliberate, decisive motions, I unwound her cravat and bared her neck.

"Delphine," Camille said, curiously anguished. "You undo me."

"I've hardly done anything yet," I said and kissed her. In the study, I'd let Camille take charge. You know that's not usually my way—or it wasn't my way with you. With Camille, I might be different. I want to find out.

Taking hold of her lapels, I began to push the coat off her shoulders. I freed her arms from the sleeves and dropped it on the floor. Her skin was warm through the fine fabric of her shirt. Untucking it from her trousers, I slid my palms up her bare back and kissed beneath her ear. "I want you naked. I want us both naked."

"I want that, too," she said.

It made me giddy with relief to hear it. When Camille

hadn't returned or written to me, and then when she'd arrived upset about Taillefer and asking about you, I'd feared she didn't want this. But by her own admission, she did.

I gave her a quick kiss on the lips and said, "Wait, I need to do something first."

I crossed the room, tossing my slippers off as I went, and tore the black drape off the freestanding psyché mirror to the side of the bed. I dumped it on the floor. In the privacy of my bedroom, my false mourning was finished.

"No more of this theater," I said. "As I am not really grieving."

Camille hummed in response to that, almost a sound of disagreement. She bent to remove her own shoes and then rolled back her shirtsleeves with care, exposing her lovely, strong forearms. She padded across the floor and the two of us stood before the newly revealed mirror. Wrapping her arms around my belly, she hooked her chin over my shoulder.

"You're a very beautiful woman, Delphine. You make me do foolish things."

"I think taking off my dress would, in fact, be a very wise thing to do," I said. "Then you could see what's under it. Even better, you could touch what's under it. I would like that very much."

"Oh, it's not wise at all," Camille said. "But I want you too much to resist."

"Good," I said. "Let's be foolish together."

I wish I could convey to you, Ari, the effervescent anticipation of having Camille's long, clever fingers unfasten every button and loosen every lace all down the length of my spine. Champagne has never gotten me so drunk. My whole body lightened and released, though that was perhaps the effect of Camille removing my corset.

I sighed with relief. "I'll have to get new things made when I'm out of mourning. I had so little appetite in my marriage. But lately I've been so happy, and you fed me so well at Verneuil, that I'm going to spill out of all my old ones."

Camille pulled my chemise over my head and let it drop to the floor. Then she kissed the back of my neck and cupped my heavy breasts, lifting one in each hand. "If you like, I could stand behind you everywhere you go."

I laughed. "A generous offer."

Camille let her hands fall to my belly, where the corset boning had left red lines pressed into my body even through my shift. Camille traced one lightly, then her fingers drifted to the silvery lines that had faded into my skin after pregnancy. Camille tugged me closer until my bottom was pressed against her clothed hips. She kissed the side of my neck, the tip of her nose brushing my ear. "I can think of nowhere I'd rather be."

I melted against her, letting my head loll back, crushing the delicate arrangement of my hair. Ari, I'd never thought to have that—the ease, the comfort, the flirtation—with anyone ever again. "If I had to walk around naked in order to have you, I think I'd do it."

Camille's low laugh vibrated against me. "You'd cause a bigger scandal than I ever have."

"You underestimate yourself," I said. Camille, neither woman nor man, but brilliant and beautiful and unflinchingly Camille at all times, irresistibly draws Paris's attention.

"I could say the same to you, Delphine. As appealing as it sounds, you don't have to go naked for me." Camille raised a hand to cup my breast again, brushing her thumb over the peaked nipple. I shivered. "You'd get cold, for one. And I am not here solely because the view is magnificent—though it is."

It had been so long since I'd laughed freely that it left me a little breathless. That, and Camille's roving hands, cupping and squeezing and massaging. She was right that we'd cause a scandal together, with Camille in long hair and trousers and myself in a pair of white silk stockings.

Even in the privacy of the room, it felt daring and obscene to look in the mirror, at this unfettered display of my body. The stockings slipping down my calves turned my nudity to nakedness. I hadn't seen myself in ages, and the sight was at once familiar and strange. Camille's hands ought to leave rosy trails of heat everywhere they'd touched, but my peach-pale skin was only faintly flushed.

Camille's eyes, glimpsed in the glass, were coal-dark and burning. I clenched my thighs together.

Camille shifted, the seams of her clothing brushing my naked skin. Whatever she was doing to me, I had that power over her as well. In the mirror, a smile curled across my lips.

"Touch me. Now."

"Yes, Madame la Marquise," Camille said, only a little mocking.

"Please don't call me that," I whispered. I wanted no trace of my marriage, neither the black drapery nor the title it had conferred, present in the room. Embarrassed by my moment of weakness, I added in a brighter tone, "I don't object to the sentiment, naturally—Ari used to call me Highness—not that you have to, forget I mentioned it, really, it's nothing."

"Your Highness," Camille repeated, amused. "You want me to elevate your rank?"

"I want you to touch me."

"Then it shall be done. I am sworn to your service, Majesty."

"Less swearing, more service," I said tartly.

I hummed happily as Camille combed through the thatch of my hair and caressed the slick folds of my sex. It was a little unfair, telling Camille to touch me like this again when I hadn't offered her anything in return, but it was worth it for the heady feeling of having all of Camille's handsome, skilled brilliance at my beck and call. I liked what she had done in the study, pinning me to the desk and telling me exactly how loud to scream, but Camille responding to my demands was perfect, too. Even if Camille was a little defiant about it. Especially if Camille was a little defiant about it.

Before the study, I'd forgotten what it was like to have someone else's hand there, to not know exactly where those questing fingers would go next. One slid in, and then a second, just enough fullness to make my hips roll in search of more. I'd coaxed Camille into pleasuring me twice already and all I could think of was more.

Camille dragged a searing, open-mouthed kiss down my neck, teeth sinking into the juncture with my shoulder. I cried out. Camille's fingers thrust into me, slow but relentless. Every touch had stoked heat in me, spark after spark, and when Camille rubbed a thumb over my clitoris, I hissed out a burning breath. It was too hot; I wanted it to be hotter. I writhed, caught between the hand clamped around my aching breast, the strong and solid body behind me, and the hand making my pussy clench until I shrieked.

I came hard and fast. When my vision fixed on the mirror again, Camille was watching.

My shoulder blocked my view of her mouth, but I knew she was smiling. A moment later, Camille lifted her chin and licked her elegant fingers clean. I stared as if magnetized.

"You," I said, breathless, "are a genius. And you're wearing entirely too many clothes."

"It's not the first time I've been called a genius, but that's not usually what the literary critics say about my clothes."

"I'm quite sure they're wrong, then," I said and turned so we were facing each other.

Camille's gaze drifted down to my bottom, now on display in the mirror, and her hands followed. "I spoke so highly of your bosom earlier. It would be a shame not to distribute my praises equally."

I imitated her gesture, grabbing hold of her firm, trouser-clad backside. "Perhaps I'll take to dressing as you do."

"God," Camille said, dropping her forehead to my shoulder, hands still kneading my flesh. "Please do."

"I like to watch you walk around, you know, especially without your coat on." I traced the outline of Camille's body with her fingers, tracking the twin curves under her ass. "These are very fitted. You give me indecent ideas."

"That _is_ what the literary critics say," Camille said. "Giving people indecent ideas never sounded so thrilling before. Do go on."

I pulled off Camille's shirt and kissed her exposed chest. Her small breasts were high and tight, each one barely a mouthful. I unbuttoned her trousers and began to push them down her hips, then reconsidered our position.

"Sit on the bed," I ordered. I knelt and removed the last of Camille's clothes, and then found myself conveniently positioned between her spread thighs.

"Lie back and let me see."

The curls there were thick and dark, and I couldn't resist petting them a few times before parting them to reveal the pink folds of her sex, swollen and glistening with desire.

I skated my finger down the seam and then into the wetness. The inside of Camille's body was warm silk. It felt nothing like touching my own. If I could have, I would have slid my whole self inside. Instead I leaned forward to taste.

There was something of the ocean to it, but it was earthy, too. Not so different from the faint salt flavor of kissing her neck or her breasts, but more powerful. I loved it.

I'd never done it, but you never missed an opportunity to do it to me, Ari. I remembered the feel of your tongue slipping over me, into me. The hot, rough texture of it. The suction of your lips. The way you'd grab me, pull me closer, and plunge inside. Sometimes you used your hand and your mouth at the same time. I imitated my memory, slipping a second finger in and drawing a little circle with the point of my tongue.

Camille sucked in a breath, and I kept going, thrilled to be the cause of such a sound. I worked my fingers in and my tongue over, making a mess of myself, and she reached down and wove her fingers through my hair, knocking all the pins askew. A chorus of little moans, sighs, and gasps colored the air, delicate and so unlike her speaking voice. The rough clench of her hands punctuated the oration, and then at last, pleasure rippled through her. She drew down tight on my fingers and cried out.

Camille pulled me up and kissed me afterward, not caring that my face was soaking wet. We tumbled into the bed together and lay there intertwined, Camille tucked into the curve of my body. The study had been earth-shaking, but it had lacked this intimacy, the quiet afterward with our naked skin touching everywhere.

"If that was foolish, Camille, then I want to be your fool all the time," I said.

"Mm," Camille said, which I found unsatisfactory and somewhat disconcerting.

"What I mean to say is that I would like to do that again," I said. "If you're not occupied with other lovers."

She huffed a sort of dried-up, hollowed-out laugh. "You think I have other lovers."

"Well, I know there was a countertenor in December, and an actress before that, and you did say you slept with Julien..." I folded my fingers back toward my palm. It was rude to count. "I don't know how these things are done, Camille. It's only ever been you and Ari. Well, and the Marquis, but I hated him."

"I know, Delphine," she said, her voice heavy with fatigue. "You've told me."

I'd hardly ever talked to her about my dead husband, so she must have meant the stories I'd told about you.

"I just... wanted you to know him," I tried to explain. I never meant to make her resent you, Ari. If I don't tell Camille about you, then how else is it possible to have both of you in my life? "He's important to me, and I wanted to share him with you."

I want to share her with you, too. These letters are the closest I can get.

Camille said, "I don't have other lovers. It's only you."

She sounded so grim about it. I tried to smile. I touched her hand and said, "It's only you for me, too."

"After Ari."

Stricken, I withdrew my hand. I know now what I should have said—Camille is <u>after</u> you only in the sense that I met her second. She made me want to live again even before she saved my life. I care for her as much as I care for you. But in the moment, I was speechless.

Camille sat up, and her expression softened when she saw me. "Forgive me. I shouldn't have said that. I'm grateful you've told me about Ari, and I'm sorry you lost him."

I didn't know what to say to that, either. Camille thinks you're dead. I understand. Two and a half years is a long absence. Sometimes in the deep, silent hours of the night when I'm alone, I think so, too.

I don't want you to be dead, Ari. Until Isabelle de Tourzin tells me she's found your bones, there's hope. But if Camille only accepts my love because she thinks you're dead, and you're not dead, what will become of us?

Dear Isabelle,

Thank you for responding to my earlier letter, though I know you don't care for written correspondence. I write again because I am still trying to respect propriety and not go gallivanting about town while ostensibly in mourning.

Perhaps you have followed the compass and are no longer in Paris. If so, I wish you luck in your quest. However, if you are still here, I could use your help.

There is a man—a friend of my late husband's—who will not leave me alone. I have politely refused him three times now, and he will not hear it.

Would you consider applying some stronger form of persuasion?


Your friend,
Delphine

Madame la Marquise,

I noticed that you wrote to Isabelle recently—I didn't read your letter, but I work at her home and she doesn't receive much correspondence, so yours was notable—and I thought I should let you know that she's traveling and won't see your letter for some time.

Perhaps you knew all of this already. If you are in need and willing to share your concerns with me, I will do what I can for you. I've enclosed some encrypted paper—whatever you write will only be legible to your intended reader—in case you need it.

I don't know how long Isabelle will be gone, or where she went, though strangely enough, in a rare moment of candor, she did mention that she was undertaking the journey to retrieve something for you.


Please accept, Madame la Marquise, my respect,
    Victor Beauchêne

III

# WIFE AND MISTRESS

1825

# PRIVATE DIARY OF ARI LAZARE, MAY 11, 1825

Prison may have driven me mad.

How would I know, though? Wouldn't madness render me unreliable? My senses can no longer be trusted. I hear the relentless rush of the ocean in the streets of Paris. Sometimes I see a guard's face in some passing stranger's half-glimpsed profile and terror closes a fist around my throat. A rational person would be pleased by freedom, but open spaces make my body sweat and quake.

That's how I showed up at Delphine's last night, fearful and filthy like a hunted animal. I would never have found her without the coin, since apparently she's been both married and widowed in the two years and eight months we've been apart. The disgusting grand mansion where she now sleeps—even more disgusting and grand than the one her awful brother has inherited from her awful parents— was new to me, and difficult to find in the dark. Knocking took all of my resolve.

It's a measure of how much faith I have in the luck coin that I even touched the door, but the coin helped me escape forced labor. If that's not demonstrable proof of its power, what is?

She looks the same, Delphine. A little fatter, maybe, and all the more beautiful for it. In prison, I never let myself think of her. That's the same as always thinking of her, in a way.

I should write to her to explain myself since I hardly had a chance. That's why I asked my host for this paper. Instead I'm using it to work out whether I'm a lunatic.

It was pouring rain when I dropped myself on Delphine's doorstep in the middle of the night. A mercy, probably, because at that point it was the closest thing I'd had to a bath in the month since I fled Toulon. That's not saying much. All this matted hair made me smell like a wet dog.

I didn't expect anyone to answer my knock, especially not Delphine herself. She always used to tease me about not knowing what was proper, but I know ladies aren't supposed to open their own front doors, especially not after midnight when there are raving lunatics and escaped convicts on the loose. (I'm one of those. Maybe both. Does this diary count as raving?)

I thought I was having a vision. Delphine haloed in the doorway, still as a painting and untouched by the rain, staring at me like—well, like she was having a vision, or I suppose like she'd seen a ghost. That's what I must be to her. After nearly three years, I would have assumed I was dead, too.

Unfortunately for me, I was alive in the worst of all possible ways. The Christians are right about Hell, I think; they're just wrong about where it's located.

Anyway. Delphine. A vision. Utterly recognizable with all that amber hair falling to her elbows, glowing in the candlelight. Barefoot and dressed in an open robe and a nearly transparent shift, she wore an equally transparent expression of astonishment.

"Ari?"

Her voice trembled. Her throat rippled with a swallow. She blinked and the candlelight caught a certain wet shine in her eyes.

Shock constricted both of us like a net.

How she recognized me under the hair and the rags and the filth, I don't know, but it stunned me as much as it stunned her. No one had used my name in a long time. She said it like a question, and I didn't know the answer.

She reached for me, her hand breaching the dark, and then drew back before we could touch. The opportunity flashed and vanished. I didn't move. Or I don't think I moved. Maybe I flinched. I couldn't imagine it, what it might have felt like if her hand had arrived.

As I write this, I see that I was afraid of her touch. I wanted it and I was afraid of it. Even thinking of it, my heart feels like a bomb. A tearful embrace might have killed me.

And I think she was afraid of me. I hate that. But she withdrew her hand so quickly, and I can't blame her.

"Don't stand in the rain," she said, cloaking herself in composure like she always used to, kind but impatient. She stepped aside. "Come in."

She shouldn't have let me in so easily. I could have been anyone. But I was too selfish to say so. I was grateful, too, that whatever fear she'd felt—entirely reasonable fear— she'd set it aside. Delphine has always been brave.

I stepped over the threshold and into the dry, warm foyer.

"I thought you were dead," she said, as direct as ever. "Where have you been?"

"Prison," I managed. I spoke so little over the past three years that my voice shocks me every time. It's like a growl from the back of a cave. I used to discuss natural philosophy at salons. I can't always have sounded like such a feral creature. "I got out, but—"

I stopped speaking as a new person descended the stairs, pale feet flicking out from under the hem of a silk dressing gown. They must know the house well to walk around in the dark, I thought, at first assuming it was her husband, and then remembering that her brother's scullery maid had told me the husband in question was three months dead.

A lover, then.

With each step, Delphine's candle illuminated more of their body, though its shape was concealed by the loose dressing gown, clasped together only by a hand at their waist. Above that was a long, thin triangle of hairless chest.

The stranger's face was the last thing to enter the light. I squinted at the strong nose and jaw and the dark hair tied back in a braid, unable to form any thoughts.

"Delphine," said the stranger. "What are you doing? Who is this?"

"Ari," Delphine said faintly. "Camille, this is Ari."

Camille—naturally the stranger would have a name that could belong to either a man or a woman. The lack of explanation for Camille's presence, or even the briefest "Ari, this is Camille," chafed. I was the intruder. Camille was at home.

"You should not be answering the door in the middle of the night," Camille said, which I approved of, though I didn't want to, first because Delphine's new lover had said it and second because I was the one who'd knocked. "And I thought Ari was dead?"

"He says he was in prison," Delphine said, casting me an expectant glance.

That shook me out of my daze. "I was, but I escaped. I need shelter. I'm being hunted—"

"And you came here?" Camille said, outraged.

That hurt, which was interesting, because after so many beatings, I didn't think I could be hurt by mere words. And of course I had thought of it myself, that my presence might endanger Delphine, but she had what I needed.

"Of course we'll help you," Delphine said briskly. "I will give you a room for the rest of the night. My friend Camille will take you to her townhouse tomorrow."

That settled the question of how to refer to Camille, but raised so many others. And it hurt, too. Delphine had a new lover and no more interest in me. She wouldn't even let me stay past dawn.

"I will?" Camille was capable of a formidable expression.

"You will," Delphine said.

Despite everything, I was pleased that Delphine has remained as commanding as always. You'd never expect it of her, with all her frills and her laughter, but she could have been a general.

Delphine escorted me upstairs to a bedroom. Not hers. Camille followed a few steps behind like a guard, staying in the hallway but never taking her eyes from me.

"I won't trouble the servants for bath water at this hour, but I think I can find you something else to wear. You'll want your things. Wait here for a moment,"

Delphine said to me, as if I might be in a hurry to leave after traveling hundreds of kilometers of wilderness in order to find her again.

When she returned, she handed me a clean shirt, one of her dressing gowns and, more importantly, a brown paper package. It weighed almost nothing.

"I've lent the compass to a friend," she said. "She'll return it soon."

Her mention of the compass nearly stopped my heart. All this time, she had it and didn't search for me. She'd given it to someone else.

Had Delphine ever loved me? Or was that memory, like the crashing of the ocean in the Rue du Bac, a fabrication of my mind? I searched Delphine's face for any sign that she felt as shattered as I did, but I found nothing. She wouldn't meet my eyes.

The presence of the stranger Camille was the only thing that kept me from an outburst, or worse, falling to my knees to weep.

Camille and I were discreetly evicted this morning, after an event I can't bring myself to write about. We took a silent, uncomfortable carriage ride. The paper package on my lap might as well have been a stone. Camille left me in this bedroom after that. Most of the day has gone by, so I've had time and solitude enough to open it. Instead I've paced and fretted, either already mad or destined to be.

# CAMILLE DUPIN TO JULIE MORÈRE, MAY 11, 1825



My dear Julie,

I will hand this letter to you myself. I know I shouldn't be writing, and I have eschewed the mail, but these pages are the best way to inform both you and Victor of what happened this morning. You have my permission to share this with him.

First: you remember Delphine's dead lover Ari? He's not dead. He arrived at her door in the middle of the night, claiming he'd been in prison—not merely in prison, but doing forced labor in Toulon—for the past two and a half years, and that someone was hunting him. Delphine seemed to recognize him. She let him stay the remainder of the night.

(Not in her bed with us. She offered him a different room. But still his presence agitated me too much for sleep.)

Second: you are aware that the loathsome Maximilien Taillefer has continued to write to Delphine despite her initial refusals and then her lack of response? Well, he also arrived at her door this morning.

His arrival woke me. I'd only fallen into a true sleep at dawn. Delphine, not habitually an early riser, had left the bedsheets to cool in her absence. She must have instructed her maid Amélie to dress her quietly so as not to disturb me. (Amélie knows about us and is unfazed by my frequent sharing of Delphine's bed.)

Delphine denied Taillefer entry, or rather she had the footmen deny him entry, and he forced his way into the foyer. The shouting drew me from her room. Reckless fool that she is, she confronted him herself at the bottom of the grand staircase. The footmen flanked her, putting themselves in Taillefer's way, but leaving enough space for Delphine to address him.

In the hall upstairs, in only my dressing gown, I nearly collided with Ari. He was in a dressing gown as well, rather than the rags he'd been wearing last night. It was one of Delphine's. Its hem only reached his calf and it was bedecked with ribbons. Ari didn't notice his own state or mine. Under his sun-leathered skin, he was grey. I can't say what he was feeling, but he looked ill. Worse than he'd looked when he arrived rain-soaked in the middle of the night, and he'd looked like a flea-bitten alley cat then.

I only stopped him from charging headlong down the stairs by saying "Ari" in an urgent whisper. He came to a halt, seemed to perceive me for the first time, and I suppose he put together that it would do harm to Delphine if Taillefer saw either of us, especially dressed as we were. In silent distress, he turned his attention once more to the argument in the foyer.

"An escaped convict was seen in this neighborhood, Madame la Marquise, I beg you, let me see to your safety," Taillefer said.

I pressed myself against the wall near the stairs, unseen

but with a view into the foyer if I cautiously craned my neck. I gestured for Ari to join me so he would be out of sight. With great reluctance, he did. He left a large gap between his shoulder and mine, unwilling to come any closer to me. I knew he was itching to take my spot closer to the stairs—closer to Delphine. He kept his posture rigid. I swear his thumping heartbeat vibrated the wall behind us.

"No escaped convicts have entered my house without permission, but one obnoxious industrialist has," Delphine said. She rarely raises her voice. She wasn't shouting, merely performing for the benefit of her household, myself and Ari included. Still, I could imagine how furiously pink her cheeks were from her tone. "I did not invite you, Monsieur Taillefer, and you assured me many times that you would do nothing to harm my reputation. Leave now."

"Delphine, I will not. Not while you're in danger."

"Madame la Marquise."

Taillefer made a sound of frustration. "Listen to sense, you impossible woman! I fear for your safety, Madame la Marquise. I didn't want to tell you this, but the escaped convict—this raving, murderous <u>madman</u>—is someone you used to know. We frequented salons with him. His name was Ari Lazare."

"None of that excuses your behavior, and none of it means anything to me," Delphine said, each word hammered like a pick into ice. I shivered to hear it.

I peeked around the corner to see her, resplendent in her severe mourning dress. A ray of sunlight from the high window over the door bronzed her hair. Standing in three-quarters view from my perspective, she stood between the footmen who blocked Taillefer from advancing any further into the house. Her eyes were narrowed. Her fingers dug into her hips so hard they were white at the tips. Taillefer should have turned and run from her. Even from a distance, I knew she wanted to strangle him.

I wondered if she'd put her late husband's pistol in her skirt pocket when she'd dressed this morning.

"I'm surprised you don't remember Lazare. Are you so heartless, Madame la Marquise? Everyone knows that you..."

"Please finish that sentence," Delphine said. "I'm seized with longing to know what salacious gossip you believe about me. Do you wish to slander your dear, departed friend Henri while you're here? Will you decorate my husband's corpse with a cuckold's horns?"

"Of course not. But before you married Henri, you were seen in Lazare's company," Taillefer said. "Often."

"Were you not also _often_ in his company, if you frequented the same salons?" Delphine asked. "Who is this Lazare to _you_?"

"A deceiver and a thief," Taillefer said. "He robbed me."

Next to me, Ari couldn't go more rigid, but it was possible he'd stopped breathing. He'd never specified _who_ was hunting him. If Ari did rob Taillefer, that puts Delphine in a precarious position. She's clearly decided to protect him regardless. I hope Ari understands what she's risking for him.

The deftness with which she deflected Taillefer's accusations stunned me. My admiration wasn't enough to mute the ominous hum of fear underlying the scene—no matter how clever Delphine was, Taillefer loomed over her.

The two footmen kept him at a distance, but they'd failed to keep him out of the house entirely. They're young. They probably didn't expect a man of Taillefer's wealth to disregard propriety and shove his way in, and thus weren't prepared to shove him in return. Next time, they'll know better.

Taillefer continued, "Whether or not you remember Lazare, he remembers you, and he was seen near here last night. You need protection from him. He might break into your house—"

"Or come to the front door and push his way past the footmen, as you have?" Delphine demanded. She pointed imperiously toward the exit. "More dangerous men than you have come and gone from this house, and yet here I remain. Get out."

"Respectfully, Madame la Marquise, refusing me is a grave error," Taillefer said. He turned toward the door and opened it a crack, his hand lingering on the handle. "I will protect you regardless. Soon enough, Lazare will come here. He never could resist you. When he comes, I will be waiting, and I will force him to give back what he stole from me and more."

When the door shut at last, Ari crumpled to the floor. He put his head between his bent knees and drank in air by the gulp. Needless to say, he bears no resemblance to Taillefer's story of a violent madman. (Nor does he bear any resemblance to the man from Delphine's stories, but that is a matter for some other time.) Delphine sat on the bottom step and tried vainly to still her own trembling until I went down to put my arm around her shoulders.

"I won't leave you alone here," I said to her.

"You have to. It's the best way to keep Ari and—" Delphine cleared her throat. "To keep Ari safe. Taillefer doesn't know about you and me; he won't look for Ari at your house."

I'm quite certain she meant to say "to keep Ari and Octave safe," but she didn't say Octave's name. Perhaps it was too frightening to mention him in connection with such a threat, or perhaps she thought Ari was listening and couldn't bear to explain Octave yet. I don't know. I do understand that she wants to keep her child away from danger, as any reasonable mother would, but she failed to address my main concern. I said, "And what about keeping you safe?"

She lifted her chin. "I told you, I will do that myself."

I won't bother to record the rest of our argument. Delphine has an iron will. I brought Ari home with me.

There it is. If you and Victor have any notion of how to keep Taillefer from his pursuit of Delphine—and, I suppose, his pursuit of Ari—please tell me.

If you have any notion of how I might extricate myself from this unfortunate tangle without ripping out my heart or abandoning Delphine to Taillefer's clutches, tell me that as well.


Your friend,
  Camille

# DELPHINE TO ISABELLE DE TOURZIN, MAY 11, 1825

## WRITTEN ON ENCRYPTED PAPER AND SENT BY PRIVATE COURIER

Dear Isabelle,

Your associate (?) Victor has informed me that you're traveling. I hope you're not still looking for Ari, as he's here.

God, Isabelle, the shock of seeing him—

You'll wonder why I'm writing to you again when we've only met once. You specifically instructed me not to write. I am contravening your wishes.

Unfortunately for you, I'm finely attuned to what I can get away with, and I know you'll permit this. You made a touching offer to do violence on my behalf. I prefer to believe it's because you're dazzled by my charms, and not because we've both worn the same undesirable piece of jewelry, but either way, it moved me.

I may still need to accept your offer, by the way. Taillefer was here again this morning. If you don't return to Paris soon, I don't know what I'll do.

Taillefer was looking for Ari.

I hid Ari at Camille's house. (Do you know Camille? Camille Dupin, that is, the novelist and beautiful genius who's having an affair with me.) Neither of them cared for my plan, but there wasn't time for a better one.

I don't know what to do, Isabelle. Not merely about Taillefer, but about Ari and Camille—and Octave.

For years I imagined my reunion with Ari as an embrace and a heartfelt outpouring of emotions, something straightforward and romantic, not shot through with doubt and fear.

Ari showed up on my doorstep thoroughly uncivilized. Possibly you're the reason he returned to Paris, though your methods are unknown to me. Anyway, I almost didn't recognize him. When I did, it knocked the breath from my lungs.

To know him despite the changes, to see him again after all these years, oh, it <u>hurt</u>, Isabelle.

And I was afraid. Of him, for him, for myself, for Camille, and even for Octave, though I don't want to be.

I want that fantasy reunion, the one where we kiss and say "I love you." But I'm not the person I was when he disappeared, and Ari—I can't say who he is. I don't know.

He's still handsome under it all—I do pride myself on my taste—but frightful. Not merely filthy, but haunted. Even scarred and half-starved, he is breathtaking. My heart aches just to think of him.

And he looks so, so much like [*this sentence is barely legible through a scribble*]

I know. I shouldn't be writing. You told me not to.

But where else am I to express all these feelings, Isabelle? I will die of it. I will explode and they will find little bits of me splattering the walls and the mess will be a terrible burden on the staff. This letter is saving my life, Isabelle.

Ideally I'd have another friend—ideally I'd have <u>many</u>

friends—to confide in, one whose heart was just gushing with compassion. Oh, that's a disconcerting image. Apologies. Anyway, all that to say I sense that you aren't at ease in the role of sympathetic listener, and I've made it worse by writing my woes in a letter, but after so many isolating years of marriage to that man, I've discovered that I don't have many true friends left. Everyone <u>likes</u> me, of course, let's not be ridiculous. I'm adorable. But nobody knows what I've been through except for you.

I've confided a great deal in Camille. I can't talk to her about this, though, because Ari's arrival has thrown everything between us into question.

Ari found me with Camille at an hour—and in a state —that made our liaison evident. So he knows. And Camille knows my history with him. I'm heartsick. What if I've lost them both?

Taillefer is a simple problem in comparison. Wherever you are, Isabelle, please come back and help me.


Your friend,
Delphine

Ari,

I notice you haven't left your room yet this morning. I had this tray of bread, butter, and raspberry jam made for you in case you don't feel well enough to come to the dining room. There is a cup of coffee as well, though I don't know if you drink it. Request whatever you like from the kitchen if this doesn't suit. You are free to explore the house at your leisure. The library is on the ground floor.

I have included a note from Delphine that arrived this morning.


Camille

# CAMILLE TO DELPHINE, MAY 12, 1825

## SENT BY PRIVATE COURIER

Delphine,

Are you quite sure this person you have foisted upon my hospitality is the Ari you described to me at such length? I feel as though I know that man, but this one is a stranger.

He's ensconced himself in the blue bedroom as a gloomy, skittish presence. I'd suspect him of being a ghost, except that he's entirely too solid. All sinew and scar, his weathered body is a knotted tangle of jute rope. So are his hair and his beard for that matter. They cloud his face like a great dark storm. I have offered him shears and a razor to no avail.

He did, at least, accept clean clothes to replace the shredded, infested rags he arrived in. He began to strip in front of me mechanically and without a care for his privacy. I had to turn away swiftly to avoid seeing more.

My trousers are too short for him and my frock coats too narrow through the shoulders, but I have not yet been able to persuade him to accept a visit from the tailor.

His sole request was a pen and some paper. He ought to be ravenous, but he's hardly eaten. I suspect he's not sleeping. What do you wish me to do with him?


Yours,
    Camille

# DELPHINE TO CAMILLE, MAY 12, 1825

## SENT BY PRIVATE COURIER

Camille, sweetness itself,

I miss you this morning. Octave has been asking for "Cami," and making such pleading eyes at me, but I told him you could not come see us today as you were doing very important work, which is the truth.

All I wish you to do is house Ari and feed him. Leave the rest to me, including Taillefer.

And if you could please not mention Octave for the moment, I think that would be best. Ari seems in a delicate state and I don't wish to give him a shock.

Yours,
Delphine

# DELPHINE TO ARI, MAY 12, 1825

## SENT BY PRIVATE COURIER, TUCKED UNDER A TRAY LEFT OUTSIDE THE DOOR

Ari,

I hope you will offer me an explanation for these last two years and eight months of absence—yes, I counted. Was Taillefer telling the truth when he said you robbed him? Once I understand, I will do my best to help you.

In the meantime, Camille is a dear friend and I know she will take care of you. Please repay her hospitality with kindness.


Delphine

Dear Camille,

What a terrible day you had yesterday.

Regarding T***, V's proposed solutions are [*a scribble renders this illegible*] On second thought, if you want to discuss that, it's best to do it face to face.


With affection,
Julie

# CAMILLE TO ARI, MAY 13, 1825
## TUCKED UNDER A TRAY LEFT OUTSIDE THE DOOR

Ari,

You hardly ate yesterday. We're in strange circumstances and I don't mean to nag you, but if I have to tell Delphine that you starved to death under my roof after miraculously escaping from prison, she won't take it well. I dread disappointing her. I suspect you know the feeling.

Here is a new assortment of offerings in the hope that something will tempt you: more bread, butter, jam, coffee, and a small pot of extra cream, with the addition of hot chocolate, tea, a little honey, a croissant, a soft-boiled egg, half an orange from this winter's last shipment, and three tiny strawberries from the kitchen garden. They are the first of the spring.

Camille

# CAMILLE TO DELPHINE, MAY 13, 1825

## WRITTEN ON THE REVERSE OF THE PREVIOUS LETTER, SENT BY PRIVATE COURIER

D—

You want me to house your wounded former lover and lie to him about your child? God knows why I put up with you.

—C

# DELPHINE TO CAMILLE, MAY 13, 1825

## WRITTEN UNDER THE TEXT OF THE PREVIOUS LETTER, SENT BY PRIVATE COURIER

Camille, my nimble, long-legged doe, we both know why you put up with me and it has nothing to do with God.

I wept in the bath tonight. It's been so long since I did either of those things. My eyes haven't produced tears since some time in 1823. Toulon created a sort of vacuum inside me. It was the only way I could go on.

And the bath—well. A kindness from my mysterious host, I think, though she didn't write me one of her little notes. Someone from her staff simply summoned me to the room where a copper soaking tub was already brimming with water. Steam clouded the air. I inhaled a huge gulp of it deep into my lungs and could have floated before I even set foot in the water.

I scrubbed myself down before I got in. I was unthinkably filthy. But sometimes it's good not to think—about how goddamn grimy I was, and how I got that way, and how long it had been since anything felt even halfway nice, and what the hell I'm doing and whether it's as doomed as it was the first time I tried it. What a relief just to scrub and rinse and sit in some hot water and not think. Let the rusty gears of my brain stop their useless shrieking and grinding. I didn't realize I was going to cry until it happened. Thought it was splashed bathwater at first, but I hadn't moved. I'd forgotten the sensation. Tears, bath, the strange, loose lightness of having cried, all of it feels so unfamiliar. Like I really did come back from the dead.

Had to sit up with my knees bent to fit in the tub. Probably for the best. Might have stayed there for hours if I'd been more comfortable.

Delphine,

It is a pleasure to write your name. I learned your new surname and title in my quest to find you, but they separate us by such a vast gulf that I don't wish to write them. For the same reason, I never cared for your maiden surname, either. Only your given name.

Was it a pleasure for you to write mine? Or did you feel nothing, as your brief note suggests?

Forgive me. I used to write you love letters and I fear I've lost my touch. This fine paper, gifted to me by your friend Camille, is worthy of you, at least.

I could not permit myself to think of you—the ring of your laughter, the velvet of your skin—in the prison in Toulon, where it is a torment to have a body, a thing for hauling lumber and taking whippings, let alone to think of the sweetness of someone else's.

But I did dream of your letters.

Of the soft scrape of the loose rock in the churchyard wall where we used to slip notes to each other, of the weight of your expensive cream-colored paper, of the faint scent I always imagined lingering there, but most of all of the sinuous line of your cursive looping across the page. Always unsigned, but so unmistakably yours. I could piece together the signature in my mind's eye, having pored over the sloping majesty of your capital Ds and the delicate tails of your final Es. The fine slant of your given name in writing, an intimacy we never risked, only ever existed in my imaginings.

Now that you've been widowed and I'm a wanted criminal on the loose, I can write it as much as I like.

Delphine, Delphine. I would have carved it into my cell wall or burned it into my skin—far better to have your name on my shoulder than the brand TFP, *travaux forcés à perpétuité*, hard labor for life—but I couldn't bring myself to sully your letters with such unworthy surfaces. It would not have brought me what I wanted: you.

Did you go to the churchyard after I disappeared? To the crack in the wall where we slid our secrets? I'm not sure what hurts more: to envision you leaving letters there and receiving no replies, or to picture the grass untrodden by your footprints.

You believed me dead. I suppose that's preferable to believing me the bastard who abandoned you.

I never wanted to leave you. I didn't want to come back to you with my reason shredded to rags, either, but it was that or never return.

You asked me to explain myself and I've dawdled for paragraphs. Here are some excuses, all genuine: I fear to commit the truth to paper; I lack important details; I worry you will judge my choices as harshly as I do; I long to write you a love letter, and this history has no place in one. But you asked, and I always want to do as you ask, Delphine.

In brief, T*** told the truth. What I did was a crime according to the law, but it was justice—or an attempt at justice—for me. Writing more about the act itself would be unwise.

Perhaps you don't recall that during those heady years we spent meeting at salons and sneaking around in other people's darkened gardens (and on one especially cherished and memorable occasion for me, on a chaise longue in the Comte de Davrance's study)—

Let me begin again.

You know I dreamed of pursuing my own researches. In the summer of 1822, I stumbled across some artifacts with unusual effects. Take, for example, the linen kerchief. It can wipe away a memory as you use it to blot your face, or to restore that same memory at its next use. These effects could not be explained by the objects' material properties. Fascinated, I needed more specimens to examine, but such artifacts are rare. When they're for sale, which they're often not, they're costly.

T*** claimed to have a collection. I didn't care for him, but my curiosity overpowered me. We spent one evening at his home. It was never my intention to keep any of this from you. Even as I was touring his house, I was saving all my snide remarks about him to tell you later. I never had the chance. The course of our meeting made clear to me that he simply could not be allowed to possess these items. I know I owe you a better truth—that is to say, a decidedly worse, but fuller truth—but I can't bring myself to write it.

I should not have eaten of that fruit, but once I had, the world was not the same for me.

Afterward, I took precautions to protect myself. You must have found the note I left you, if you had my compass. None of it mattered. I was discovered, waylaid by masked men, interrogated, beaten, and then handed into the custody of the police along with a considerable bribe. Then I was chained by my neck to a parade of other unfortunate souls and marched to Lyon. From there, we were put on a boat and taken down the river to Toulon, where I spent an eternity. It took three weeks to travel there and longer to travel back to Paris, sleeping rough and stealing what I needed to survive. The time in between those journeys is marked for me by only two things, one of which is that I still limp from the iron manacle that was once locked around my ankle, and likely always will.

The other is that every month for the first six months of my captivity, and once every six months thereafter, one of T***'s men of business came to see me. A slight, middle-aged clerk in a modest but neat brown suit, he didn't seem like a servant of evil. We had the same conversation every time: he offered my freedom in exchange for the where-abouts of what I had stolen. I never answered. As much as I would like to believe in my own steadfast commitment to righteousness, I owe you honesty, Delphine. I neither knew the location nor believed his offer. So I remained in Hell. When I left that place, it was by a plan of my own devising and a great deal of luck.

This is not the letter I dreamed of writing. What I wanted most was to die or come back to you. In both cases, <u>almost</u> fails to satisfy.


Yours,
  Ari

# DELPHINE TO ARI, MAY 15, 1825

## SENT BY PRIVATE COURIER

Ari, darling,

Reading gave me a strange, doubled sensation of being who I was in the summer of 1822, wildly in love with you and untouched by the grief of your loss, and at the same time being who I am in the spring of 1825, hurt and angry that we were separated, that you suffered so, and fragile like hope has split me right down the middle.

Even when you are recounting the direst of things, it lifts my heart to see your handwriting. I am so, so glad that you're alive. Please come see me as soon as you can do so safely—I have faith that between you and Camille, the two of you can work out how to get here unseen.

Of course I remember the chaise longue. I remember the tree trunk in the Baron de Sainte-Claire's garden, too.


Yours,
Delphine

To myself at some future date,

I'm enclosing this note with a particular linen kerchief and leaving both in Delphine's care. Anyone who touches the kerchief will remember where I hid something—at the price of one of their own memories. It is possible to select a memory by meditating on it. If your concentration fails you, one will be taken at random. Don't hold the kerchief to your brow for too long.

I know nothing of your circumstances except that you are alive to read this letter. There are very few instances in which I would advise remembering what this kerchief holds. If Maximilien Taillefer is dead, or if you know a reliable method of destroying cursed artifacts, it is safe to do so.

Or if you haven't escaped Taillefer, and you need to arm yourself with anything available—in that case I leave you the only weapon I have.

# PRIVATE DIARY OF ARI LAZARE, MAY 16, 1825

I tried to leave Camille's tonight.

Pacing the luxurious room she's provided me accomplishes nothing. Taillefer had me thrown in prison, he knows of my escape, and I can't see Delphine again until I know he won't hurt her. I waited until three in the morning. It was easy to slip out, as I own nothing. The clothes I'm wearing belong to Camille, and thus might constitute another theft, but I didn't think she would send me back to Toulon.

My feet were quiet on the stone threshold, or at least as quiet as my strange, shuffling walk can be. I reached for the door and found Camille instead.

She stopped the progress of my hand by wrapping her fingers around my forearm.

Her grip startled me. Knowing where her hand was, I was able to make out the contours of her figure. She's not as tall as me, but something about the way she carries herself makes her seem tall. Perhaps it's just that she's not a trembling, flinching, sweating mess.

"Why are you leaning in your own doorway in the dark at three in the morning?"

"That's the longest sentence I've ever heard you say," she replied. "Leaning is more comfortable than standing. I'm here to stop you from sneaking out of my house—in the dark, at three in the morning, I might mention. Are the sheets not soft enough?"

The caustic tone of her question made me reconsider the notes she'd sent with breakfast. Perhaps they hadn't been as sweet as I'd assumed. The last of the winter oranges and the first of the strawberries spoke for themselves, though.

Camille's grip loosened as she spoke, but her hand remained. I found it curiously reassuring. She didn't want me to leave, but she wasn't chaining me.

"Delphine asked me to give you shelter," she continued. She said it like anything Delphine asked for was a sacred charge. I know that feeling, and in a less pitiful condition, it might have sparked jealousy. Instead, my heart curled in on itself with despair while she spoke. "If you want shelter elsewhere, that's fine. I'll help you find it. But I can't imagine you're going somewhere safer if this is how you're choosing to leave."

Her words snagged my mind like a bramble by the side of the road. I couldn't pull myself free to form a coherent response. "You... what?"

"Perhaps we could have this conversation sitting down," she said. "With a lit candle, or a glass of brandy."

She led me to another room and retrieved both for herself. I shook my head at her offer of brandy, feeling too dazed already. Shadowed arrays of books surrounded us. Her library was large, its luxury obvious even in the light of one candle, the parquet and the polished wood of the tables and armchairs gleaming. The light caught on a mirror extending from the fireplace mantel to the high ceiling. I avoided my own dim reflection and studied Camille instead. She was wearing the same silk dressing gown she'd had on at Delphine's, an embroidered purple thing that made her look like a debauched prince. It was closed this time, revealing nothing below her neck, which was something of a relief. Her brown hair was braided and her feet were bare.

"I can't stay here," I said before she could start.

A slow sip of brandy and an uncomfortably long regard later, she said, "Not that I'm eager to have you as a guest, but why not?"

"I need to stop the man who put me in prison." I worried she would ask me about my reaction to his intrusion at Delphine's. I couldn't bring myself to say his name. Even writing it is excruciating.

It also seemed imprudent to tell her I was going to the woods to dig up what I'd buried there.

"Certainly," she said, sparing me an interrogation for the moment. "I'd like that as well. Who else in Paris can shelter you?"

A cruel question. I'm an escaped convict, wanted by the law, and far worse, hunted by Maximilien Taillefer. My presence endangers anyone who offers me their home— not that there is anyone else.

In response to my silence, Camille pressed, "Family? Friends?"

"My parents have been gone for years, I have no siblings, and everyone I used to know thinks I'm dead." I could scrounge up some cousins, perhaps, but we were never close. I was an apostate then and I'm worse now. Besides, they're poor and would have no defense if the law came to trouble them. And by now they'd likely have little children, another vulnerability. My various colleagues in science might not remember me, not even Hassan, with whom I'd had a more intimate friendship. Even if he does remember me, his work for the King's menagerie makes him both too visible and too difficult to visit. Delphine is a rich Gentile, and from what I can tell, so is Camille. That affords them some protection. "I remind you I was in prison."

"So it's only me, then," Camille said.

All my possible replies scraped my throat as I swallowed them. I yearned for Delphine, who was closer to me than she'd been in years, yet still unreachable. She'd stuck me with this stranger. I thought fleetingly of all the friends I'd chatted with at salons in another lifetime, people who wouldn't recognize or remember me, people who'd be disturbed by a bedraggled ex-prisoner at their door, and wished I could rely on anyone but the quiet eccentric in the chair across from me.

Camille said, "Your entry into prison is as interesting to me as your exit, and you've said nothing of the latter."

"How I got out?" I used to be a scholar, damn it. Rephrasing her statements as simple questions made me feel like I had jelly sloshing around inside my skull.

"Yes, Ari. How you got out."

Camille had taken my shredded rags and given me clothes, so she'd likely seen the brand on my shoulder that marked me for life in prison. Even if she hadn't, the filthy uniform and snarled hair didn't grant me the appearance of someone who'd been allowed to stroll freely out of Toulon.

"It will be difficult to believe," I warned her.

"I've encountered my fair share of unbelievable things recently."

Her calm made me grit my teeth. I wanted to unsettle her. It's unfair of me to take against Camille as I have, but I can't help it. She has everything: food, clothing, shelter, money, health, reason, <u>Delphine</u>.

And the capacity to extend hospitality to Delphine's feral, presumed-dead ex-lover. I wish Camille was unkind; my resentment would feel less petty.

"I found a coin in late March," I said. "A five-centime piece from the Revolution. It's marked Year 8."

Instead of wondering why I was offering her such irrelevant information in response to her question about my escape, Camille asked, "You <u>found</u> it? Who has coins in prison?"

"Guards, of course, but it could have been anyone's. We worked in the shipyards, you know. One day I was working and the toe of my shoe scraped something in the dirt, and I picked it up. I don't know why I kept it—as you said, I had no use for money—except that it was odd, finding such an old coin, and it was one little thing to distinguish that morning from an endless string of similarly miserable mornings. It felt... lucky."

I paused. I wanted to explain to her how strange—how absurd and impossible—it was for anything to feel <u>lucky</u> in that place, but I couldn't find the words. Dark-eyed in the candlelight, she watched and listened, and I had the inexplicable impression that she understood at least a little of what I'd left unspoken. No doubt that's part of my loss of reason, to imagine a person such as Camille, in a silk dressing gown and an upholstered chair, soft slender fingers wrapped around a glass of brandy, understanding the hopelessness of Toulon.

Surprising me yet again, she said, "The feeling you had,

can you describe it? Was it a sensation? A warmth, a vibration?"

She'd said she'd encountered unbelievable things recently. Perhaps she'd found an artifact like the ones I'd upended my life stealing. Or something better, like the coin.

Maybe it was the hour, or the darkness, or the fact that my life was already in ruins. I said, "You know about magic."

"Not much," she said and offered nothing further.

"Yes, the coin was magic," I said, answering the question she hadn't asked aloud. I hid my disappointment. What did she know? Did Delphine know it, too? "But the magic didn't manifest as a sensation. I just wanted it. I hadn't wanted anything in a long time. Finding the coin felt lucky, and then when the guards and other inmates didn't find it and take it from me, that felt luckier still. I was familiar with other unusual artifacts, so I wondered about the coin. I had nothing better to think about. I took to touching it all the time, and sometimes flipping it, if nobody was looking. Childishly wishing for things like 'Heads, and that guard doesn't notice me.'"

"It worked," Camille guessed.

"It worked. If the coin showed tails, I knew something unlucky was about to happen. Heads, things would go well for me. The chain to my ankle manacle had a weak, rusted link. The most incompetent guards were on duty. Someone was drying laundry that happened to fit me just as I needed to change out of the uniform that identified me as a prisoner. It took days of testing and waiting, but I was able to choose the moment of my escape just as everything aligned."

"And you still have it?"

I didn't want to hand it to her for inspection, so my response was grudging. "Would you throw away something like that?"

"Perhaps one of your unlucky flips caused it to fall into the Seine and you lost it," she said. "You don't have to show it to me. I believe you. But why didn't you flip it before attempting to leave tonight?"

"I did," I said.

Using the coin has become a habit. I'd never have tried to slip out of her house without checking its prognostication. I'd chosen a fortunate moment to escape, at least according to my flip. Then again, supposedly I'd chosen a fortunate moment to knock on Delphine's door, and Camille had been there, too.

Maybe I'd worn through the coin's charm and it had stopped working.

"So encountering me constitutes good fortune for you. It would be gratifying if only I felt the same." Camille set her brandy glass on the table next to her armchair and stood up, stretching like a satisfied cat. "In that case, I suppose you'd best go back to bed."

Her insult slid over me with no effect. What irritated me was that I'd told her so much and I still knew nothing about her.

She sauntered off. I came back to the guest room, but sleep remains impossible, so I've written instead.

Ari,

It brings me such relief to see that you've been eating a little. Thank you for saving me from Delphine's disappointment. Perhaps you would be kind enough to continue to do so?

Not to diminish your efforts, but I am obliged to point out that three strawberries, half an orange, and a cup of coffee is not, in fact, a sustaining amount of food. I don't wish to overwhelm you, but a normal adult needs to eat not only more than that, but also multiple times a day, every day. It is also considered beneficial to leave one's room, and even one's house, though that latter may be unwise in your case, and I have been known to ignore such suggestions myself.

(You may wish to point out that I foiled your sole attempt to leave the house, but I think the restorative effect of an outing comes from sunlight, not skulking in the dark.)

Here is a reprise of yesterday's offerings, though there are no more oranges. My cook wanted to add a small selection of charcuterie, but I advised against it. Delphine had mentioned to me that you were Jewish, and it is my understanding that Jews don't eat such things. Though I also recall her reporting in shocked, delighted whispers that you had a certain philosophical tendency toward deism—something we share—so perhaps you do. My only concern is, as I have mentioned, that you not wither away while under my roof. If you do eat charcuterie, there is plenty in the kitchen, but you will have to leave your room to get it.


Camille

Is tomorrow's breakfast going to come with a whole essay?
Stop treating me like a child.

Camille, my handsome genius,

I worry my last letter was too flippant, and failed to convey how concerned I am for both you and Ari. I miss you every minute and never stop wishing I could be there.

Being trapped in this house and powerless recurs far too often in my life. I hate this place. Divesting myself of it through the solicitors is taking too long. Perhaps while Octave is napping today, I'll start ripping down wallpaper and prying up floorboards.

Do you have any news? If there's anything I could possibly do for you, please tell me. I want to help so much.

Could we devise a way to meet without being seen?


Yours,
Delphine


P.S. The enclosed drawing is Octave's work. He instructed me very firmly that it was a gift for Cami. The horse—yes,

that indistinct mass of lines is a horse, how could Maman
even need to ask such a silly question?—is Lancelot.

# CAMILLE TO DELPHINE, MAY 16, 1825

## SENT BY PRIVATE COURIER

Delphine,

I miss you as well, though in honesty I am not sure what we are to each other, or what our future holds. But I do miss you.

I will consider how I might arrange for you to see Ari.

Ari and I have discussed how he came back to Paris. There is still much he hasn't told me. He has, at least, bathed and taken a few meals, so I hope that eases your worries.

I also hope you haven't had any unwanted visitors since we departed, and that you would tell me immediately if you did.

Octave's portrait of Lancelot is a masterpiece. He truly captured his subject's attitude. Please express my gratitude to him, and tell him I will frame it and hang it in my study.

Yours,
Camille

# PRIVATE DIARY OF ARI LAZARE, MAY 17, 1825

I didn't even make it to the door last night. Camille was waiting for me in the foyer. This time, she'd already lit a candle. "You're trying to go somewhere," she said. "I thought you were simply fleeing before, but you have a destination in mind."

"That's not your affair."

Impatiently, she said, "Did you flip the coin?"

I should never have told her about the coin.

"You did," she guessed. "So it's good luck that you've found me again. Where are you going?"

I bristled. "Who are you to ask me that?"

"Your host, to begin with. And your lover's lover, or perhaps your former lover's former lover. We'll see. But I suppose Delphine didn't formally introduce us," she said.

It is maddeningly impossible to unsettle her. Worse, she was right: I didn't know her family name, or how she came to be living alone in relative luxury. Her Latin Quarter home is not so opulent as Taillefer's Right Bank monstrosity or the ancient Faubourg Saint-Germain pile of stone where Delphine now resides, but it's more than comfortable. The library alone is worth a fortune.

"My name is Camille Dupin."

"Like the novelist?"

"Oh, very much like."

The words landed like she'd smashed her elbow into a cluster of piano keys, though the blunder was mine. My ears rang. How had I failed to see it? Camille Dupin had written <u>Virginie</u>—the last novel I'd read before being abducted, imprisoned, and separated from the wonders of fiction for years. Delphine and I had read it together and discussed it endlessly. That reading had sweetened the book for me so it was almost inextricable from my love for Delphine.

And while I was gone, the author had fucked her.

How enormously unfair that Camille has slipped not only into Delphine's bed but also, somehow, into my memories of Delphine, leaving traces of herself everywhere. Like a cat pissing to mark its territory. She has my beloved and my beloved novel.

I gaped at her. Those teasing notes she'd left outside my door had been written in the same hand that had composed <u>Virginie</u>.

Before knowing that Camille was Camille <u>Dupin</u>, novelist, jealousy and antipathy had little hold on me. That Delphine had chosen someone else in my absence was a source of despair, and I felt a childish resentment of Camille and her good fortune and her generosity, but I couldn't hate anyone for the circumstances. I'd disappeared. If I'd been dead in truth, I would have wanted Delphine to find happiness without me.

I decided to hate Camille entirely for herself. For the

smug angle of her smile as she'd said "Oh, very much like." For the way she'd been unfailingly kind and hospitable to me out of loyalty to Delphine. For the way she moved and spoke with calm ease while fear dogged my every breath. For the way she leaned gracefully against the entry, her silence like a cloak and mine like a swarm of gnats. For the way the candlelight praised her untangled hair and unscarred skin. For the way she'd ruined my favorite book by having written it.

"Did you think Camille Dupin was a man?" she asked.

"I didn't give it much thought," I lied. Delphine and I had wondered for weeks before the papers had revealed Camille's idiosyncratic person, and we'd both been delighted to learn that the novelist was somewhere in between a man and a woman. Now I could never, ever tell her how many nights I'd lain hopelessly awake in prison retelling myself the love story in <u>Virginie</u>.

As with everything else, my dismissal didn't bother her. She said, "How did you arrive in prison? What can we do to keep you, and thus Delphine, from further danger? And, I ask again, where were you planning to go?"

"We," I repeated.

"We've established this. You're in my house. You are now my problem."

Bitterness coated my tongue. "You plan to solve me, then?"

"If it's possible, yes. And if it's possible, I'd like to keep Delphine out of this."

With reluctance, I said, "Keeping Delphine out of this may not be possible."

"She's very strong-willed," Camille said in a tone of agreement.

"Yes, but that's not why," I said, realizing that I was going to tell Camille the story despite my new commitment to hating her. Needing her help is another reason to hate her, I've decided. "But can we walk while we talk? I was on my way to retrieve some of my belongings."

"You're permitting me to accompany you," she said, entirely too smug. "Where are we going?"

"The woods. Southeast of the city."

"That will be a slow journey on foot. Do you ride?"

I thought about lying that I knew how, just so she wouldn't have the advantage, but she'd discover the truth soon enough. I spoke it as sharply as possible. "My father was a cobbler in Belleville. No, I don't ride."

"No matter, I'll give you a gentle horse," she said. "I suppose you want the cover of darkness and I won't be able to convince you to wait until morning."

"You have the right of it."

"It's a clear night. Good weather for an outing. You know where you're going?"

"I'd better," I said, and she took me to the stables, where I tried not to be impressed by how quick and thorough she was at checking over the horses and finding all the equipment we needed. The rich don't deserve praise for learning to do simple tasks without the aid of their servants. As she cinched the saddle on the chestnut gelding she'd called Arthur, I coughed. "We, ah, might need to bring a shovel."

"Oh, <u>might</u> we," she said and gave me a lopsided smile. "When you said you were retrieving your belongings from <u>the woods</u>, I assumed you'd left them out in the open."

She dutifully found and packed a shovel for me, and thankfully did not ask me what I would have done without her help. Then she dragged a wooden block next to Arthur the horse. Compared to my experience of the horses that draw carts through markets and shipyards, he'd seemed small. When Camille gestured for me to step on the block in order to get on top of him, it struck me that he was an enormous and powerful creature who could crush me beneath his hooves. It was impossible to say so to Camille, who'd promised me that Arthur was a good-natured, hard-working horse. I sweat fear into all the layers of my clothes (_her_ clothes) as I put my foot in the stirrup like she said to. Then I threw my leg over the horse's haunches and hauled myself onto his back. Camille corrected, or attempted to correct, a dozen things about the way I was sitting and holding the reins, then shrugged and said, "If you fall, just let yourself slide to the ground. Don't try to catch yourself with your arm, you'll break your wrist."

"How reassuring," I said, and kept my mouth closed while she swung herself onto her horse, a long-legged black stallion called Lancelot, in a single, effortless movement.

"Arthur will follow Lancelot," she told me. "You shouldn't have to do much."

"Isn't that backwards, Arthur following Lancelot?" I asked.

She smiled. "Usually they both follow Guinièvre, but she's at my house in the country."

The sky arched above us as we departed the city, only a few grey wisps of cloud strung between the stars. Cool and windless, the night furnished only the muted buzz of insects to accompany our horses' hooves and Camille's contented silence. Since my escape from prison, sometimes a fear of open spaces seizes me, but the darkness helped. So did Camille's presence.

It was an odd thing to see her lift her face and bask in the moonlight. In Toulon and on the long road back to Paris, I'd only considered the weather if it threatened my life or augmented my suffering. It had been years since I'd thought any day or night beautiful.

It would have been more beautiful without Arthur's allegedly placid walk heaving me from side to side, but I must not make the perfect the enemy of the good.

"I'll allow what you hid in the woods to surprise me," Camille said. "Let's return to the question of how you arrived in prison."

Here was a way to ruin what little enjoyment I'd felt. I didn't sigh. It was best to get through the story and be done. "I collected a few things, objects with strange properties, like the coin, with the intention of studying them."

"Ari," Camille interrupted. "By 'collected,' do you mean 'stole'?"

"In one case, yes," I said.

"From Taillefer?"

"Yes," I said tightly.

"What was it?"

"Well," I said. "I don't know."

The brim of her hat shadowed her face, which was just as well, because she was likely narrowing her eyes in suspicion or outright glaring.

"Truth-telling artifacts are common, whether they force people to confess the truth or simply identify lies. I knew he was likely to possess something of the sort, so as a precaution, I made myself forget what I'd taken and where I'd hidden it. I planned to remember once a suitable amount of time had passed. If he found me and asked me questions, I could say honestly that I didn't know."

"How can you make yourself forget something? Another artifact, I assume."

I explained about the kerchief, then said, "I, ah, gave it to Delphine."

A long, measured breath. I don't think Camille has decided to hate me as I've decided to hate her—most likely because I'm too pitiful—but in that moment, I sensed her wrestling with anger. "I see."

"I told her to keep it a secret and not to touch it, which she did. She gave it back as soon as I returned. I've already used it to restore a memory."

"You left her with something potentially dangerous and didn't warn her of any of this," Camille said.

I didn't have a good response to that, because Camille was right that I'd put Delphine at risk, so I said, "I did warn her. In my defense, I didn't know I'd be gone for years. Being abducted and imprisoned was not part of my plan."

"You knew what you were doing was dangerous," Camille said. "And yes, it's clear that all your plans failed spectacularly. Were you caught in flagrante delicto?"

This was unnecessarily insulting on her part, but chiding her for rudeness felt like admitting a weakness. I have too many of those already. "I wasn't caught in the act. I had time to bury something in the woods, as you can see."

"But not time enough to tell Delphine what had happened," she said.

"It took about fourteen hours from the time of the theft to the moment that two men grabbed me, hauled me to a dank little room somewhere, and interrogated me. They had a flute that would play true if I told the truth. I volunteered my truths quickly."

"And did they respect your honesty?"

I swallowed. "You already know that they didn't. They knew I was telling the truth, but they also knew I'd taken something. When I couldn't tell them what they wanted to know, they beat me. The next morning, I was in chains."

Triumph filled my chest at her sharp intake of breath. Finally I'd wielded some of the violence of my life against her. I deflated when she posed her next question so carefully.

"It <u>was</u> Taillefer who arranged for you to go to prison, wasn't it? You haven't said his name."

Camille asking gentle, perceptive questions about Taillefer made me desperate to slide bonelessly from Arthur's back, just as she'd advised, and then to sink into the dirt beneath his hooves, never to be seen again. To prevent that, I kept my hands clenched around the reins. "Yes."

She hummed, and thankfully said no more of him. "So you'll dig up your stolen treasure, and then we'll... handle the rest."

How exactly the two of us—a novelist and a cowardly escaped convict with nothing to his name—might "handle" someone powerful and cruel enough to condemn me to forced labor for life remained unspoken, as I'm sure neither of us could conceive of a solution.

Camille's shoulders slumped. I felt a twinge of regret for wanting to disturb her composure; once it was gone, I realized I'd been focusing on rattling her so I wouldn't have to think about just how badly I'd fucked up.

With a note of worry, Camille asked, "But you <u>do</u> remember how to find whatever it is you buried in the woods?"

I reassured her with more confidence than I felt. A fading footpath, hidden under the encroaching grass, marked the place where we turned from the road. The ground was less packed, and Arthur's hooves sank into the soft, muddy earth, slowing our progress through the pastures. Tree by tree, the forest surrounded us. Branches interlaced overheard and the moonlight thinned.

We dismounted before it became too dense to ride through. I removed myself from Arthur's back without tangling myself in any of the tack, kicking him, or bashing my head into the ground, but my method looked nothing like Camille's smooth descent. She handed me the shovel, then held both horses by their bridles. To my relief, the oak with the round burl protruding from its trunk hadn't been cut down. I dug in silence until I'd unearthed the wooden box. Uncovering it was as taxing as burying it, though I'd spent the eternity in between doing hard labor. If only it were my lack of sleep making my hands tremble as I lifted it from the dirt.

I didn't undo the latch, telling myself it was too dark for any useful examination of the box's contents. I held it under my arm as we walked the horses back toward the footpath. The night had grown misty as we emerged from the woods. The moonlight caught on drifts of air.

The first thing I pulled from the box was a letter.

(Hand cramping. Have to come back to this later.)

Even in the dark, I know my own handwriting. My hands shook. This was what I had come here for. After a glimpse, I folded the letter and put it back in the box for later, more private reading. Whatever it contained, I wasn't prepared to suffer it in front of Camille.

I ran my fingers over the worn brown leather cover of the journal where I'd kept my notes. A few extra pages stuck out beyond the edges—letters from Delphine I hadn't been able to part with. Underneath it lay a slim volume marked <u>A Catalog of Artifacts</u> by J. L. A. Malbosc, a frustratingly incomplete treatise that had cost me far too much money and taught me half of what I knew about magic. Next to the journal and the book, wrapped in canvas to prevent them from rattling, was a small ceramic jar.

"Is that jar for something cosmetic?" Camille asked, peering into the box. "Do you remember?"

I'd forgotten the jar was in the box, but I recognized it. "Yes, there's kohl in it. I don't know how old it is. The oil would've gone rancid by now if it were normal, but its properties seem to have altered."

"Is that the magic, then? Oil that doesn't go rancid? Magnificent and terrifying."

"Oh, no, the magic is enhanced vision. Or perhaps it's the everlasting oil that's magic, and the vision is an unintended consequence, but I'd been assuming it was the other way around. I wore it several times, but I'm not very good at applying it and after an hour or so, I'd forget it was on my face and walk out into the street with huge black smudges circling both eyes."

She laughed, and I forgot that I'd vowed to hate her. I wasn't very good at it.

"Does it have ill effects?" she asked. "Other than the smudges. Will you lose your vision if you wear it too much, or something of that nature?"

"You think I would have worn it if that were true?"

"I just thought... I thought most of these things were evil."

It was rare to hear Camille hesitate. "What sort of artifacts have you encountered?"

She shook her head. "It's not my story to tell. From what you're saying, I gather some artifacts are benign."

"People create them, and much of what people want is benign—blankets that always stay warm and dry, water flasks that never empty. The trade among the wealthy considers those objects less powerful, and therefore less desirable." After a moment, I said, "Do you want to try it?"

"The kohl?" Camille's voice lifted in surprise. "If you're sure it won't cause me harm."

The blunt, flat stick I'd used to apply the kohl wasn't in the box, but Camille slid her hand from her glove, swiped a finger through the jar, and held it in front of her face to squint at it. "Will you do it first?"

"Yes," I said, preparing to hand her the box so I could apply the kohl.

Instead, she reached toward my face.

Unaccustomed to gentle touch, I froze in terror, moving only to squeeze my eyes shut when her finger approached. All the unused, coiled energy of my body sprang into my heart, which jumped and beat against my ribs.

"My apologies, Ari," she said. When I opened my eyes, she'd withdrawn her hand without touching me. "I wasn't thinking. You should do it yourself."

"Yes." If she'd phrased it as a question, "would you prefer," I don't know if I would have had the courage to say that. Was I more afraid of her touching my face, or of her knowing that I was afraid of such a trivial, harmless thing? Did she already know I was afraid, or had she stopped simply because we were closer to strangers or enemies than friends? She'd called me <u>Ari</u> with such ease. To avoid further thought, I added, "Though you likely have more skill at applying it than I do."

"I might resemble a woman on occasion—emphasis on <u>might</u>—but applying makeup without a mirror is not among my powers," she said.

She accepted the box from me. I dipped a shaking finger into the kohl and dabbed my eyelids. The moonlight whitened, distinguishing the black shadows of the forest behind us from the silver-blue of the pastures and the grey of the road. The elegant lines of Camille's face sharpened. Her gaze flicked across my face, searching for some hidden consequence of the magic. Her pupils were large against the thin ring of her irises. Their color was difficult to determine in the limited palette of night, but my mind readily supplied that they'd been a warm brown in the library's candlelight, a detail I couldn't remember noticing and ought to have discarded. I could have counted her eyelashes.

"You don't have to," I said.

Bizarrely, that goaded her into dragging a dark line of kohl over each eye. True to her word, she'd done a slapdash job. I wish I'd laughed, but laughter no longer comes easily to me. It would have disguised my real reaction, which took me by surprise: the effect was fetching. The smudges made her eyes even more luminous. I could never, ever tell her that.

She blinked several times, stared at me, then turned to take in the night's new gradations of color and texture. "This is marvelous," she said. "I didn't know magic could do such things."

"Each object is as individual as its creator. While you might come across two with a similar effect, but they'll have entirely different methods and limitations. The variety is astounding, and as far as I know, there's been very little study. It's unclear how one would even undertake such a study, as people create them at random, they're scattered all over, and their owners tend to keep them secret. But like the kohl, they're not all malevolent."

"Wait." With undisguised suspicion, she asked, "Where did you get it?"

"The kohl I bought from a curio shop on the Quai de Voltaire. It was costly to me, but compared to the rest of the shop's wares, it was inexpensive," I said. "There was also a compass, but I gave it to Delphine."

"Oh," Camille said with an air of sudden comprehension. "I never understood why she had that with her all the time. When her husband was alive, she couldn't leave the house without a great deal of coaxing and scheming. What use is a compass when all you do is go from the bedroom to the nursery to the parlor?"

"She... kept it?" She'd told me she'd lent it to someone and I'd mistaken that for a lack of care. Because Delphine hadn't found me, I'd assumed she hadn't looked—after all, I'd been trapped in the same place for years.

So had she.

Camille said, "She had to take care to keep it from her husband. Any time we were out together, she'd take it from her reticule. I didn't realize it was magic. What does it do?"

"Do you know about Ørsted's compass?"

Her lips pursed for an instant. "I suppose I ought to?"

She was never uncertain or startled when I tried to make her so, and this time I hadn't intended to. I shook my head. I'd always hated it when people at salons tried to make themselves seem incomparably sophisticated by mentioning thinkers and ideas without explaining them, as though everyone who mattered would already know. "Ørsted is a Danish physicist. Utterly brilliant. A few years ago, he demonstrated a connection between magnetism and electricity using a compass."

"I recall hearing about this now. He made the compass needle point toward an electrified wire, is that correct?" At my nod, she said, "What does that have to do with your compass?"

I cleared my throat, slightly embarrassed. "Before I was an escaped convict, I made my living translating scientific texts. It wasn't what I wanted—I wanted to study at the École Polytechnique, but I couldn't afford the fees. Translation was adjacent to my real interests and it paid.

When I read about Ørsted's experiment, it was such a revelation, and it seemed like something I could recreate myself. I couldn't resist. Once I had the copper and zinc for the battery, all I needed was a compass, some wooden clamps, and a wire. It should have been simple. But I'd just met Delphine the night before and I was distracted. I couldn't stop thinking about her. My attempt to recreate the experiment failed. Soon after, it became clear that the compass I'd used no longer reliably pointed north."

Camille blinked her kohl-shadowed eyes. "Are you telling me your compass always points to Delphine?"

"It points in the direction of one's thoughts," I said, "which, in my case, is usually Delphine. She was the one who solved it. I was wandering around Paris in circles, following the compass on some inscrutable path, trying to understand what I'd done, if anything, and I kept running into her. She thought I was following her. She was right. I didn't know it until she said so."

"I'm sure she was modest about that discovery," Camille said.

The memory suffused me with warmth. "We saw each other four or five times on different days, and she winked every time. The last time, she was out for a stroll with her mother—I don't know if you've been subjected to Delphine's mother, but I hope not—when our paths crossed on the Pont Royal. We knew each other from attending the same salon, but I didn't want to let on in front of Madame de Montfleury, and apparently Delphine didn't, either. She bumped into me on the bridge. I dropped the compass, and while I was apologizing loudly and profusely for jostling her, she bent to pick it up and said, 'Sir, I think you dropped this. Oh, but look at that, it's broken. It doesn't point north.' In her hand, the compass needle spun languidly and slowed to a stop when the arrow was aimed at me. I'll never forget the way she smiled—as slow as the compass, but so deliberate, like she was drawing back a bow. My face reddened so much I'm sure people in the Tuileries could see the glow."

Camille laughed. Though the kohl didn't aid in discerning color at night, she could probably guess that a new flush had risen to my cheeks.

"Delphine kept hold of the compass and said, 'How fascinating. I wonder what happened to make it so. Well, my mother and I must go now, we're late to see our friends.' When she said 'my mother,' the needle moved toward Mme de Montfleury. I asked Delphine later how she'd figured it out so quickly and she shrugged and told me she hadn't had anything else of interest to think about. Before she left, Delphine pressed the compass firmly into my hand—her mother must have scolded her for days about the audacity, the impropriety—and of course, as soon as she did, the needle jumped. It landed on her so hard it was quivering. 'There,' she said, 'now you know where to go.'"

"I see why she carried it every time she left the house," Camille said. There was a note of sadness in her tone.

"I tried to make one for her, too. Not in anticipation of my own disappearance, but so she could find me for…"

"Illicit trysts?" Camille suggested.

"So she could find me when she wanted to," I finished. Certainly there'd been plenty of illicit trysts, but that wasn't all we were to each other, and Camille's joke nettled me. "My room at the boarding house was littered with compasses. Whatever I did, I haven't been able to reproduce the results. Magic is like that, I think. It emerges from some unknowable confluence of factors at a single instant, never to be replicated. Plenty of other people have successfully recreated Ørsted's results. I couldn't even recreate my own. Not that it mattered—when I did disappear, the compass was no help. Do you happen to know who has it? Delphine said she lent it to someone."

"I have a guess." Camille closed the box and placed it securely in one of the saddlebags.

She handled that box so lightly, as if it didn't contain the unknown terror of my past.

"Ari," she said gently, interrupting my dread. "We should ride."

I eyed Arthur with trepidation. Camille knelt in the mud next to him and formed a cradle with her hands.

"What are you doing?"

"Being your mounting block. Step here."

It was easier to put my boot in her hands than to let her touch my face, but the action still brought us closer together than I'd been to another human in years, not counting instances of violence. Her proximity set my insides churning, but I hid my reaction. Camille's gloved hands on my muddy boot didn't spark desire so much as loneliness. It's been too long since anyone touched me. Someone who came near enough could shiver in the absence wafting from me, like I'd entered a warm room still carrying a winter chill on my skin. I want closeness so much it terrifies me. Sex, too, but I'll scald myself if I start there.

And I want it with <u>Delphine</u>, not Camille.

Camille boosted me onto Arthur's back with ease. She mounted Lancelot without help, though he was the taller of the two horses. His long legs kept a graceful gait even over the soft, wet ground. Camille moved with him so well that she hardly seemed to move at all. They were gliding together effortlessly. I imagined Lancelot providing a smoother ride than the uneven one I was enduring, though it's probably unfair of me to blame Arthur for my own clumsiness.

Camille said, "Do you think you'll return to your research—once Taillefer's dealt with, that is?"

Her tone contained unmistakable disapproval. I said, "There is no future until Taillefer's dealt with."

Since she posed the question, I've reflected on it. I can't stomach the thought of studying more magical arti-facts if we survive this ordeal. That's not the life I want anymore. If Camille meant to taunt me about how I'm a penniless outlaw with nothing to offer Delphine—if any of us even lives through the threat I've brought—then she succeeded. So many doors are closed to me. The ones that remain open are just barely cracked; my former translation work, as poorly paid as it was, might be possible under a new identity. But even with a false name, I could never ask Delphine to tie herself to me through marriage. The risk is too great. In our life before, even though such a union seemed impossible, I used to dream of having children with her. That's all I've ever really wanted—a family with Delphine. The closest I can come now is to help her survive Taillefer and not screw up the rest of her life. It doesn't matter what becomes of me as long as Delphine lives.

Still, there is a grief for our old selves, for what could have been.

Once we'd been on the road again for a while, Camille frowned at Arthur's legs and asked me to stop and dismount. She dropped to the ground more fluidly than I did, then asked me to stand aside and pressed Lancelot's reins into my hands, as if I could possibly have stopped that enormous horse from fleeing if he'd had a mind to try.

Arthur agreeably lifted his hoof to show it to Camille and she murmured, "Damn."

"I don't like the sound of that," I said.

"It's not terrible—he's lost a shoe. I checked before we left, but it's been a long ride and there's been a lot of mud." She searched through a bag attached to Lancelot's saddle to retrieve a small metal tool, and then set about removing the other three shoes from Arthur's hooves. Knowing nothing about horses or their shoes, I was nevertheless entranced by her competence. As she worked, she said, "He'll have to walk home barefoot. We can walk or ride Lancelot. Your choice."

It would take us twice as long to return on foot, I knew. Camille was proposing that we ride the same horse. My tongue tied itself in knots. I wanted to insist that we walk. I wanted to say yes to riding with her. She knew well enough that I was in shambles, as I'd been shut up in her guest room and she'd been nagging me to eat. She'd perceived my fear when she'd tried to touch my face.

She was careful and kind. That mattered. So did the journey we'd undertaken together. I'd showed her things she'd never seen before and answered her questions. For a little while, I'd felt almost like the old Ari. He wouldn't have flinched from her touch. He would have been delighted to share a horse with such an adept, experienced rider as Camille, not least because she was, I had to admit, very handsome. He would already have flirted with her. I could hardly bring myself to answer a simple question.

I wanted very badly to appear unafraid. It would allow me to prolong this dream of being my old self, unaffected, and the two of us could continue for another few hours as we were, not Ari the ruin and Camille the genius, but two people closer to equal footing. Camille on the road didn't seem like Camille in her splendid house full of silk and strawberries and sentimental novels, my smug, patronizing rival for Delphine's affections. She'd become someone different, this amiable stranger who'd accompanied me into the woods to retrieve some artifacts and notes.

"Can Lancelot carry us both?"

Her mouth twisted like she was on the verge of making a joke, but all she said was, "He'll be fine."

Camille helped me mount. If anything remained of my dignity, it wouldn't have survived that farce. I managed to seat myself behind her. She calmed the horse and kept us from toppling to the ground.

A deeper and more private humiliation than dragging myself onto Lancelot's back was that I'd initially imagined myself in front of Camille, cradled in the strong V of her thighs, like a rescued damsel or a child in need of comfort. I said nothing and let the fantasy fade with only a brief pang. There were practical considerations: I was taller than her, and she needed to ride in front to direct us.

"Be passive," she told me. "Try not to touch your heels to his flanks. It's confusing for him to have two of us riding."

It was confusing to me, too. Delphine hadn't embraced me on the night of my return, and I'd spent the years before that in stark loneliness, untouched or chained and beaten. Clinging to Camille's waist represented such a reversal that it set me reeling. The brim of her hat poked me. My beard brushed the wool of her greatcoat. I breathed in the chill night air and the smell of her hair and skin.

She wasn't the person I most wanted to touch, but it

had been so long since anyone had willingly, peacefully put their body in contact with mine. Pressing myself to her back was like coffee quickening my senses and soothing some clawing need inside of me. In the end I was glad to be behind her, where she couldn't see my face and whatever trembling, wide-eyed mixture of awe and relief passed over it. If the kohl around my eyes revealed tear tracks when we returned to her stable and she lit a torch, she didn't mention it.

# ARI LAZARE TO ARI LAZARE, AUGUST 9, 1822
## UNSIGNED

To myself at some future date,

If you dug up this box in the woods, Maximilien Taillefer hasn't killed you yet. I hope he's not looming over your shoulder. With every fiber of my body, I hope you don't believe you're in love with him.

I am burying this box to keep one particular item out of Taillefer's disgusting clutches. It is so important to me that he never use it again that I shattered my entire life over it. I'm writing—and you're reading—this letter because you learned where I hid it, but you don't remember what it is.

If Taillefer is behind you, swing your shovel at his head. Don't stop until you're sure. A forest is a good place to leave a corpse, unlike the luxurious bed where I awoke next to him this morning.

Would I have killed him if I'd worked out a way to flee the scene of the crime? My nerve might have failed me even if I hadn't been addled. Emotionally, that is. As of this letter, my memory is in unbearably perfect condition. I remember last night's every excruciating caress and whisper. I remember so well I am sick with it. I remember the cloying, false desire thick in the back of my throat and heavy on my thoughts, and suffocated underneath it, the last clear breath of my real self—the knowledge that I did not want him.

I remember how we lay together afterward and he told me, idly dragging a finger from my collarbone to my navel, that he'd do the same to Delphine.

As it was, the best I could do this morning was to take his weapon and disappear.

He knows it was me who took it. There was no way to prevent that. If you lived to read this letter, you are undoubtedly suffering the consequences of my choice. I'm sorry for it, but it was hardly a choice at all. Some things are simple: Taillefer cannot have what is in this box.

To be precise, the item he cannot have is a fire striker. You will find it wrapped in chamois cloth under this letter. It is flat, sized to fit in the palm, and utterly ordinary in its appearance—a curved piece of steel with a break in it to fit the flint, though I removed the flint. A fire lit with this striker will produce an intoxicating smoke, rendering anyone who breathes it powerless to resist the one who lit the fire. It counterfeits not merely desire, but love.

It works best in a hearth. That was Taillefer's method last night. We had no need of a fire in the sticky summer heat, but I'd come to see his collection and he insisted on a demonstration. After that, it was too late. A candle or a cigar lit with a spill from the hearth fire can continue the effect—under the bile, I can still taste the cigar smoke he breathed into my mouth. This morning the hearth held a pile of cold ashes. The striker's effect ceases when the fire goes out. That's how I escaped.

I think it would be hard for Taillefer to use the striker

against you out here in the woods where the wind can dissipate smoke, but he has so many other resources.

All I can offer you is time. Between my writing and your reading, perhaps enough has changed that you'll now be able to solve the problem. I wish you luck.

# DELPHINE TO CAMILLE, MAY 18, 1825

## SENT BY PRIVATE COURIER

Camille, my artful sestina,

I don't know what we are to each other or what our future holds, either, but your absence makes me ache. I want to see you again. Yes, you <u>and</u> Ari, not Ari alone. Please don't write yourself out of the story just yet.

Do you think you could sneak in? At night, perhaps, or using one of the carts that delivers food in the morning.

No need to worry about me. I promise to tell you if that man comes to my door again. He hasn't. A couple of letters have arrived, but that hardly signifies. I declined to respond.

Octave has become passionate about drawing, so we are putting my late husband's correspondence to better use. Leaving behind such a trove of paper—and pencils, what a marvelous invention—is one of the best things that man ever did. Anyway, Octave insisted on gifting you another drawing. As I'm sure you can tell, this one is a portrait of Arthur.

I miss you. Come see me if you can.

. . .

Yours (I mean it),
Delphine

# CAMILLE TO DELPHINE, MAY 18, 1825

## SENT BY PRIVATE COURIER

Delphine,

You've made my life rather complicated, asking me to host Ari. He's in difficult circumstances, and I don't want to worsen things. I think the best solution for all three of us—the quickest, simplest way through this—is for me to help Ari extricate himself from danger. Then we will see where we stand.

Ari and I discussed the items that he left in your care. You returned the kerchief to him, but not the compass. What did you do with it?

Camille

# DELPHINE TO CAMILLE, MAY 19, 1825



Camille, my melancholy villanelle,

What's this about you helping Ari extricate himself from danger <u>without</u> me? I don't care for that at all. Let me help. You didn't respond to my suggestions about sneaking into the house. Shall I come to you instead? I think I could do it.

Regarding the compass, I lent it to my terrifying new friend—I told you about her, Victor and Julien's mysterious acquaintance Mme de Tourzin—in exchange for her aid finding Ari. Apologies for the undisguised bleakness of this thought, but I expected her to locate a grave. Evidently, she didn't find one. She simply left Paris with the compass and has not communicated with me since. I wrote to her about Taillefer in March, and again right after he came to the house. Victor told me she was traveling, and I think she's still traveling now. She needed the compass for an important purpose, and now that I know Ari is safe under your roof, I no longer have need of it except as a cherished souvenir. (Since I know you worry, let me assure you again that Taillefer has not come to the house since that morning a week ago. He persists in writing to me like a mosquito buzzing next to my ear.)

Octave has completed his trio of horse portraits with the enclosed drawing of Guinièvre. I think it's his best work yet.

Yours,
    Delphine

# CAMILLE TO DELPHINE, MAY 19, 1825
## SENT BY PRIVATE COURIER

Delphine,

There's no need to endanger yourself so recklessly by going out alone. I will bring Ari to you. Be patient.


Camille

My dear Julie,

Delphine and I are hardly seeing each other because her profoundly unwell former lover is haunting my house like a hairy ghost.

God, Julie, I'm trying to be thoughtful and responsible and I hate it. I've never hated anything so much. Delphine keeps asking me to come see her and I keep declining.

I've been avoiding her <u>in order to help the man she loves more than me</u>.

What is wrong with me, Julie?

I know what's wrong with Ari and Delphine—they've both suffered terribly—but I'm wealthy and famous and pampered, blessed with intellect, artistic genius, and rakish good looks, and nothing bad has ever happened to me. There is a straight and simple avenue to getting what I want, and it's evicting this man from my life and returning to Delphine's bed, and I can't understand why I'm not doing that.

. . .

Your foolish friend,
    Camille

Camille,

You have such a modest opinion of yourself, my friend. I notice your list of good qualities doesn't include a conscience, but you do have one. I know because you're trying to do what's right even though it's making your life worse.

As for nothing bad ever happening to you, I know you wish you hadn't told me about Lucien and Félix, but I haven't forgotten. That qualifies. I think you still carry it with you. Why else would you be so certain that Delphine will choose the long-absent Ari over you, the self-professed wealthy, handsome genius who saved her life?

I'm sorry that this has been so hard. If you want to come over and drink until you weep, I'll tell V to leave us alone.


Julie

I've avoided Camille since our ride, but she did inform me that Delphine requested that both of us visit her. "Discreetly," she said. She meant I ought to shave and do something with my hair to make me look less like a wild animal, and I did try. It wasn't even the blade of the razor that perturbed me.

It was the mirror.

Camille knocked several times, I think, before she opened the door and found me stuck in a chair transfixed by my reflection like the world's ugliest Narcissus.

"Ari," she said, and I have to credit her that she didn't sound exasperated that I'd made us late by staring in horror at my own reflection. Indeed, her voice was so gentle that it was unbearable, which would be a good reason to hate her, if I weren't failing at that, too.

"I can't," I said.

Camille removed the wet towel from my hand and set it on the table next to the untouched razor, brush, soap, shears, comb, and basin of water. A still life of defeat.

Then she sat on the edge of the bed, a careful distance away from me. "What is it that you can't do?"

Her interruption had broken the mirror's spell, but I didn't want to look at her or the abandoned tools. The blue bedding seemed a safe enough place to affix my unfocused gaze. "Shave. Leave. Any of it."

After a moment, she said, "One thing at a time, then. We'll start with shaving."

"Are you suggesting I let you hold the razor?"

"I'm in a better state to do it than you."

"I neither like nor trust you," I said, though this wasn't strictly true. Our midnight ride had thrown us into disarray, and now I didn't know what we were to each other. "Why would I let you near my neck with a blade?"

When she spoke, she didn't sound hurt, but I noticed the slight tightening of her fingers in the bedspread. "You don't have to like or trust me. Trust that I want Delphine, and she would never speak to me again if I hurt you."

She'd made an inarguable point, so I switched tactics. "Do you even know how to shave?"

"Yes," she said.

I scoffed. Camille wears trousers, but she doesn't have facial hair. "Why in the world would you know that?"

"I had a... lover," she said at length. "Or perhaps he was more of a friend. He was ailing, and was sometimes too sick to do it himself. So he taught me and I did it for him."

The sadness in her tone didn't feel like a victory. Whatever grim pleasure I'd taken in shocking and unsettling her with the horrors of my own life, there was none to be found in reminding her of her own suffering. I could tell she'd suffered; this friend and lover was gone. Thinking of her grieving made it even more difficult to hate her.

The idea of hating her had enticed me with its simplicity. So few things in my life are simple. I wanted this one to be. We are rivals, therefore we hate each other. Or, at least, I hate her. (See how it's already falling apart?) She doesn't hate me, not with the kind of devotion one might demand in a rival. She might feel some resentment or annoyance, but she gives me shelter and food. She takes me on midnight rides to help me dig up things I buried in the woods. She asks fascinating questions. She smells like soap and sweat and leather and woodsmoke. She's good with horses. She has nice eyes.

She stole the love of my life.

I might not hate <u>her</u>, but I hate this. I feel at sea.

"One of the household staff could shave you if you object to me," Camille offered. "Or I can find a barber."

"No," I snapped. Then, panicked and embarrassed—I intended to reject her help in a civilized, sneering way, not stomp my feet like a child, but these days I careen from one emotion to another with little control over what comes out of my mouth—I added, "They used to shave us. Like shearing sheep."

Camille made a small noise with her lips closed.

"They'd leave one sideburn long so we could be identified if we escaped," I mumbled. My hair had grown wild over the course of my journey across France on foot, so the asymmetry wasn't as obvious.

"You freed yourself," Camille said. She stood, took the towel from where she'd laid it on the table, and handed it to me. When I held it to my face, it was still warm. Perhaps not as much time had passed as I'd thought.

She passed me the brush next, already lathered with soap. I accepted it, the motions of this small daily task familiar to my hands. My thoughts quieted and I ceased to notice her presence, though she continued to stand nearby, taking tools when I finished with them and handing me what I needed next. I pulled at my cheeks and my upper lip with care, regarding myself in the mirror only as a series of planes, a problem in need of solving. The razor whispered over my skin. The long sideburn disappeared as though it had never been there. I dipped the razor into the water and washed the black stubble away, then blotted myself clean.

Slowly, my face emerged.

The sight transfixed me as much as before. There's a passage in <u>Virginie</u> where Virginie encounters her long-lost love and they leap into an embrace after the instant of recognition. Not that I could leap into an embrace with myself, and besides, it wasn't like that. Certainty slips out of my grasp these days, so it felt more like passing someone on the street and wondering where I'd seen them before. Were my brows always so dark, so thick, so drawn into a permanent scowl? Was my jaw always set so grimly? My skin wasn't so leathery from the sun, that I know. There wasn't a pale scar cutting from my forehead down toward the corner of my eye and another slashed across my chin. I didn't used to look so angular, so hollow.

I shook myself out of it and noticed Camille staring. Her lips were slightly parted. She averted her gaze as soon as our eyes met in the mirror, which seemed unlike her.

"You know if we're going to solve your problem, we'll have to go out, and it would be easier if your hair looked more... unobtrusive," she said, reaching for the comb and the shears.

"Fine," I said, scraped too raw to protest or question her skills. The haircut had to happen at some point, and I'd make a mess of it. If she did the work, I could close my eyes.

Dryly, she said, "You're not worried I'll stab you with the shears?"

"The razor would have been easier, you know."

"You're critiquing my choice of weapon?"

"I'm telling you that you missed your best chance," I said. "Or I suppose you could have staged an accident with the horses."

"You think Arthur might have snapped your neck while sweetly plodding along? You esteem him too highly. Besides, I haven't missed anything. You sleep in my house," she said, and it was such an outrage to decency, such a wildly wrong and terrible joke to make to the perpetually frightened wreck of a man taking shelter under her roof, that I let out a creak of laughter. It wasn't funny. A sharp-edged joke makes me feel like her equal, her adversary, a person. Gentle sincerity reminds me of everything I'm not.

I squinted at her in the mirror. My own reflection elicited too many feelings, but Camille's was a welcome respite from looking directly at her face, especially when it was lit with mischief. Her chestnut hair was coiffed today, piled on top of her head except for a few glossy spirals that fell around her face. It made a strange but handsome pairing with her grey waistcoat and trousers. She'd come into my room in her shirtsleeves, which seemed a breach of etiquette, though what etiquette exists for an androgynous novelist paying a visit to the escaped convict she's hosting at her lover's request, I don't know. Certainly it doesn't include threats of murder, even in jest. The shirtsleeves hardly mattered.

I said, "Who sleeps in this house? I don't, and based on our meetings in the middle of the night, neither do you."

Then Camille ruined the moment by frowning and

saying softly, "I've been meaning to ask you about that, Ari."

I tossed the wet towel at the mirror. It left a splotch. "Cut my damn hair."

She paused to roll up her sleeves and to call for more hot water and clean towels. The sight of her bare wrists distracted me for a moment. They were paler underneath than on top, the tendons and bones standing out in relief as she adjusted her sleeve. Her wrists were as strong and elegant as her long fingers with their neat, oval nails. She'd used her hands to write <u>Virginie</u>, and now she was going to use those same hands to touch the tragic bird's nest of my hair. Shame warmed my skin.

I shouldn't have agreed so easily to the haircut. Shaving had been such an obvious moment of vulnerability—the blade, my neck.

Camille washing my hair was worse.

It wasn't dangerous in the same way. There was little risk of injury. But my life has been devoid of pleasures these past few years, so I'm not prepared for them when they arrive. If I'd known, I would have guarded myself better against Camille. I unwittingly leaned back and placed myself in her hands, braced for the scornful, punitive handling I'd grown accustomed to in prison.

Instead, she made me feel good.

What comfort I'd derived from touching her during our return from the woods was my secret, and I could tell myself that sharing the horse had been a necessity, and Camille hadn't done anything other than ride. This was different. More frivolous. More obvious. More intimate.

Once she'd poured warm water over my head and begun to work her fingers through my tangled curls, it was too late to protest, and in the privacy of this journal, I can admit that I wouldn't have had the strength of will. I let her do it. I wanted her to do it. I bit the inside of my cheek to stifle a moan.

She wasn't lingering or being particularly sensual. I'm sure if she'd washed Delphine's hair, it would have been a more languorous experience. I was so pitifully deprived of normal human touch that even her brisk, practical movements overwhelmed me. Closing my eyes, I tried to pretend it was anyone but Camille making me feel this way. My efforts failed. Delphine would have been slower, sweeter, more playful. Camille was merely trying to make me slightly more presentable without hurting me, and still I could have melted.

It would always be between us now, this moment. She'd made me feel something I hadn't felt in years. That was a power she'd always have over me, and I'd yielded it to her.

She snipped at the ends of my hair, turning the shapeless, shaggy mass into something more acceptable for walking the streets of Paris. I didn't look quite so much like I'd spent a month sleeping in roadside ditches or piles of straw. The loose black curls of my hair never sit neatly in any arrangement, so she couldn't stamp out every trace of wildness, but she successfully tamed it from "vagabond" to "poet." Or some other eccentric, intellectual salon-going type, which is who I used to be.

Camille set the shears on the table and turned my head toward her. It was only the barest brush of her fingers against my temple and my chin, but I felt defenseless and sensitive. She was assessing her own work, not peering into my eyes to divine my secrets, but all the same I examined my feet.

"You'll do," she said.

"Not so hideous that children will run when they see me?"

"Children are braver than people give them credit for," she said. "Could I convince you to allow my tailor a visit? You're stretching out my clothes."

Only in the shoulders. Her trousers sagged at my hips and ended above my ankles, which probably gave the effect of a scarecrow—especially before my haircut—but I hadn't ventured beyond my face in the mirror. Once I would have cared about the fit of my clothes. In that other life, I'd dressed with the utmost care any time my path might cross Delphine's.

I yearned to see Delphine again but feared what might pass between us. We were hours late already, I knew, and I could feel the day dragging on and my lack of rest creeping up on me. Perhaps tomorrow would be better. If I agreed to see the tailor, would Camille know I was stalling? She always seemed to know everything. "Aren't we supposed to go to Delphine's?" My voice wasn't as steady as I wished. "Call the tailor if you wish."

"Delphine waited for you for three years," Camille said. "One more day is nothing."

"But she didn't," I said. "She thought I was dead. She got married. She found you."

It was weak and I shouldn't have said it. People of Delphine's wealth and class don't marry for love. I knew that then; I never forgot it. Whatever Delphine has with Camille is not my affair. And, as I'd said myself, Delphine had thought me dead.

"None of that stopped her from waiting for you," Camille assured me. She touched me under the chin, lifting my face. "Believe me, Ari, I wish it had."

And then she left.

My dear Julie,

I've made everything worse. Far too late, I understood that Delphine would never have fallen in love with Ari if he wasn't devastatingly handsome, something I helped reveal by obtaining a shave, a haircut, and new clothes for him. That's an error I won't make again. Should I find myself sheltering my lover's ex-lover in the future, I will leave them in their filthy rags.

I don't mean to malign Delphine as superficial. She also has a taste for brilliance, it seems. Humor, kindness, other good qualities I will make myself sick listing. He's intriguing and so pitifully haunted that even I want to take care of him.

And by total coincidence, he strongly resembles her darling child.

Life was simpler when I'd never met him and I wanted to push him off a cliff.


Camille

Camille's tailor came by a few hours after the haircut. We could have gone to Delphine's this evening, but instead Camille withdrew to her room, claiming she was tired.

I didn't believe her. For further proof that I am losing my mind, I knocked on her bedroom door at an hour when sensible people are asleep.

"If you don't like or trust me, the least you could do is leave me alone," she said once she'd opened the door. Slightly rumpled and red-eyed, she was wearing the purple silk dressing gown again. I'd never seen her hair loose before. It's longer than I suspected and it doesn't form those spirals on its own. It falls in gentle waves. Nothing else about Camille looked especially gentle at that moment.

"I'm sorry. I... don't know how to feel about you," I said. "But I know you're afraid to see Delphine."

"And you're not?"

"Of course I am. I'm also afraid of walking through open spaces and going to sleep. It's because I spent the last few years wishing for death in a hellish prison. What's your excuse?"

Camille's tired glare spoke obscenities, but she didn't slam the door. After a long moment, she said, "The woman I love is in love with someone else, and I don't want to see them together."

"I could say the same to you," I said.

"I really don't think you could," Camille replied. She pushed past me and shut the bedroom door behind her. "If you insist on talking to me at this hour, I will be getting drunk in the library. You can berate me there."

"I'm not berating you here or anywhere else," I said, but followed.

Our previous meeting in the library had only been lit by a single candle. Tonight Camille lit some of the wall sconces, drawing my eye upward. The bookshelves extended to the ceiling and lined every wall. They were all full. She'd bound most of her books in green leather and stored them with the gold-lettered spines facing out.

A perusal of the room made clear that she read Latin, Italian, English, and German, in addition to French, and she liked history and natural philosophy as well as fiction. I brightened, questions on the tip of my tongue, and then I saw a set of her novels and remembered who she was.

Camille was sprawled in one of the armchairs, sipping her cognac morosely. I sat and she poured a glug into a glass and shoved it toward me.

"I'm afraid to see her," she said. "But I wish she was here."

I raised my glass to that. We drank in silence for a few minutes and I said, "This would be more fun if Delphine were here."

"Everything is," Camille said. "It's too bad she goes for

gloomy intellectual types instead of people more like herself."

"You're not that gloomy," I said, and amended, "Usually."

Camille threw back the rest of her brandy. "According to her, you didn't used to be."

It was like being offered the apple from the Tree of Knowledge. I wasn't strong enough to refuse. "What did she tell you about me?"

To my surprise, Camille gave me a bright smile. Then I realized she was performing. "Ari is so <u>smart</u>, Camille. He's curious about everything. He's read as much as you have, in as many languages, and he can quote it from memory. And the way he reasons—" Camille paused to touch her sternum with a delicate gesture that was remarkably evocative of Delphine. "We asked so many questions together. What stuff thoughts might be made of, or feelings. Do you think some day we'll find them in the nervous fibers of the body? Does my affection for you exist somewhere in the particles that compose me, or is it intangible? He explained the steam locomotive to me, and the camera obscura as well. We wondered about the nature of sound and whether we'll ever capture it the way we can light and shadow in photograms. Oh, it might not sound like much to you, Camille, but even after attending dozens of salons, nobody treated me like I was worth talking to about such interesting things except for Ari. And now you."

This was a far longer answer than I'd expected from Camille, and it was strange to hear it coming from her in an imitation of Delphine's voice and manner—somewhat like the captured sound Delphine and I had once discussed, a years-later echo—because I remembered all of those conversations.

Camille wasn't finished.

"He was so quick-witted. Biting, sometimes, but you know I like that in a flirtation. And when a man is that beautiful, I take everything he says as a flirtation. I know I'm supposed to praise a man's shoulders or his muscular thighs, but Ari wasn't that sort of man. It was his lips and his eyelashes that I loved."

I shifted in my chair and began to regret my question.

Camille continued her recitation. "Ari liked to listen to me as much as I liked to listen to him, even though my areas of expertise are so few. I taught him about fashion— I think he would have been quite a dandy if he'd had more money. As it was, he did admirably with what he had. I also taught him what I knew of gossip and sentimental novels. Oh, Camille, he loved <u>Virginie</u>. We read it together and both wept at the end."

She turned a wicked smile on me, fully herself. The whole time I'd lived in her house, she'd known my love for her work—among far too many other things. I was grateful there hadn't been any details about what I was like in bed, although knowing Delphine, she might well have shared those.

"I must have disappointed you in so many ways," I told Camille.

"It's some consolation that you were equally disappointed to meet me."

"I'm baffled that you retained all those details. You thought I was dead," I said. Then, with another sip of brandy to warm my throat, something dawned on me that warmed my heart: Delphine had talked about me a <u>lot</u>. Another realization followed. "You were jealous."

"Delphine vastly overstated your powers of observation." Camille dropped her head to rest on the back of her chair. "It's a good thing you have impeccable taste in literature."

I drank instead of responding to that, wondering which of the things Delphine had loved were qualities I still possessed. I'm reasonably certain my eyelashes haven't changed.

"You know, Delphine pretended not to know who I was when we met," Camille said. "She was beautiful, so I introduced myself. I'd grown accustomed to some fawning by then. Even people who haven't read a word I've written usually know my reputation. The way I dress makes me especially easy to recognize. I'm controversial, but people are usually flattering in person. I said my name and Delphine said 'And what do you do?'"

Camille's imitation of Delphine's sweet, light, suspiciously innocent voice almost brought her into the room with us. It was so perfect that I laughed. The rough sound shocked us both.

"Oh, it gets worse," Camille said. "I stumbled over the sentence 'I'm... a novelist?' and then couldn't remember the title of <u>Virginie</u> for a moment. She pretended not to know that, either, so I gave her a terrible summary. I think I said 'There's a dog in it.'"

"Well," I said, smiling so broadly my face ached. "There <u>is</u> a dog in it."

"My friend Julien witnessed the whole thing and teased me relentlessly afterward," she said. "So did Delphine, naturally."

"Our first conversation was about pigments," I said. "I was talking with a small cluster of people at a salon about Thénard's discovery of cobalt blue, and Delphine asked whether we thought any of these new pigments could ever be used to dye fabric. I wasn't sure, but I don't know much about dyes, so I started asking questions. She knew a lot about various dyeing processes—how different fibers require different methods, what plants and animals produce what colors, that sort of thing."

"Your sudden interest in dyes had nothing to do with how pretty she was," Camille said.

I spread my hands. "When a beautiful woman wants to talk to me about something interesting, I listen. It's not a crime. But you know, she thought the same thing you did. After we'd been talking for a while, she said 'I hope you don't think you'll obtain anything other than conversation from me this evening.' I told her primly, with as much offended dignity as I could, that I hoped she didn't think she'd obtain anything from <u>me</u> other than conversation, and she laughed."

I paused, lost in the memory. That was another life. It saddened me to linger over the details. "We encountered each other many times over the next few weeks—the compass, salons—and eventually she obtained a great deal more than conversation."

"<u>She</u> obtained? Not you?"

"I didn't pursue her. She was too beautiful and too far above my station. I just enjoyed her company when I could. When she made it clear that she wanted me, I was too surprised to answer for a moment, and she thought I was declining. Can you imagine? Even in our first meetings, she could have had anything she wanted from me. I would have done anything for her. Ultimately, I did."

"Oh, don't," Camille said.

"Don't what?"

"You told me why you stole those cursed things. You did it to satisfy your own curiosity. To further your own ambitions. And then you disappeared and abandoned Delphine. It wasn't for her; it was for you."

"I suppose it was, but——" I took in and released a slow, sad breath. The brandy had loosened my tongue enough to tell the truth. "I have to tell you what happened with Taillefer."

My tone or my posture alerted her before I said another word, and she softened. "Oh."

"Mm."

"He cornered me and assaulted me at a salon once. Put his hand between my legs. Over my clothes, but it was still awful. I know he's assaulted other people, and if that's how he behaves in public, he must be worse in private," Camille said.

Quietly, I confirmed, "He is."

"I'm so sorry, Ari," she said. Forcefully, she added, "I wish I'd hit him after he touched me. I could have gotten away with it, I think, thanks to my reputation. But I was stunned and violence doesn't come naturally to me."

"Nor to me—or it didn't used to," I said. "If it helps, you were likely under the influence of some kind of magic when he touched you, something that would make it diffi-cult to fight back. He has a collection curated for his particular tastes."

I thought Camille might hurl her empty glass at the bookshelves, but instead she squeezed it until her knuckles went white. "That is vile. Why hasn't anyone stopped him?"

"I tried."

"Shit," Camille said. The soft click of a swallow broke the silence. "You robbed him to remove some power from his hands, then."

I suspect she knew by then what I would say, but I had

to say it. I was draining a wound. "Taillefer knew—everyone knew, anyone who'd been in the same room knew —that I loved Delphine. He told me he'd do to Delphine what he'd done to me. I thought if I robbed him, if I removed the power from his hands, he wouldn't be able to. I know I made the wrong choice—I suffered for it—but there didn't seem to be a right choice."

"You knew it was a risk and you judged that it was worse to do nothing," Camille said. She reached across the space between us and rested her hand on mine. "That's courage, Ari."

"It didn't feel like that," I said. "I was terrified, but I couldn't stand not doing it."

"That sounds exactly like courage to me," Camille said. "Taillefer hasn't been pursuing Delphine for long, you know. She may have unknowingly protected herself from him by marrying the Marquis, although that was Charybdis to Scylla, I think."

I waited, but Camille offered no more information about Delphine's marriage. She squeezed my hand and said, "What Taillefer did to you is monstrous, and I'm sorry. Robbing him was brave. You've suffered too much for trying to do the right thing."

Camille's words ought to be gratifying, but her respect cannot protect me. Taillefer is still alive.

A pounding knock at the door made me jump. Camille stood with only a little wobble, grabbed the fire poker, and went to answer.

Even from a room away, even when she's speaking softly, I know Delphine's voice. I relaxed, relieved the person at the door wasn't Taillefer, but my shoulders tightened an instant later. What emergency had brought her here?

The two of them entered the library. I should have stood to greet them in some fashion, but they were engaged in an argument and paid me no mind. Delphine shed a voluminous black cloak and said, "I'm sure I wasn't followed, I took a circuitous route—"

"You wandered around Paris alone in the dead of the night," Camille interrupted before I could.

Delphine shrugged and pulled a pistol out of her skirt pocket.

"A pistol is not protection against everything," Camille said, keeping her voice low but not steady.

"You didn't come," Delphine said mulishly. The soft glow of the wall sconces caught shadows of anger and fear on her face. "You were both supposed to come see me today. I thought something had happened."

Delphine turned to me. Her mouth dropped open. "Ari, you look—"

Enough like my old self for her to see how changed I am—I assume that's what she couldn't bring herself to say. The shave and the haircut make the scars and the weathering more obvious. I used to have, if not beauty, at least a sort of youthful sweetness. It's gone now.

Delphine slowly closed her mouth instead of finishing her sentence. She must really have wanted to say something, since I had time enough to think about the delicate pink of her lips. Mourning black might make some people look stark and severe, but for her it only emphasizes everything lively and colorful it's meant to restrain.

Her gaze dropped from my naked face to the pair of brandy glasses on the table. "You've been drinking," she said. I heard it as an accusation, but she sounded delighted when she added, "You two are conspiring."

"Commiserating," Camille corrected. "Would you like a

drink, Delphine? On the condition that you will absolutely not be walking home alone in the small hours. Taillefer <u>told</u> you he was watching your house."

"Which is why you two were supposed to sneak in," Delphine replied.

"It's my fault we didn't come," Camille said, surprising me. She easily could have blamed me. "I apologize. I should have sent my excuses. I didn't intend to scare you."

"Forgiven," Delphine said immediately.

I tensed at her approach, but the armchair where I was still seated wasn't her destination. She took the bottle from the table and poured some into the empty glass that had been Camille's. She drank without asking which of us it had belonged to. Like everything she touched, it was hers now. Her lips caressed the rim and her throat pulsed with a swallow. I averted my eyes, which didn't save me when she sat at my feet.

No part of her body came into contact with mine. Her nearness made me aware of all the places we could.

She leaned her head against the armrest. Her hastily pinned knot of hair flopped to the side, the same color as the cognac sloshing in her glass. The high neckline of her mourning dress revealed nothing, and still I felt I shouldn't look. Why hadn't she dragged another armchair over? She'd sat in this utterly improper position that practically begged me to lay a hand on her shoulder, or take down her hair.

The silk of it would catch on the roughness of my fingers.

I reached for my brandy and bumped my hand against Camille's. She was pouring more liquor into my glass. She must have intended to take it for herself, having lost hers to Delphine. Her expression was distant. When she finished pouring, I pushed the brandy toward her and she took it.

"What were you discussing?" Delphine asked.

Over the glass, Camille met my eyes, a silent cue that she would let me decide what to share. I wanted to tell Delphine everything, but I wanted sobriety and daylight for that. The thought of telling the story a second time tonight—of dodging, for a second time, the question of what exactly I'd dug up in the woods, and what I might do with it—made my insides slither and crawl.

Delphine was nearer to me than she'd been in years. Underneath the sweet-sharp scent of the liquor, I could smell her. In this softly lit corner of a place neither of us should have been, we'd found a fleeting, precious peace. I couldn't let the world intrude.

Camille was still watching me. I offered her a smile. In answer to Delphine's question, I said, "You."

"Camille said you were commiserating."

"Not about you," I said. To avoid other questions, I added, "We had good things to say about you."

Delphine hummed. "I do have many wonderful qualities."

She twisted toward me. I was so entranced by her face that at first I didn't see that she was offering me her glass. Camille's glass. Both their lips had touched it.

"You can't drink to me without a glass," she said, her eyes sparkling.

I lifted it and was surprised when Camille clinked hers against mine.

"To Delphine, who makes us forget what we've written and where we were going," she said, and Delphine laughed, bobbed her head, and delicately pinched her skirts as though preparing to curtsey.

After a sip, I lowered the glass to my lap. Delphine reached for it. I was tired and half-drunk, but not drunk enough to imagine her arm moving so slowly—that was real. She was really reaching toward me, centimeter by centimeter, with painstaking precision, her gaze never leaving my face. I didn't understand at first, but afterward, I did. It was care. She was letting me see, giving me time to withdraw, making sure that if our fingers brushed when she took that glass, it was something I'd permitted.

I hadn't told Delphine what I'd told Camille. All I'd said was that I'd gone to Taillefer's house, discovered he owned something he couldn't be allowed to have, and stolen it. And then Toulon.

Perhaps she moved so slowly because she guessed how brutally I'd been treated in prison, or perhaps she knew enough of Taillefer's character to fill in what I hadn't said. Perhaps so much time had passed that she didn't know if she still had permission.

She didn't know everything, but she knew enough.

It was only hands. I'd accidentally bumped hands with Camille mere minutes ago and it hadn't destroyed me. I wasn't that fragile. Delphine's caution wasn't necessary. But her small, discreet effort to ensure my comfort betrayed a depth of concern that had been absent from my life for a long time.

And she wanted to touch me. I hadn't been sure. My eyes stung. Perhaps I was fragile after all.

When her fingertips alighted on the glass, I pressed it firmly into her palm. Our fingers met. I touched Delphine for the first time in years. The glass grew warm between us. She made no move to break away.

I wanted more. I traced the ridges of her knuckles with the pad of my thumb. She parted her lips. I slid my fingers along the back of her hand until my fingertips met the bones of her forearm. Her long sleeve stopped my progress, but I enjoyed lingering. She'd only been inside for a short while, but her skin was warm. That warmth passed into me, heated me, made me imagine running my fingers up the tender skin under her wrist, up to the inside of her elbow, up the soft swell of her arm until I grazed the side of her breast. Instead I tracked a circle around her wrist until I found her hammering pulse, a match for my own, and slid the tip of one finger inside the tight cuff of her sleeve. Pressing gently into her delicate skin let me feel the throb of heat surging in her veins.

Desire glazed her eyes. She might as well have been a mirror.

I wanted to touch so much more of her. I wanted her to toss the glass aside. It wasn't the time or the place. For Camille's sake, with a drunkard's determination to walk straight, I ignored what had stirred in my lap a mere hand's breadth from where we touched.

"Delphine," I said. "I missed you."

A laughable understatement, but I couldn't come up with better words. My tone, at least, was sufficiently reverent.

"I missed you, too," she said, and there was yearning in it.

She broke our contact at last, taking the glass with her. It glimmered as she raised it into the air. "It's not right that you two have toasted me and I haven't returned the favor. To Camille and Ari, my favorite mysterious conspirators, whose absence makes me wander the city like a forlorn ghost."

At that, I heard the muted thump of the cork coming out of the bottle and the splash of a stream of liquor.

Camille was refilling her glass. I wondered how much of my moment with Delphine had been visible. Had Camille found it excruciating? I hoped not. I didn't want her to suffer.

"We should all do each other," Delphine said, and before I'd fully understood, she'd pushed the glass back into my hand. "Ari, drink to Camille."

My head swam with a memory of clinging to her on horseback. Her competence. How safe I'd felt. I thought, too, of lying awake in prison and revisiting <u>Virginie</u> through the clouded lens of my own memory. I wasn't drunk enough to confess all that. I stumbled through a less revealing toast. "To Camille, the best novelist and the best host."

I drank. Camille tipped her glass toward me in acknowledgment. Delphine held out her hand and I passed her our shared drink, which she savored at length.

Camille and I had fought, or something like it, before we'd entered the library tonight. She hadn't wanted to see Delphine with me, and we'd reunited in her home. Now Delphine had asked her to drink to me. Camille had good reason to resent me, and she'd witnessed some of my more pathetic behaviors over the past few days. I braced for a cutting remark.

"To Ari," Camille said, swirling the amber liquid until it lapped at the rim, never splashing her hand. Even after all that cognac, her dark eyes were only a little hazy as she addressed me. "To your courage."

She drained her glass. Delphine did the same. In the absence of the insult I'd expected, I wasn't sure what to do with myself.

Delphine, thankfully, yawned instead of asking what Camille meant. "Oh, I wish I could stay awake all night," she said. "I've wanted you two in the same room for such a long time and I finally have it, but I feel like I could fall asleep on the floor."

"You've had a lot of cognac," Camille said.

"Not as much as you."

"You aren't accustomed to it," Camille said. "Let's find you a bed."

"Yours," Delphine said, unmistakably drunk and enamored.

Her tone made my heart sink. I was drunk and enamored, too.

"Not tonight." Camille stood.

At my feet, Delphine had oriented her whole body toward Camille. "Your hair is so beautiful like that," Delphine said with a gesture at the loose, brown waves falling over Camille's shoulders.

I'd never seen a man with hair that long and I'd rarely seen a woman with unbound hair. Camille in her dressing gown seemed to have some of both about her. It was alluring. Delphine's supplicant posture and dreamy speech made a little too much sense to me.

"You know," Delphine said, the tone and volume of her voice bobbing in some unseen current of alcohol. "My late husband had a wife and a mistress. Many men do. I don't see why I shouldn't."

Even writing it down gives me a blunt shock. Delphine never fails to astonish.

Camille said, "It isn't usually a happy arrangement."

All I could think to say, after a stupefied pause, was, "Would I be the wife or the mistress?"

Delphine dissolved into giggles. Camille offered her hand, but in the end she had to bend down and haul her upright. A drunken wobble made Delphine careen toward my chair. I caught her arm to steady her. I tried to exchange a glance with Camille over Delphine's head, but Camille refused to look at me.

Rising to my feet gave me no trouble, though I hadn't had a drop of brandy in years. Delphine had arrived long after we'd begun drinking, so I don't know how she could have imbibed more than either of us.

It's not impossible that she simply wanted Camille on one side and me on the other. If Delphine played at drunkenness to arrange that, I find it hard to object. She leaned into me as we went up the stairs, and though I couldn't sleep and wrote this instead, the memory of the soft weight of her body kept me company for hours afterward.

# IV
# NECESSARY RISK

1825

Dear Isabelle,

I've heard nothing from you and thus assume you're still traveling. I'm writing to tell you that in your absence, I've decided to take matters into my own hands. Here is how it happened.

I spent last night at Camille's, having slipped in under cover of darkness to find her drinking with Ari. The three of us retired to bed separately despite my efforts, alas.

We breakfasted together in Camille's dining room, the clear morning light doing me no favors after such scant sleep. I do miss Amélie's talents dearly when I have to dress without her.

Camille and Ari, both tired but radiant, studied their coffee like its dark depths could foretell the future. They could have seated themselves at opposite ends of the long, polished wood table, but they sat side by side. Any sign of ease between them delights me. I dabbed a napkin over my smile.

We'd avoided all serious topics during our late-night

gathering, but I couldn't indulge that desire in the light of day.

"I wish I could stay here," I said, not mentioning that the reason I couldn't was my son, whose existence remains a delicate matter. "As I must return home, we should use this morning to plan."

Camille turned to Ari as though waiting for him to speak. Eventually, he said, in the low rumble that is now his voice, "You want to discuss Taillefer."

A frustrating response. What else could I possibly have meant? Something was troubling Ari, evidently, so I remained calm. "I cannot lock myself in that house forever, especially as I plan to rid myself of it, and neither can you hide indefinitely. What do you suggest?"

"I'll do it," he said.

"Do what?" I asked.

"Handle Taillefer," he said, not making any suggestion and thus not truly answering the only question I'd posed. "I don't want you to have to go near him."

"Ari," Camille said gently. "That doesn't seem... prudent."

I didn't show it, Isabelle, but I was startled that Camille seemed to know more than me. From the points available to me, I've drawn the contours of what passed between Ari and Taillefer; Camille may have the full picture.

She displayed such concern for Ari. A soft, feathery hope fluttered inside me.

I think Ari and Camille like each other.

"Nothing's prudent," he muttered.

"What, exactly, do you intend?" I asked.

"I don't want to talk about it," he said. "It makes me

sick, but I'll do it. That's it. That's all that needs to be said."

"It absolutely is not," I replied. "And if you're talking about murder, I'd be perfectly happy to. Why not let me do it, if it makes you sick?"

That woke them both from their bleary morning stupor. Round-eyed shock, my name in scolding tones, choruses of fragmented questions and protest. How funny that both Ari and Camille would describe <u>me</u> as the one who exaggerates.

Please understand, Isabelle, it's not that I take joy in distressing two of my favorite people in the world. Had we not been pressed for time, I would have broached the subject differently.

People like Taillefer and my late husband—and Malbosc, I assume, since he was rich enough to acquire an emerald necklace—hardly seem to have trouble violating the less powerful <u>without</u> magic. It is already obscene. That they seek more power through magic is unconscionable. My husband had near total control of my life <u>before</u> he used the necklace to own my will itself. (Excuse this rip in the page. I was writing with more force than I knew.)

Living under my late husband's rule gave me some experience with reasoning through such problems. I had already determined in my own mind that the only way to keep us safe would be to separate Taillefer from his power, that is to say, not only his collection of artifacts but also the wealth and status that protect him from consequences.

I strongly suspect there is only one way to accomplish that.

Even without his riches or his name, at heart Taillefer would still be a predator. If we save ourselves by ruining

Taillefer's fortune and reputation, he will be friendless and impoverished and free to continue his monstrous habits. The cobblers and laundresses and paupers of Paris deserve better than to be subject to his abuses. Even if we were to put him in prison, the other prisoners would deserve better.

When Ari and Camille had ceased their appalled protests, there was a silence.

Camille said, "Could we take some time to think about this?"

Ari said, very quietly, "I didn't even tell you the whole story."

"You didn't have to," I said and felt my shoulders curl inward with the weight of my own secret. Of course Ari hesitated to tell me how Taillefer violated him; he wouldn't want to dwell on the details. Meanwhile, I am keeping our beautiful child from him.

I've guarded that secret for so long. I don't know what my late husband would have done to Octave—or to me—if he'd discovered the truth, and I'm grateful I'll never find out. But now I fear I've forgotten how to unlock this door.

I want to tell Ari that Octave is his. It will be painful, but I want to.

We were discussing Taillefer and how to kill him, though, and that took precedence.

To Camille, I said, "I've already taken a great deal of time to think about it."

"My objections are logistical, not moral," she said. "I don't care what happens to him, I care what happens to you."

Camille is a marvel. Though I hold myself in very high regard, sometimes I still wonder whether I deserve her. It's not every day you meet someone who hears you threaten to kill a man and then patiently explains that they are worried about <u>you</u>, not him. I must do everything in my power to keep her.

"There is another detail I should mention," Camille said. "This strange state of affairs hasn't removed all my other obligations, and I do still have books to write, and more relevant to the two of you, a reading to give a week from now, on May 27 at the Comtesse de Davrance's salon."

"Don't go," I said immediately. For Ari's benefit, since it had been years since he'd attended a salon, I added, "Taillefer is usually in attendance. Camille, pretend to fall ill. Invent an emergency."

"I'm going," Camille said. "I was invited, and I promised I would, and I'm looking forward to it. Taillefer doesn't know of my liaison with you, and even if he did, we'll be in a room full of people. I won't be alone with him. I'm telling you two my plans in the interest of honesty, not because I intend to change them."

"Could someone accompany you?" Ari asked. "Not me —I'm too recognizable and too hard to explain."

"I'm supposed to be in mourning, I can't go to a salon," I said.

"Both of you presume you would be invited, which you are not," Camille said.

I laughed, but Camille merely waited until I stopped.

"Putting aside that neither of you is safe in the same room as Taillefer <u>and</u> that I would find your presence distracting, the two of you need to speak to each other," she said. "At Delphine's house. Without me present. I want to give this reading and I don't want you there. Use the time wisely."

"At Delphine's?" Ari asked. "That seems an unnecessary

risk."

"It's a risk," Camille agreed. "But it's a necessary one."

She stared me down. I couldn't argue without making it seem as though I was afraid to be alone with Ari, or as though as I was hiding something from him, which, of course, I am. Resigned, I said to her, "If you insist on doing this, could Julien go with you? Or is there some artifact that could protect you?"

"I asked Victor about that," she said. "If I'm willing to do my reading in plate armor, he could provide me with a cuirass that returns projectiles, or a very scorched pair of leather boots that would render me invulnerable to flame. Not especially useful for the Comtesse's parlor. In terms of more offensive protection, there was a perfume that would make everyone like me, but I don't want Taillefer to like me, and I'd rather not influence the innocent. Victor also offered me a number of options for altering my appearance. I think becoming invisible would make the reading somewhat unsettling."

Invisibility would be an excellent way for me to attend the salon, but Camille had so bluntly rejected my presence. I'm unaccustomed to feeling unwanted, Isabelle. I don't think I managed to hide my hurt and disappointment.

More importantly, I have no experience in plotting violence, and am not sure I can arrange to remove Taillefer before Camille's reading. My decision is not in question, but I need time to consider my approach. If only you would write back, I'm sure you could advise me.


Your friend,
Delphine

Camille,

"Devastatingly handsome"? I see what you mean about making everything worse—_you_ like Ari.

Julie

# CAMILLE DUPIN TO JULIE MORÈRE, MAY 21, 1825

## SCRAWLED AT THE BOTTOM OF THE PREVIOUS LETTER AND SENT BY PRIVATE COURIER

Fuck off.

# PRIVATE DIARY OF ARI
# LAZARE, MAY 21, 1825

I went to Delphine's today.

Camille's reading isn't for a week, but our conversation at breakfast yesterday left us miserable and antsy. Delphine went home and we made arrangements for me to be unobtrusively carted to her kitchen along with a delivery of cheese.

It didn't matter what the cart smelled like, what the kitchen smelled like. I was still breathing Delphine from our night in the library.

Her scent lingered on my skin. I was feverish to see her again, by turns flushed with heat and chilled with the idea that she might now treat me as some broken object of pity.

I _am_. But I don't want to be. I want to live like the man I was, to do what he did. That's another way of saying I've recently remembered how good it is to be touched, and I'm dying for more.

She met me in the kitchen, which is half a step from me sneaking in or her sneaking out like we used to. Fresh-faced and in new clothes, she must have slept serenely. She bore no trace of our cognac-soaked late night. Though that was two nights ago, I couldn't say the same for myself.

Delphine should have looked totally out of place among all the potato peels and chicken bones, wearing some extravagant thing of deep blue. Instead, pale golden light from the high window made her shine and left everything else in shadow. Excessive, really—I can never see anything else when she's in front of me, anyway.

If she could read this, she'd chide me for not remembering all the words she taught me about sleeves and skirt shapes and fabric types, but when presented with the sight of her cleavage, it's a wonder I remember any words. Soft, maybe. Warm. Who needs words when I have two empty hands and a ready mouth?

It's a good thing she isn't going to read this.

Though she's the one who grabbed my hand and led me from the kitchen to her bedroom, so I can hardly be blamed for getting ideas. And if Delphine were holed up somewhere privately recording all her most inappropriate thoughts about me, I would be ecstatic.

It was crushing when she shut the bedroom door, backed against it to block us in, and said, "I suppose we should talk."

Seeing Delphine in the midst of that disgustingly decadent room didn't put me in the mood to talk. I wanted to rip down all the drapery and spread her across that bed that could have slept five people. I wanted to push her against the brocade wallpaper and slide her skirts up her thighs. Restless, adrift in the space between the bed and the door, I paced the plush carpet and found myself inexorably pulled back to Delphine. Not close enough to reach for her. I wasn't that bold.

I said, "Ask me anything you want."

In the old days she would have smiled and told me to get on the bed, and my back would have hit the mattress before she finished her sentence. Her shoulders slumped a little and she said, "We've been through a lot."

Lightly, I said, "Well, I haven't been sleeping in a place like this."

Delphine couldn't be deterred by such a weak attempt at a joke. "Do you want to tell me about it?"

"No."

"What happened to 'ask me anything you want'?" She smiled then, so my belligerence was almost worth it.

"You asked if I wanted to talk and I answered you truthfully. You'll need better questions if you want better answers—or I can tell you it was hellish and I never want to think about it again, and we can spend our time in some other, more enjoyable way."

My face or my tone of voice must have been wrong; pity furrowed her brow. Things had been easier in Camille's darkened library, all the rough edges smoothed by alcohol and the late hour. Maybe Camille's presence had helped us somehow. I don't know. In Delphine's bedroom, I felt rusty with disuse.

Maybe the two of us just didn't fit together anymore. Delphine would have seized that opening in the old days. She never missed a chance for lasciviousness.

Camille entered my thoughts suddenly. I found myself angry that Delphine would shut herself in this bedroom with me while Camille pined for her, angry that Camille had forever changed things between Delphine and me, angry that I couldn't have Delphine without hurting Camille, angry that Delphine wanted Camille, angry that I wanted Delphine despite everything.

"If you don't want to talk, then should I tell you about the last few years of my life?" Delphine asked.

I gestured at the suffocating adornments of wealth. "What's to tell? Instead of looking for me, you married a rich man, had his babies, he died and left you dowager marquise, and now you're fucking Camille. Everything worked out perfectly."

"I didn't have his babies."

"Fine then, one baby," I snapped. "What does it matter? Why am I here, Delphine? You could have found me at any time in the last two years and eight months if you'd wanted to. If you'd been willing to leave all of this behind, we could have made a life together years ago—but you didn't want that."

Unlike Camille, Delphine reacts easily. I've always loved how quickly her feelings surface. Her eyes spark and she flushes. She speaks like she's biting off every word. It's beautiful. Writing about it, I see that I must have provoked her on purpose. I hadn't realized how much I wanted it until it happened. She stopped treating me like I was made of glass once I pissed her off.

It started with a harsh bark of laughter. "You think I didn't <u>want</u> you?"

She strode forward so fast that I took a step backward without meaning to, so I was off-balance when she grabbed me by the lapels of my coat. I stumbled into her and she dragged me down until our noses nearly touched. Softly, in a tone that might have been anger or regret or affection, she said, "You don't know anything."

She kissed me like a slap. The sharp edge of her teeth landed in my bottom lip, and I let her bite me. I swayed into her like it was a caress. My pulse sang in my ears. I would have let her hit my face in truth if she'd wanted.

We'd never been like this with each other. Before, it had always been gentle, laughing, nothing but pleasure. It's not that I crave pain, but right then, I needed the sting of her anger. It tempered her pity. I wouldn't have known what to do with pure pleasure, but this lust, crude and messy, fierce and furious, was what I needed. It let me be human—crude, messy, angry, lustful—in return. Subject, not object.

Still kissing, we moved until the backs of my thighs hit the carved wooden foot of her bed. She balled the wool of my coat in her fists and trapped me there, her knuckles pressing into my chest and her lips hot against mine. Half-perched, I was uncomfortably hunched over and my collar was cutting into my neck; I would have stayed there for hours just tasting the sweet-salt, velvet slide of her tongue. It was perfect. It was everything I hadn't let myself dream of, and it was happening, every catch and rustle of our clothing and every little suck and sigh making it real.

I pulled her closer by her hips, my fingers crumpling her skirt and digging into the flesh beneath. She rubbed against me, luscious, abundant, and let out a little sigh into my mouth. At that sensation—that sound—a dam broke inside me. All I wanted was more. Years since she'd kissed me, years since she'd pressed her body to mine, but there was no drinking it in slowly, no savoring it sip by sip. A wave of lust crashed through me. I dragged my lips downward, my stubble rough against the smooth column of her neck, and she groaned. I kissed my way to her collarbones and the rounded tops of her breasts. She smelled delicious, like luxury, like comfort, like some perfumed elixir concocted to make me lose my mind. I inhaled her to the very depths of my lungs.

Her hands released my coat and plunged to my

trousers. A shudder shook the whole length of my body when her fingers brushed my cock through the fabric. That single, light touch almost undid me.

She made quick work of my buttons. I scratched and groped at her clothes like an animal, desperate to get under her skirts to the feel of her skin. At last the silk of it met my fingers, smooth and warm, her soft thighs dimpling under my grip. The curls between them were wet already, clinging as I slid a finger along the lips of her cunt. She spread her thighs and let me in. That slick heat surrounding my finger stole my breath.

I was so hard I was lightheaded. Delphine rocked her hips and wrapped her hand around my cock and I made a wordless, obscene noise. I wanted to fuck her. The memory of how much she used to love it made me press forward, but she kept her hand on me, stroking me relentlessly, and that was good, too. I was close and I wanted her to finish first, or at least with me, so I touched her wrist to slow her.

She did slow. She stopped entirely, removing my hand from her body and separating us. Then she dropped to her knees, her shimmering dark blue skirts pooling on the carpet, and kissed the head of my cock. It wasn't what I'd intended. The hand I'd touched her with was cooling in the air, making the lack of her warmth that much keener, but when she slid her mouth along my shaft, I couldn't imagine asking for anything else. I sucked the taste of her from my finger. She sucked the life out of me.

The little death came fast and hard, everything rushing hotter and brighter toward that single point where overwhelming sensation drops into release. Some kind of low, raspy sound shuddered out of me. My hand fell to her shoulder for support. I spilled pulse after hot pulse into her mouth. She swallowed. She didn't let go until long after I'd finished. I felt liquid, boneless, brainless.

Delphine delicately wiped a hand across her mouth and stood.

I reached for her hand. "Delphine, please, let me," I said, thinking of her sweet, wet, untouched pussy. I'd hardly even tasted her.

"Don't ever tell me I didn't want you enough," she said. "I wanted you to the point of madness. I still do."

I gaped at her. "Did you suck my cock to win an argument?"

"I sucked your cock because I wanted to," she retorted. "And I would happily have run away with you instead of marrying that unspeakable man, but I needed time to plan so we wouldn't all starve and freeze in your leaky garret, and there wasn't any, because you <u>died</u>, Ari. You vanished and I had to fend for the two of us. And I looked for you, of course I looked for you, I never stopped looking for you. Even a few months ago I was bargaining your compass in exchange for your location. My late husband didn't allow me much freedom. I couldn't climb out a window while pregnant or roam the countryside alone with an infant, and I had no notion of why or how or where you'd disappeared."

I hadn't recovered my faculties from the onslaught of pleasure, and I was still caught up in yearning to touch her, so all I could think to say was, "I didn't do it on purpose."

"I know," she said softly. "But it happened, and not just to you. It happened to us, too. I need you to understand that I didn't have a choice, either."

"Your parents forced you to marry," I guessed, though I wasn't sure what she was talking about.

"That's the least of it," she said. "Ari, there's something I need to tell you."

Has anything good ever followed a sentence like that? Cautiously, I asked, "What is it?"

In the thick silence between us, it was easy to hear the patter of little feet running and a high-pitched voice squealing and calling "Maman!" from outside the room.

A woman chided, "Octave, your mother is busy."

"It's no trouble, Marthe," Delphine said, her voice raised to carry. "You and Octave wait there a moment. I'll come out."

The room held a stand with a basin and a ewer of water where Delphine cleaned her hands and face with hardly a glance in the mirror. She smoothed her skirts and walked to the door, the flush still high in her cheeks. The door clicked shut behind her. I staggered a few paces. The bed caught me as I sat.

Several things fell into place at once. Delphine had brought up her pregnancy and her child as reasons she couldn't look for me. My abduction and her marriage had coincided. The pregnancy must have followed soon after.

Or maybe it hadn't.

She'd said "You vanished and I had to fend for the two of us." The bizarre construction of her sentence had flown over my head in the moment—the two of whom, exactly? —but it stuck out now. "It happened to us, too," she'd said. And earlier, before we'd started kissing, she'd said "I didn't have his babies." In my irritation, I'd mistaken it for a trivial correction about the number of her children. But she'd been saying something else entirely. She hadn't had <u>his</u> baby.

She'd had mine.

I felt a hot flare of anger—why hadn't she just said so? But that first spark was quickly drowned in sorrow.

A child. My child. Our child.

Octave.

Delphine must have been keeping the secret for his entire life. It would be hard to break the habit. And in her way, she'd been trying to broach the topic, and I'd been too preoccupied to listen.

I wished she'd told me before I'd died, as she put it. Before the fiasco with Taillefer. I didn't know how old Octave was, what month he'd been born. When had Delphine discovered she was pregnant? Would I have behaved differently if I'd known?

The child outside that door was my son. To have a child with a woman I loved and admired as much as Delphine was a miracle, a dream, something I'd always wanted. To have inadvertently abandoned Delphine and that child, to have lost the first days and months and years of my son's life to the time I'd spent in prison, time we could never get back... I clutched at my head and let out a ragged breath.

Delphine should hate me. How could she not hate me?

No wonder she'd kicked me out when I'd dropped myself on her doorstep, trailing trouble behind me. She was protecting her son. Our son.

Camille had known, I realized. When I said it was a risk to come here, she told me it was a necessary one. She wanted me to see him. That knowledge was one more piece of detritus caught up in the whirlpool of my emotions.

I could hear Delphine talking to Octave outside. Mechanically, I cleaned my face and hands. I restored my clothes to order and wished I could do the same for my thoughts. Opening the door took all of my strength, but crouching came easily—too easily, as my knees failed me when I took in his big dark eyes and mop of black curls. He had round cheeks and chubby hands and was sucking intently on two fingers.

"Fingers," Delphine whispered, and in tilting his head to gaze up at her, Octave let his hand fall from his mouth. He gave her a stunned, adoring smile that cinched painfully tight around my heart.

"Hello," I said, steadying myself with a hand on the carpet, trying not to think of Delphine spending the past two years grieving, being reminded of me every time she saw her son's face. It was hard to breathe. I forced air in and a smile out. "My name is Ari."

"Ari," he repeated, dodging the R in the middle so my name was only vowels. In a better world, this little one would be calling me Papa. I ache for that world. It hurts to think of it.

"What's your name?"

"Otav."

I gave him another wobbly smile. Who could have imagined that any child of mine would be named Octave de Tousserat, Marquis de Quennetière?

"Beard," he said, or some approximation of the word, and reached for my face. His small hand touched my stubble, exploring the short, scratchy points.

I didn't weep, but it was a near thing. My eyes watered and I dashed my hand against them. I want to see him again. I want to see her, too. The two of them. I hope we can find a way. I hope she deems me worthy of the privilege.

"Ari needs a moment, Octave," Delphine said. "Go play with Marthe and Caro."

She nodded to the slim, brown-skinned young woman who was standing off to the side with a little girl who must be her daughter. Octave ran to the woman in his uneven child's gait and threw his arms around her legs, and I felt a deep pang of envy. Marthe laid a hand on Octave's dark curls and ushered the children away. Delphine and I watched them go. My thoughts crashed together and my insides tangled so nothing worked right anymore: everything jittery, stuttering, disconnected, heart in my stomach, eyes leaking again. I couldn't let him see me cry. I didn't want him to leave.

My joints protested as I stood, but it was good to take my time. I was searching for something to say. There was so much between us, and we'd been interrupted, and everything was new, tender, fragile. We stood side by side, painfully aware of each other, not touching. She didn't even know if I knew the truth yet—but how could I not?

Octave is beautiful. He looks like Delphine.

I would want to be his Papa even if some other man had fathered him. In a sense, some other man did. Ari-before-Toulon is a different person, a person I can't be. I'm Ari-after-Toulon, and I didn't know it until just now, but I'm Ari-after-Octave, too.

My throat felt thick and closed. When my voice emerged, it shook like a reed. "I knew your late husband by reputation. I saw him once, too. As I recall, he was blond."

"Yes, he was," Delphine said softly.

I wrapped my arms around her. Both of us burst into tears. I tried to cry less violently than her, to be the one holding her instead of the other way around, since I hadn't been there to hold her for any of the rest of it. Instead we clung to each other like survivors of a shipwreck far from the shore.

Had her husband known? Had he been cruel to her or Octave because of it? I held my tongue and didn't ask. There were more important things to say first.

"I'm sorry," I began, speaking softly near her ear. "I don't know that I'll ever be able to express how sorry I am for leaving you. Or how much I want to make it better. To be there, in whatever way you'll have me. For you and for him."

"Oh, Ari," she said, and when I dared to glance at her, tears sparkled like gems in her lashes. "I already know."

"You... do?" I'd been composing whole speeches in my head, drafting reams of love letters, planning a hundred ways to prove myself worthy.

She nodded mutely. I wondered if her throat felt as closed as mine.

Delphine drew a trembling breath and stepped back from me. "I loved you. I still do. And I knew you loved me. I kept you with me in the only way I could. That's not to say I never had doubts or cursed your name. It's been a hard few years. But in my heart, I knew you would have chosen us if you'd had the chance. It doesn't matter if you don't have the words now. You'll show me in acts. I don't know the shape of our future yet, but I know that."

"I won't let Taillefer hurt any of us, not again," I promised, thinking of all the obstacles to our happiness and starting with the most insurmountable.

"Oh, it's not Taillefer that worries me." Delphine waved a hand in the air. "I know how to solve that problem." That blunt reminder of her offer to do violence passed quickly. Instead of elaborating, she continued, "I want you in my life, Ari. I want Octave to know you. But I want Camille, too. I've already hurt her, and I can't bear the thought of breaking her heart further. She saved my life and I've treated her callously."

"Ah," I said. It was all the eloquence I possessed. "So you intend to... choose between us?" I couldn't bring myself to say "choose Camille," though that's what I meant.

"No, that's not what I intend," Delphine said fiercely.

My sunken heart lifted a little, but I still didn't know what to make of our conversation.

Delphine opened the doors of her wardrobe and sorted through the rainbow of fabrics like she was paging through a book. Then, finding the dresses she sought, she dove between them and pulled something from the depths of the cabinet.

When she stood, her dainty hand was wrapped around a dark piece of metal.

"I didn't know what a crowbar was until I had to pry up one of the floorboards at the Maison Laval to get your compass," she told me. "So it was you who taught me this."

She flipped up the edge of the carpet and set to work prying one of the boards beneath it. Her skirts pooled around her. I tried not to gape.

She retrieved a bundle wrapped in coarse cloth. Unwrapped, I could see it was a packet of letters.

"I shouldn't have written these, or kept them, but I couldn't bring myself to burn the pages and he never found them. They were always meant for you, Ari."

She pressed the whole thick packet into my hands. Then, after biting her lip, she untied the cream-colored ribbon around the packet, flipped through the pages, and extracted a few after skimming their contents. These, she retied with the ribbon, wrapped in cloth, and clutched to her chest. "I think Camille isn't ready for you to see these yet."

"Camille read your letters to me?"

"No," she said. "But I wrote some private things about her."

My gaze strayed to the cloth-wrapped bundle. "You wrote private things about her in letters you addressed to me?"

"I thought you were dead and I didn't have anyone else to tell," Delphine said lightly, or as lightly as it is possible to say such a thing. She tucked the letters under her arm as though that might cause me to forget their existence and continued, "Will you come here again tomorrow? With Camille. The three of us need to talk. You can spend time with Octave, if you like."

"I'm staying with Camille because Taillefer has someone watching your house," I reminded her, though the need surged through me to tell her I'd return whenever she wanted, that I'd stay as long as she asked, that I'd never leave her again. It would be unforgivable to put her in harm's way. To endanger our child. "I risked coming here today because I couldn't resist, but I can't make it a habit, not until we know we're safe. You might not be worried, but I am."

"Will you write to me, then?" she asked, laying a hand over mine, the paper crinkling beneath my fingers. "It's lonely to know that you're in the city and not be able to see you."

There was only one possible answer. "Always."

ARI TO DELPHINE, MAY
22, 1825
SENT BY PRIVATE COURIER

Delphine,

I can't express how moved I am by your letters, and how sorry I am for doubting that you wanted to find me. Thank you for letting me read these pages. I have already returned to them twice.

Your descriptions of Octave as a baby are dear to me, since those moments are past now and your writing is the only glimpse I will ever have of what I missed. A small consolation. A greater one is that I hope not to miss his future, or ours.

I am gutted to learn that you were as imprisoned as I was—perhaps more, for those nine days you had that necklace around your neck. That should never have happened to you, and I am relieved that the man who inflicted it on you is dead.

Enclosed are two brief notes I wrote to myself before my disappearance. I will entrust Camille with their delivery, as she can move more easily around the city than I can, and I will ask her to read them as well. You two must know what happened so we can prevent it from happening again.

You gave me something wonderful to read, as bitter-sweet as it was. I'm offering you something ghastly in return, but I can't allow myself to contemplate the future fully until we've dealt with the past. Rest assured that I do want one. I have gone without dreaming of the rest of my life for years now, so trying again is a sweet ache.


Love,
    Ari

# PRIVATE DIARY OF ARI LAZARE, MAY 23, 1825

It has been a very strange few days, with Delphine sucking my cock and telling me I was the father of her child and giving me all those letters to read, and yesterday evening Camille knocked on my door and made it stranger.

My presence startled her, though she was the one who'd knocked. From her slow blink and her dazed chocolate-brown stare, she'd expected me to ignore her. Her fist, poised to knock again, hovered at shoulder height.

"I," she began. Her hand drifted to her side. "I wanted to ask if you were... I thought I should ask how things went with Delphine. You've been quiet since you came back."

"Come in."

I stepped aside so she could enter the room. The box of my possessions that we'd retrieved sat open on the writing desk next to all my scribblings, which I'd wisely turned over so Camille could neither see my irretrievably bad handwriting nor read my uncontrolled thoughts. The former would prevent her from the latter unless she was very dedicated, but I'd rather not discover that.

My letter to Delphine, and the old notes I'd enclosed, lay folded on top of the pile.

"Delphine told me about Octave," I said, since that was clearly the question Camille had been working toward. "I met him."

Camille stood by the desk with one hand on the back of the chair. It was the only seat in the room other than the bed, and I hadn't offered it to her, though it, like everything else, was hers to begin with. I didn't want to sit while she stood, so we simply faced each other on our feet. The shift from conversing in the doorway to conversing in the room granted her enough time to recompose herself, and she said, "I didn't ask what happened. I asked how it went."

I made a helpless gesture and then let my shoulders fall. "How can it go when someone reveals to you that you have a child you never knew about?"

"Will you see Delphine again? And does Octave know?"

"We exchanged names and he remarked on my beard—well, my stubble, really. Maybe we'll broach the topic of his parentage when we've spent more than ten minutes together."

She sighed in relief, and I realized she cared for him. She knew him in a way I didn't, and that, like everything else about his existence, made me sad and happy.

"And I didn't spend every day in Toulon desperately thinking-and-not-thinking of Delphine only to come back and stop speaking to her," I said. "I can't imagine anything that would make me do that."

"I suppose if surprising her in bed with me and then discovering your secret child didn't do it, nothing will,"

Camille said. "So you and Delphine are in love and you're happy about Octave."

"Well," I hedged. "Happy, yes, but devastated to have missed so much—"

I stopped when Camille turned to leave. My emotions weren't the matter here. She thought I was telling her that there was no room left for her in Delphine's life.

Without thinking, I laid a hand on her upper arm. She had the grace not to recoil in surprise. There was hardly anything untoward in it, as we were both fully clothed despite the late hour, but it was the first time I had touched her instead of the other way around. It was just my palm against the wool of her navy frock coat, which had those newly fashionable sleeves that are full at the cap, puffing almost like women's evening dresses and giving everyone the appearance of broad shoulders and thick arms.

Camille, I discovered, actually does have muscular arms.

That nearly caused me to forget the subject we'd been discussing. With effort, I recalled what I'd intended to say. "I was hoping you'd deliver that letter to her next time you go out. You should read it, too." I nodded at the folded papers.

Camille tucked it into the inside pocket of her frock coat. "I will."

"Delphine thinks the three of us should talk."

"I'm sure she does," Camille allowed. "We can, of course. I wouldn't leave her without saying goodbye."

"I never meant to do that to her," I protested.

"Oh, Ari, I wasn't—you made the only right choice."

"Maybe, but I shouldn't have done it all myself," I said. "If I'd involved Delphine more..."

"You can't know what would have happened. She might have gone to Taillefer to bargain for your freedom," Camille said immediately. "Or perhaps I'm underestimating her cleverness. If she'd been free to follow your compass, she would have found you by other means. Probably she would have ridden a string of stolen horses across France."

"Delphine would never have to steal a horse," I said. "People would just offer them to her when she asked."

Camille laughed, rich and full-throated. Her arm shook a little, and I realized she hadn't shrugged off my touch. "You're right. She would have arrived in a palanquin carried by six strapping young men she'd met on the road. The warden would have personally escorted her through the gates, apologizing for not tidying."

"Speaking of Delphine's resourcefulness, she gave me some old letters, ones she'd written to me years ago and hidden under a floorboard. She pried it up with a small crowbar she'd stashed in her wardrobe," I said. "When she went hunting among her silks, that wasn't what I expected her to retrieve."

"A crowbar," Camille enthused. "God, I love that woman."

"Me too," I said, and before I could regret saying it, Camille beamed at me and I found myself smiling back. She clapped me on the shoulders.

I had two equally strange thoughts at once. The first: if Camille were gone from my life, I would miss her.

The second: Camille almost kissed me.

I can't be sure of that. It was only a fleeting expression, something in her posture, in the shape of her mouth, in the instant before she'd clasped my shoulders. And after all, she didn't.

"It's late," she said. "I should sleep."

"Good luck with that," I said and meant it sincerely.

As usual, my own efforts at sleep met with little success. I dressed in my night shirt, extinguished the candle, and lay still in bed. Nothing happened. I rolled over. Nothing happened. I tried both approaches again until I had twisted the bed covers into a nest. Thinking of Delphine's touch made me hot, but thinking of Camille giving her reading in the same room as Taillefer doused it quickly. Neither thought was restful.

A knock came some time later. "Ari, it's Camille," she said, as if I didn't know.

I sat up and told her to come in. The light of her candle flickered under her tired eyes. Her hair was loose and she was wearing the purple silk dressing gown again. It lay open over a long, thin linen shirt, identical to the one I was wearing. Her tailor had made me new trousers, waistcoats, and frock coats, but there'd been no need for new shirts. I hardly even thought of them as Camille's clothes anymore.

I had the stray thought, then, that the boots I'd been wearing must have belonged to someone else. Her feet would swim in them. But she'd never said anything about their former owner—unless it was the ailing lover or friend who'd taught her how to shave his face.

"I can't sleep," she said.

"Misery loves company."

I was briefly ashamed of the wreck I'd made of the bedding. Camille's hunched shoulders moved me to pity, and I patted the bed beside me, carefully not thinking of what we were doing, or why we might be doing it. She blew out her candle, leaving us with only the scant blue moonlight slipping through the curtains. The mattress dipped under her weight. She made no comment on the state of the bed, just stretched out flat on her back with her hands joined over her stomach, like a sculpture on a medieval king's tomb. She could have been holding the hilt of a sword. I wondered if she slept in that pose.

"Why can't you sleep?" she asked.

"Tonight in particular, or every night?" I leaned back, letting my head fall against the headboard. In the daytime I might not have answered, but the inky darkness wicked the truth from me. "I suppose the answer is 'Taillefer' either way. But it's also... Toulon was noisy. So many men tossing and turning and clanking—they chained us to the beds—and every snort and groan echoing off the walls. We worked to exhaustion every day, so it almost didn't matter. My mind and body simply quit at night. Except it's quiet here, and soft, and my thoughts never cease, and I don't think I know how to fall asleep anymore."

She let this hang in the silence, and I knew without her saying so that she wanted to tell me again how sorry she was. "Is there anything I can do?"

"Are you offering to write me little notes encouraging me to sleep?"

"It worked with food," she said.

Until then, I hadn't realized she was right. I'd been so distraught in those first few days that nothing had appealed to me, but her persistent coaxing had given me one small thing in life that was dependable and expected. That had made it easier.

"You annoyed me into it," I agreed. The word was enticed, or tempted, but I couldn't bring either to my lips. Camille's presence in my bed had already quickened my pulse in the nervous way that I knew could easily become excitement. What was between us was fragile and uncertain. I didn't want her to leave. "Why can't you sleep? Is it Taillefer?"

"Among other things."

"Is it me?" I asked.

She sighed. "Not in the way that you think."

"I hardly know how I think, and I certainly don't know how you think I think, so I can't even begin to untangle that."

My protest must have surprised her. She huffed in amusement and then was quiet for a long time. "The man who taught me to shave," she said at last. "His name was Lucien."

Her lover or friend who'd been ailing. Likely the previous owner of the boots I'd been wearing. In a softer tone, I said, "You lost him. I'm sorry."

"Thank you," she said. "We weren't... in truth, I lost him a long time before he died. He didn't love me like I loved him."

"But you took care of him in his illness."

"I did. He'd left his relations in the provinces to come to Paris, and he had no intention of ever going back. The man he loved, Félix, was more interested in wine and sex than broth and cold compresses, so there was only me."

"That sounds difficult." Miserable for both Lucien and Camille, more like, but she'd lived it. There was no need to point it out. "My return isn't the first time that you've found yourself unexpectedly sharing a lover, then."

"Not the first, and probably not the last." She sighed. "Can we really call it sharing? In my experience with Lucien, there was no sharing. There was only my slow-dawning understanding that I had always been his second choice. In Félix's absence, Lucien was inconsolable. He didn't love me anymore, if he ever had, and yet I was still there, loving him."

How Camille had entangled herself with two such unworthy men mystified me. Even when I'd set my mind to hating her, I'd seen how brilliant and compassionate she was. But it wasn't the past that mattered now, so I returned us to the present. "Does Delphine know all this?"

"It never came up," Camille said shortly.

"You should tell her. Delphine loves you and can't live without you—she said that to me."

"That's sweet of you, Ari, but I already know how this ends. Don't worry about me. I'll live. I always do. It's some consolation to me that I actually like you, and I think if Delphine got sick, you'd stay for her convalescence."

"You deserve better than consolation, and I don't think you do know how this ends," I told her. "I like you, too. I was just thinking that if you were gone from my life, I'd miss you."

"Huh," said Camille. "I suppose I'd miss you, too."

"I wanted to hate you."

"I wanted to push you off a cliff," she said, surprising a laugh out of me. "You'd be much less handsome at the bottom of a cliff, Ari. I'd have a better chance."

Camille's teasing made me slide down into the sheets and draw them over myself. Delphine used to call me handsome, but it's her habit to call people meaningless endearments. Besides, I look different now, all scars and bones and calluses. Camille, on the other hand, wears trousers with aplomb, rides horses with heroic grace, and smiles like she knows all the best secrets. Of the two of us, I know who's better described as handsome.

Embarrassed enough without saying all that, I quipped, "You're the one who cut my hair and paid for my clothes."

"To my profound regret," she said. "You do smell a lot better, though. It's easier to be next to you."

"It's easier to be me, too."

"I imagine," Camille said. She rolled onto her side to stare at me, and I was thankful for the darkness and the sheets drawn up to my chin. "Though it doesn't sound easy to be you, Ari. How long has it been since you've slept?"

"I sleep sometimes," I protested. "I just have to wait until it's impossible to stay awake any longer, and then it comes—like a dead faint or a punch to the face. That happened last night, so tonight's for lying awake."

Camille hummed in response, dissatisfied. "Well, I'm not going to chain you by your ankle—"

"Wouldn't work. This bed's nothing like what I had there. Too soft."

"I categorically refuse to chain you to anything, soft or otherwise, Ari. And I certainly can't snore and groan as much as a whole prison dormitory. So I can't do much to help you sleep, but perhaps you could help me, if you'd accept me staying here."

Unwilling to admit how much I wanted that, I asked, "So you can sleep while I lie awake?"

"I haven't been able to fall asleep yet tonight," she reminded me. "My only intention is to be quiet and lie still in the dark, which I think is within your power as well."

"You think too highly of me," I said. "But fine. This can't go any worse than usual."

Trying not to disturb each other made us both acutely aware of every twitch. Were we too close together? Should I scoot farther away, or would that bother her more? After a long few minutes of listening to Camille breathe and resisting the sudden urge to scratch my nose, I revised my opinion: this could, in fact, go worse than usual.

Camille sat up. I expected her to leave, but she shrugged out of her dressing gown, dropped it on the floor, and slid back under the sheets.

Then she rolled onto her side to face me and laid a tentative hand on my hip. "Come here."

I could have asked for clarification. I could have declined. I could have asked her to leave. I could even have pretended, very badly, to be asleep, and I'm sure she would have let the whole thing pass. What I did instead was to roll onto my side, facing away from her, and let her fit her knees into the crook of my own and her front against my back. It had been a long, long time since I'd lain like this with anyone. Delphine and I rarely had the opportunity to use a bed, or spend our limited private time together on anything so indolent, and the two men I'd taken to bed before her had both been quick, friendly affairs.

Camille, a little shorter than me, pressed her face against my shoulder blade and wrapped an arm around my middle. It was only through watching her ride and touching her that I'd learned the surprising strength in her arms and thighs, invisible when she's dressed and at rest. Having her clamped around me, I could feel that strength in the most pleasant and comforting of ways. Her compact body radiated warmth. Once we were touching, the sound of her breath and the rustle of the sheets became something to settle into. Knowing she was there eased the tightness in my lungs and my jaw. Camille's presence transformed lying awake in the dark from my habitual nightly failure into a peaceful way to pass the time.

It doesn't matter if I sleep, I recall thinking, but in the

end I must have. At my next slow, groggy blink, honey-colored morning light pooled on the dark wood floor. The mattress shifted. Cool air replaced the heat at my back. There was the barest brush of lips on my temple, so brief I might have imagined it, and then, in a minor miracle, I drifted off again.

# PRIVATE DIARY OF ARI LAZARE, MAY 25, 1825

Camille and I have fallen into the habit of sleeping together. Only sleeping, that is, not having sex. We don't discuss it. She simply crawls into the bed and wraps herself around me and I let her.

I ought to tell Delphine, I think, but our unfortunate circumstances mean I can't invite her, and I suspect she'd want to be invited.

Camille, my lost turtle dove,

I write to wish you luck for your reading, since I won't be there to applaud wildly or swoon out of my seat. You don't need luck from me or from anyone, as there is no better writer alive, but I wish it regardless. It's rude of you to need so little from me, you know. If you were nervous about reading in front of a crowd, I could offer you suggestions of what to picture to distract yourself, but you love crowds and orations and they love you in return, as they should. Are you sure you don't want me to come sigh dreamily over the sound of your voice as you read? It will come quite naturally to me.

More seriously, Camille, I owe you an apology. Two, in effect.

First—and simplest—I shouldn't have summarily thrust you and Ari together in the way that I did. Panic is no excuse. I ought to have considered the matter more carefully and come up with a solution that would have caused you less pain. You handled my rude blunder with such competence and kindness, and I can hardly express my gratitude. You are a saint, Camille. Please don't get all shot through with arrows or cut into bits. I like you alive and whole.

Second, I must address a deeper wound. When we began our liaison, I lied to you by omission. I allowed you to think that you came second in my affections and that what was between us was, for me, an amusement. A friendly sort of lust, but lust alone. Nothing that touched my heart. Having loved and lost Ari, I was afraid to love and lose you, too. I thought perhaps if I didn't say the words, I could avoid the risk.

That silence is the most damning lie I have ever told. By the time we kissed, I was already in love again —with you.

If it hurts, it is my own fault. I feared heartache so much that I brought it on myself, which I perhaps deserve, and on you, which you do not and never will. You were never a dalliance to me, Camille. You were never just a friend that I happened to fuck. You gifted me your time and your body and your precious self, and I was too weak to accept their full weight. It was cowardice that made me fail to see how much I need and cherish you. Every hour that passes without you is a lonely one.

Even if Ari and I make a family together, a man and a woman and their child, everything as society tells us it should be (except that he's a Jew and an atheist and an escaped convict, while I am an adulterous whore who cuckolded her husband and destroyed his legacy, and everything about us is thoroughly disgraceful and I won't pretend to be ashamed)—even then I will always miss you if you are not with us. I love Ari. I can't tell you that I don't love him, or that I love him less than you, because those are lies and I don't wish to lie to you again. But I love you, too, Camille.

If you cannot accept that, I will always be grateful for what we had. I simply could not let you go without telling you the truth.

I would promise not to repeat the first error for which I apologized above, but I don't have any other long-lost loves who might return from the dead, which I think is a relief to all of us. I can promise, should you wish to keep me, to treat you with the care you deserve in the future.

I know you don't wish me to come to your reading, but if you'll permit me to call on you beforehand, I'd like to offer you a kiss for luck. As discussed, you certainly don't need luck, but you can have the kiss for its own sake.


Yours,
    Delphine

Delphine arrived at Camille's in the late afternoon. I'd glimpsed her handwriting in a letter that Camille read yesterday, but hadn't expected her.

Delphine and Camille kissed on the cheeks, and Delphine said, as though continuing a conversation, "What will you wear?"

"I would like to try a few things," Camille said and looked at me.

I didn't understand why. Delphine's advice about fashion is far more valuable than mine.

Delphine beamed at her. "Trying things _is_ the best way to know if they suit you. Let's go upstairs."

Though Camille comes to my room, I've only been to the threshold of hers. I hung back, unsure if I was invited to follow them, but Camille cast me a glance and tipped her head toward the stairs. She didn't say as much, but I suspected she was seeking support. Whatever passed between Camille and Delphine in letters, Camille wasn't yet prepared for them to be alone in her room. Besides, I thought Camille might want someone there who could put an end to the trying of clothes if it went on too long.

I was ill-equipped to be that person. When Delphine had played this game with me in the past, it had resulted in more undressing than dressing, and I had always encouraged it to go on as long as possible. I resolutely thought nothing of this as I sat in an armchair. We weren't there to have sex. Camille had never said anything to indicate that she was attracted to me, and she'd expressed only doubt when Delphine had made that comment about having both a wife and a mistress.

We were there to try on clothes, like Camille had said. I wasn't sure why I'd been included, but whatever was happening, I wanted to stay.

Camille's room is grand, but not so excessively opulent as Delphine's bedroom. The soft red drapes were thrown open. The last of the afternoon light glossed the wood floor and layered luster over the thick carpet, woven with all colors of flowers against a white background. On the bed were covers of that same pink-red color. Delphine spread her striped blue-and-white skirts over them like the whole thing belonged to her.

She'd probably spent time in it, but I didn't think about that, either.

The whole room glowed pink. It felt warm and cozy, or it would have if Camille hadn't been fidgeting with the contents of her wardrobe, holding tension in her shoulders. The armoire was a beautiful but imposing piece of furniture, and when its doors were opened, I was surprised to see dresses as well as suits inside. In our short acquaintance, Camille had only worn trousers.

She pulled out a deep brown dress and laid it on the

bed next to Delphine. I've never been good at envisioning how any garment, shapeless when unworn, might transform once draped over a body. The dress might have been daring or modest, staid or fashionable, but it flopped onto the bed just the same.

"I won't know until I've seen you in it," Delphine said, which made me feel a little better. "I'll do your buttons. Do you want Ari to leave the room for this part?"

"No," Camille said, which made me blink in surprise.

I was already half out of my chair and I sat back down. I expected Camille to add that I should avert my eyes, but she said nothing more. I averted them anyway.

I reminded myself that Camille was here to try on clothes. I still didn't know why I was there, but an invitation into her room wasn't the same as an invitation to admire her nakedness.

Her frockcoat landed on the bed, and then her waistcoat. I didn't look. The muted tap of Camille's boot soles on the floor as she removed them and the rustle of wool as she slid her trousers down her legs were as loud as a siren's song. I dug my fingers into the chair's velvet armrests and didn't sneak a peek at Camille's thighs. They were rounded with muscle, I knew from riding with her, and they likely had that lovely, long channel running down the side, a perfect handhold.

When her stockings whispered to the floor, I didn't look at her knees, her calves, her ankles, her feet. When her shirt billowed across the bed, I didn't look at her chest, which I remembered from my first glimpse of her as smooth and nearly flat. I didn't look at her belly, which might be furrowed with strength or softly padded. Her hips, the slant of her hip bones, the dark triangle of hair between them—I pressed my lower lip into my mouth and didn't look.

She pulled on a shift and Delphine did her corset laces, and then there were layers of fabric all brushing against each other, and finally the dress covered Camille and I could look.

It was revelatory. I stifled my reaction so as not to offend anyone.

Camille is radiant in suits. The dress hid her athletic body and sapped the confidence from her stance. Her mouth settled into a flat line of boredom or irritation. Camille's beauty is understated and unconventional, conveyed in her motion and expressions, and when she doesn't feel at home in her clothes, it's dimmed.

Not extinguished.

I'd spent the past few minutes trying hard not to think about what freckles or moles or scars might form constellations on her naked skin. It would take more than an unflattering dress to douse my interest.

Delphine smirked at me. She knew.

She'd always known when I liked someone, before. Either I make my feelings too evident or her perception is uncanny. She'd teased me about my infatuation with Hassan every time we'd seen him expound on his vast knowledge of animal behavior at a salon, and I'd slept with him at her encouragement. He treated sex like a rousing match of tennis, and never had any patience for holding each other afterward, but that wasn't Delphine's fault.

I already knew what it felt like to be held through the night by Camille.

But she might prefer Delphine to me, and prefer to have Delphine to herself, and perhaps that was why her mouth was still stuck in that line.

Delphine asked, "Do you <u>want</u> to wear a dress?"

"I don't know," Camille said.

"Are you, perhaps, a little nervous about this reading?" Delphine asked.

"No. I like reading my work. I'm nervous about everything else."

Taillefer in the audience would make me afraid—but I wondered if it was the thought of me and Delphine spending more time together in her absence that made Camille want to disappear into that dress.

"Choose a dress you <u>like</u>," Delphine ordered.

The second one was a rich, glossy purple, more red than blue. The neckline dipped far below her collarbones and left the tops of her shoulders bare, ending in short, puffed sleeves. The hem of the skirt was almost sculptural, row upon row of triangles of fabric overlapping like dragon scales. Camille picked up her skirts in a curtsy, first to me, and then to Delphine. That simple movement made her seem so much more at ease.

It also gave me a glimpse of her bare feet sinking into the carpet, meaning she had no stockings beneath her skirts. That was knowledge I should not have.

"This one's better," I said, though nobody had asked for my useless opinion. "The color suits your complexion, and the skirt... well, it looks a bit like armor."

"Thank you," Camille said, sincerely accepting my stumbling commentary. I wondered again why she'd asked me here.

She turned toward the window rather than toward me, silhouetting her form against the light. As I studied her, it struck me anew that Camille was only a little taller than petite Delphine. I think of her as towering, though of course she's shorter than me.

"This dress is better," Delphine said. She arranged Camille's skirts in some minutely different way and brushed lint that wasn't there off her bodice. Her fingers stroked Camille's cheek and then gently raised her chin. "But we can't be satisfied with merely 'better.' I want 'perfect.' Superb. Resplendent."

"An achievable aim for you, but the rest of us are mortal, Delphine," Camille said.

"You know my imperfections all too well," Delphine said and grasped both of her hands.

"I love your imperfections."

They held each other's gaze, Camille's chestnut-crowned head bent toward Delphine's amber one.

When Camille turned toward me, I felt it like an arrow. Like she'd shot right through me and pinned me in place. The sudden awareness of my thumping pulse stung and quivered.

She hadn't forgotten me. This wasn't a private moment I was witnessing by accident.

This was a private moment I was witnessing on purpose.

Camille curved a hand around Delphine's hip and slid the other into her hair, pulling her into a kiss.

She was staking a claim. Instead of jealousy, I felt lust.

The kiss was so deep and searching I could almost feel it. The firm press of her lips and the rough slide of her tongue. The dig of her grip on my scalp. The pressure of her body against mine.

I was imagining myself <u>as</u> Delphine. I ought to have imagined myself as Camille, kissing Delphine. The sweet floral scent of her perfume, the softness of her breasts and belly, all of that was fresh in my memory. But I only know how to kiss Delphine reverently or desperately, even furiously, like I worship and crave her. It's not in my nature to kiss Delphine with anything resembling calm control.

Camille was one long, fluid line of power, from the tilt of her head to the tips of her fingers. The kiss was decisive. Commanding. I was seated, yet my knees went weak.

When Camille finished, Delphine's hair was coming loose from its pins and I was breathless.

"Does this mean—" Delphine began.

"We are not discussing that now," Camille said, exactly as firmly as she kissed. "We are here to decide what I will wear tonight. I am trying on clothes."

"Ah," Delphine said, her voice ragged around the edges. She glanced at me and bit her kiss-reddened lips. It was impossible for her to miss my arousal. Even if she hadn't lingered over my lap, my face was on fire. She said nothing to me, only swallowed and forcibly composed herself. She squeezed Camille's hands. "The dress is excellent, as Ari said, but you should wear a suit."

"And why is that?"

"Aside from my own personal lusts, and aside from the expectations of everyone attending this reading to see eccentric, androgynous genius Camille Dupin—expectations you are free to ignore as you wish, naturally—there is Taillefer to consider," Delphine said. She moved behind Camille and began unbuttoning her dress. "We all know he will attend. He will talk to you, and I know you will let him. Not because you wish to hear him speak, but because you think you might learn something useful. If you wear a dress, he will treat you as a woman, and he won't say anything interesting. If you wear a suit, flouting convention, that will allow him to flout it as well."

I would never have thought of that.

Camille laughed at the "huh" sound I made. "This is why we need Delphine, Ari."

Something about that harmless little sentence, with its <u>we</u>, with my name and Delphine's sitting right next to each other, made me almost as flushed with heat as when Camille dropped her dress to the floor. She shed her undergarments like they were nothing. Then, before I'd had the chance to take her in—because her practical actions had nothing to do with what I wanted—she pulled a white shirt over her head. Its hem hung to her thighs and its collar lay open, tantalizing me with little revelations as she walked. She opened the wardrobe to search for a suit.

"Black," Delphine said as Camille's hand hovered. "With the beautifully embroidered silk waistcoat, you know the one."

Laid out on the bed, the waistcoat was indeed eye-catching. Elaborate floral designs cascaded through many colors. Camille's suits were often less ostentatious, as it was enough of a statement for her to wear one in the first place. This ensemble managed to be beautiful and confrontational all at once. Fearless. A stroke of genius on Delphine's part.

"Yes," Camille said, regarding the clothes on the bed. "You're right about this."

"I'm right about many things," Delphine said, and only a person who knew her intimately would catch her faltering. She should have said <u>everything</u>. That was the sort of thing Delphine loved to say: <u>I'm right about everything</u>. She might have evened her breathing, but Camille had knocked her badly off-balance with that kiss.

"Perhaps I'll try your other ideas as well," Camille said mildly, and I had no idea what she meant, but Delphine gave her the widest, most brilliant smile in response. Then Camille said, "I want to take off your dress."

"Yes," Delphine said, so fast it was barely a word. "Yes, yes, yes."

They moved toward each other. It was almost like the two of them had forgotten I was watching, except Delphine's gaze kept cutting across the room to where I was seated, and once—only once—Camille made just enough eye contact, and quirked one corner of her mouth just enough, to let me know that nothing escaped her notice.

"Do you want Ari to leave the room for this part?" Camille teased Delphine.

"God no," Delphine said.

"And you?" Camille lobbed this question with such nonchalance that I almost didn't catch it.

A nod in response was all I could manage. The only way I was leaving was if one of them told me to get out, and I knew Delphine wouldn't.

Silent and intent, Camille removed every article of Delphine's clothing, baring her beautiful body. It had been too long since I'd laid eyes on Delphine naked. Even when we'd been together, seeing all of her had been a rare pleasure. Memory and imagination, which I'd only recently permitted myself to use, couldn't possibly do her justice. In the golden afternoon light, she was divine. I wanted to kiss her breasts and the luxurious curve of her belly. I wanted to grab two handfuls of her bottom and drag her close to me.

When Camille glanced at me, I was relieved that my hands were still clutching the chair armrests rather than on my cock. I'd thought about undoing my trousers. She had to know that. Touching Delphine in front of me was a taunt.

A single light press to Delphine's shoulder sent her to her knees beside the bed, as wordless and fluid as choreography. My blood ran hot with lust and envy. Every fiber and stitch of my clothing was rubbing my skin. It shouldn't be possible to feel so much all at once. My hands itched to take hold of my eager, aching cock while I watched Camille, still in her shirt and nothing else, lay back on the bed with her knees up.

Propped on her elbows, she was looking right at me. Her hot, dark gaze caressed my lips and throat. I'd thought I was watching her, but we were watching each other.

She spread her legs and all I could see between her thighs was the back of Delphine's head, no matter how I craned my neck. If I stood, or walked closer—but no. I held firm against desire. This was her bedroom. Her choice. She'd invited me here. If this was a test, I wanted to pass. I had to behave as an exemplary guest. Permission, even if it never came, would be worth the wait.

Camille slid her fingers into Delphine's mussed hair, removing the last few pins and sending her bun toppling down her back in cognac-colored waves. She pulled Delphine's head forward. Every little movement offered me the tiniest snatch of a vision: her thighs, the dark hair between them, a sliver of pink.

In a gesture that combined casual grace and possession, Camille hooked one ankle over Delphine's shoulder. The naked arch of her foot echoed the curves of Delphine's back and hips behind the curtain of her hair. How maddening that I'd been allowed to witness this, but from a distance and an angle that obscured everything I most wanted to see. I didn't dare leave my chair, though it was impossible not to adjust my position ever so slightly. With minute movements, I loosened my cravat. I longed to strip off my hot, confining frock coat, but fear of disruption kept me from doing so. Camille was still watching me.

Any sound I made might prevent me from hearing the wet lap of Delphine's tongue, or the low, satisfied hum in Camille's throat. I couldn't see the point of contact between them—barring Camille's foot over Delphine's shoulder, and Delphine's hand wrapped around Camille's thigh—but in the yearning silence, I could hear it.

It might've been delirium from all the blood in my body coursing to my cock, but I imagined I could smell it, too. Delphine had barely let me touch her when we'd been in her bedroom. I'd tasted her, but it already seemed long ago, and before that, it had been years since I'd been so close to the scent of pussy. Did I even remember it? A little like the ocean, but warm and tangy. I inhaled so deeply that my mouth watered. I could almost remember the silky, slick feel of it against my tongue. That had been Delphine; Camille would taste different. I wanted them both.

My right hand unclenched from the armrest and drifted, so slowly, toward my lap.

"Ari," Camille said. That single soft utterance was a thunder clap. When it faded to silence, I felt her attention like a graze of fingernails down naked skin. "Not yet."

I put my hand back. The velvet pricked my palm. The barest hint of a smile played at Camille's lips when I did as she asked, and I experienced a flood of shame and pleasure and yearning all at once. I thought I might burst from it, and then, impossibly, my cock grew harder. It strained at my trousers. Not touching myself required a force of will I wasn't sure I possessed.

"Wait," Camille said. "And watch."

She had a strong grip on Delphine's hair. Delphine's pretty toes curled against the bare soles of her feet, both tucked neatly under her luscious bottom. I would have wagered anything that she was dripping; I was, and I wasn't even the one with my tongue in Camille's cunt. A wet patch had formed on my trousers. I didn't care. I was probably drooling, too.

And then Delphine, whether from charitable whim or devilish impulse, spread her knees and raised herself just enough to show me her slick, glistening cunt. It was beautiful. Pink and ripe. The sight made me exhale like I'd been hit in the stomach. She was so close, only a few paces from me. Nothing was keeping me from standing, walking those few steps, and sinking my fingers into her, or better yet, kneeling behind her and pulling her onto my cock.

Except that Camille had told me to wait, and I wanted to please her.

Camille closed her eyes in ecstasy and let her head fall back. She wouldn't know if I touched myself now. As unbearable as waiting was, disappointing her would be worse. What if she never allowed me this again? I squirmed and sat on my hands. Even the friction of my clothes was almost too much.

Camille's foot jerked. Her knuckles went a shade whiter. She let loose a sound from deep in her throat and then her hips thrust up and her thighs clenched as she came. Delphine never stopped. An erratic crescendo of gasps filled the room. The air was fragrant with sex. I sucked it desperately into my lungs.

Delphine pressed her cheek to Camille's thigh. Camille stroked her hair.

Then she untangled herself from Delphine and stood,

her shirt falling to her thighs. She looked more dressed than I felt. Her long perusal lingered over my lips, red and bitten, and then my lap, where my cock was thick and stiff under my trousers. The longer she stared, the harder I got. The terrible anticipation of not knowing what she would say or do next constricted my chest. Perhaps I'd been wrong to wait. Perhaps she'd laugh and tell me to get out.

Delphine was still kneeling by the bed, though she'd twisted to see both of us. Camille lifted Delphine's chin with two fingers. Light glinted on her glossy, wet lips.

Camille tipped her head at me and said, "Kiss him."

A smile flashed over Delphine's face and then she was across the room and halfway into my lap, her hands gripping my shoulders and one knee thrust between my thighs. Her mouth was hot and soft against mine. My face quickly became as slick as hers, the faint but unmistakable taste all over both of us.

She was so, so marvelously naked. I ran my hands all over her and buried my face in the crook of her neck.

"I want you to fuck me," she said, which nearly made me burst, except she was still talking. "But we can't, not without a sponge or a sheath or preferably both."

She'd been so eagerly obedient and quiet for Camille that it stunned me to have her on top of me, efficiently taking my clothes off while telling me exactly what she wanted, even though that was much more like the Delphine I knew. She whipped my cravat off and started pulling at my sleeves like I couldn't undress myself, and she was nearly right. I shrugged out of my coat and my shirt. She kissed me again.

"I have a sponge and a sheath," Camille said. I'd been too entranced with a lap full of naked Delphine to notice Camille, but her sudden entrance into our conversation made me flush with heat. She'd been watching. I liked that she'd been watching.

Delphine studied me, a question in the shape of her eyebrows, so I said, "I'll do anything you want." It was a truth so obvious to me that it seemed impossible for her not to know it, but I said it anyway. I couldn't risk leaving it unspoken.

Delphine nodded. "And Camille, you'll... watch, like Ari did?"

Camille made a sound almost like a laugh. "No," she said. "Not like Ari did."

I understood right away what she meant—Camille wouldn't keep herself in suspense, not when all of this was happening at her whim—and Delphine must have, too, because she bit her plush bottom lip and said, "Of course." And then, with uncharacteristic hesitation, "You don't mind?"

"If I minded the two of you fucking in my bed, it would have been very foolish of me to let things progress as they have," Camille said, which seemed like an answer, but wasn't exactly. She opened a drawer in the table next to her bed and handed a sponge and a sheath to Delphine, who put the sponge in right away. To me, she said, "Take off the rest of your clothes and lie on your back."

I moved as fast as I could without ripping a seam. Camille directed Delphine to fit the sheath onto my stiff, aching cock, and I shivered at the first brush of her fingers. Even through the sheath, it overwhelmed me, like no one had ever touched me before.

"Straddle him," Camille said.

Delphine smiled and mounted me. Because I was losing my mind, I thought of the night I'd gone riding with Camille, except in this arrangement I wasn't the rider. I wondered if Camille would describe me as good-natured and hard-working.

Thankfully, Delphine sank down onto my cock at that moment and stopped me from thinking further. I've never been so grateful to be rendered breathless. The sweet, snug heat of her surrounded me. The sound that released from the back of my throat was ragged, half-relieved and half-wanting. I could come at any moment.

"Delphine," Camille said. She was standing next to us, still dressed only in her shirt. She'd rolled the sleeves up to her elbows. Her fingers traced from Delphine's cheek to under her chin, drawing Delphine's attention away from me and toward her. "Do you think Ari liked watching you put your tongue in my cunt?"

"I do."

Camille's hand wandered down Delphine's throat and idled possessively between her breasts. She cupped one, and the weight of it spilled out of her palm. Envy had me clutching fistfuls of the bedsheets. "Do you think he'll like watching me make you come on his cock?"

Delphine made a sharp little gasp, then darted a glance at me. I nodded as vigorously as I could. She said, "I do."

"Lift up a little, Delphine," Camille instructed. "Ari, spread your legs."

My whole body thrilled to the sound of my name in her mouth. Even to be included in the conversation made me vibrate with eager need. When Delphine raised herself so only the tip of my cock was still inside her, I groaned at the slick clench of her running up my shaft, at the singular movement, at the return it promised. I quivered with the effort of not thrusting upward. My legs jerked apart.

Camille ran her hand from Delphine's breasts down her

belly and into the red-brown curls underneath. She kept going, touching the shaft of my cock, sliding her finger through the wetness coating the sheath, then returned to the place our bodies met and went just a little higher. From the way Delphine sucked in and sighed out a breath, Camille's long, elegant finger hadn't missed its mark.

With her other hand, Camille plunged two fingers into herself. They came away wet. Her hand disappeared behind Delphine's back. I thought she meant to fuck Delphine in the ass while I fucked her in the pussy. The thought of Delphine writhing with pleasure on my cock made me bite my lip and lock all the muscles in my hips.

Camille's fingertips made gentle contact with the inside of my thigh.

My eyes went wide. She meant to touch me. To fuck me. A frisson of surprise and excitement ran through me. It must have been obvious, since Delphine smiled at me. Not smugly, but with sympathetic understanding—she was trembling in anticipation, too.

By gradual exploration, Camille found my balls, the tender spot behind them, and then the sensitive rim of my hole. I was still shaking a little, trying not to think of the head of my cock in Delphine's pussy and how good it would feel when she sank back down. Camille's touch struck me like lightning. I twitched.

Camille said, "Ari."

My voice emerged like a rasp. "Yes?"

"Do you want this?"

"Yes," I said. "Please. Please fuck me, Camille. Use me. Anything you want."

"Good," she said. Her hands were engaged, but it felt like an approving caress. "You don't need any coaxing to talk, do you? You waited a long time for this, Ari. Say anything you like. Move, Delphine."

I swore and groaned wordlessly as Delphine enveloped me in her cunt. Camille approached with more caution, circling and applying gentle pressure. I could see her other hand buried in Delphine's curls, rubbing her clit, and I wondered if she was working us at the same pace.

"Up, Delphine," Camille said. "And down again."

I couldn't write down what I said even if I did remember it, some mixture of panting and grunting and "Delphine—Camille—please—"

"Touch her tits, Ari," Camille said.

My hands snapped up. There they were at last, Delphine's breasts, gloriously heavy and soft, undersides smooth against my palms and nipples peaked and stiff under my thumbs.

"Perfect," I mumbled.

She leaned forward, pressing them toward my face. I craned my upper body to put my mouth on one. Delphine moaned happily and Camille said, "Just like that, Ari. Keep going. Don't come. A little faster, Delphine."

Had she known I would love this? Had Delphine told her? Delphine and I had never done anything like this. I wasn't even sure I'd known I would love it. Maybe Camille had learned from observing me during our weeks of living together, or maybe this was what she wanted—to taunt me, to take charge, to take me apart—and she'd wagered that I wanted her and Delphine badly enough to go along with anything.

She'd wagered correctly, but with her finger in my ass and Delphine riding my cock, I didn't feel like I'd lost.

There was something perfect about the complexity of it, not just that there were three of us, but that I was feeling everything at once. Out of my mind with lust, wanting desperately to come and wanting desperately to make it last, at once restrained and free, wanting to fuck Delphine so hard she'd scream my name and wanting Camille to do the same to me, and maybe, somewhere deeper, still a little envious and just a touch ashamed of how much I loved making myself vulnerable to both of them, how much I longed to please them, how much I wanted them to overpower me. But Camille had granted me permission to be shameless, too, and it all mixed together. A little salt in the sweetness for depth. It was real. Genuine. It sprang from learning each other, knowing each other, from loving Delphine and waiting such a long time to have her again that I would share her with anyone she wanted—and from loving the person she'd chosen. From loving Camille.

No artifice could compare.

"Camille, I want to come, let me come," Delphine said. A flush colored her pink from her face down to her navel. She slammed her hips down and rose up relentlessly. Her voice was all plea and air, hitching with her rhythm. "Make Ari come. I want to feel it. I want him to feel me."

"Oh, he will," Camille said. "Keep going, love."

Camille kissed her. They broke apart quickly as Delphine sped up and Camille pressed her fingers deeper inside me, stroking a spot that made me shudder and shout.

"Come," she said, addressing Delphine or both of us, and it was only by the finest fraction of a second that Delphine toppled first, letting loose a high-pitched cry and clenching so hard around my cock that my eyes rolled back in my head. I felt it ripple through her in wave after wave, and then through me, as Camille kept up her slippery, stroking touch. I thrust hard into Delphine and lost myself to sensation, feeling everything so fully that it released into nothingness.

Afterward I felt pleasantly liquid. Camille slid out, and then Delphine slid off and collapsed beside me, and as she clamped her arms around me and nestled her head against my chest, my eyes drifted shut.

# CAMILLE TO DELPHINE, MAY 27, 1825
## LEFT ON THE BEDSIDE TABLE

Delphine,

You and Ari are both sweetly asleep and I don't wish to wake you before I leave. Your letter moved me, and I owe you a better response than this hasty little note, but I hope we will have time to talk tomorrow, or after we've resolved some of our more serious troubles.

Pressed for time, I confine myself to the essential: I do not—have <u>never</u> wanted you to let me go.


Yours,
Camille

Delphine didn't wake first. She never fell asleep in the first place.

(I know because she—you—told me. I shouldn't interrupt your reading, but you might find this strange, these words that represent your thoughts and your senses that come from my pen and not yours. But neither you nor Ari wrote about this moment, so I had to. It's too lovely not to include. Lacking a letter, I've resorted to fiction. It's not the first time I've been inside you, but it's the first time I've felt anything less than confident about it. Turn the page if it doesn't suit you, and I promise I'll never do it again.)

Delphine lay quiet in Camille's bed, next to Ari, and listened to Camille dress and scratch out a little note and depart for the reading from which Delphine herself had been so bluntly, unwaveringly banned. The urge to detain Camille—for more time in bed, or to impress upon her more firmly the urgent truth of Delphine's own feelings, or preferably both at once—was strong, but not unconquerable. A passionate, pleading letter along with a desperately needed, joyful fuck made a good argument, and sometimes a person needed time to reflect after such an experience. Not Delphine. But in theory, it was possible that someone might.

Camille guarded her heart very, very carefully. Today she'd said yes, but would she say yes tomorrow? Delphine picked up Camille's note, read it, and pressed it to her chest. The paper crinkled. She wanted to read it aloud, to sing it, to show it to Ari and ask what he thought.

She had to let him sleep. It had been so long since she'd seen him with any slack in his shoulders, and she'd never had the pleasure of seeing the lush black crescent of his lashes lie peacefully against his scarred cheek. Age and hardship had worn away the roundness there, had scraped and roughened his skin, and still he looked like Octave. As a baby, Octave had slept pillowed on her chest, warm and serene, for enough hours to memorize the lay of his solemn little face, but not enough hours to satisfy her.

Ari had missed it. She would take that kerchief of his and wipe away precious minutes of her own memory and give them to him, that he might know some fraction of those sweet and aching months.

When Ari stirred an hour later, she told him so.

Dismay furrowed his brow. "No—as much as I want to know what I missed, I can't take anything else from you." He twisted toward her, lifted her hand, and kissed it. "You already gave me your letters. Let's say instead that I will make my own memories."

"Yes," Delphine said, dabbing at an errant tear. "I'm so sorry we couldn't make it work the first time. If I'd been free to search for you—"

"If I'd never gone to his house in the first place—"

"If I'd agreed to run away with you—"

"It would never have worked," he said suddenly. "We were naïve, with the whole world against us, and if it hadn't been Taillefer and Toulon and your parents and your ogre, it would have been something else."

She huffed. "I wish you were wrong. I hope that's not true for us now."

"It isn't. We won't let it be," he said. "We're different, everything's different. There's Camille—maybe. I hope."

Delphine passed him the note.

He smiled at her when he'd finished reading. What a rare pleasure it was to see happiness crease his beautiful face. Delphine brushed her fingers against his stubbled cheek. He caught her hand, then drew her into a kiss. There was so much promise and warmth in it that she thought of a sunrise, or the first day of spring. The end of an enduring, cold darkness. They were going to live, Delphine thought, they were going to live *happily*.

He kissed his way down her body, another wordless promise. This one, he made good on immediately, with the devotion of a man who had been waiting a long, long time.

Delphine replied in kind.

Afterward, sated in the way of lovers who will always want more, they needed nothing but to entangle their fingers and gaze at each other.

Ari said, "You know, Camille asked me what kind of future I imagined for myself, and whether I intended to continue my research, and I told her I couldn't imagine a future until Taillefer was dead. And I'm still afraid, and I don't know what to do about him, but I've been thinking about the future."

"You mentioned that," Delphine murmured, and then said, "*Do* you want to continue your research?"

"No," he said forcefully. "No, I never want to touch a

magical artifact again—well, except the coin. I can't imagine life without it."

Delphine shivered as Ari recounted his escape from Toulon and the coin he'd used to determine his luck. "What an unsettling object. I'm grateful you escaped, but I like to make my own decisions."

"I make my own decisions," he protested.

"Of course you do. I'm sorry. I've developed a horror of these artifacts because of what my late husband did to me," she said. "I'm very glad you don't want to do any more research. I want a future untouched by these damned things."

"I understand that," he said. "It's funny that you brought up remembering Octave as an infant. Because I looked at him and I want to know him now. I want to know who he'll be next year, and the year after that. Who knows where I'll be living or what I'll be doing, but if he's there, and you're there, and Camille, too—I think I'll be happy. I haven't permitted myself that possibility in years. It's terrifying. But I want it."

Ari returned Camille's note to Delphine, and she squeezed his hand. "I want it, too."

Dear Isabelle,

You are a sly creature. Your actions might have escaped my notice entirely if Ari and I hadn't—well, it's not important what we were doing at the time. Or rather, it's very important to me, and also to him, but I don't think a detailed description falls within the bounds of my new friendship with you, and I want you to keep reading this letter.

Though I must say, since our friendship is founded on having suffered the same rare torture, as you put it, that I hope you have also reclaimed yourself, and enjoyed your body in any way you wish to, as it belongs to you and no one else. Whether that means walking freely through the world, dressing and eating and speaking however you want, taking no one or everyone to bed, I hope you have arrived there, or will arrive there soon. Myself, I think I <u>could</u> have reached that destination alone, but it would have taken me longer and been a lonelier journey without Ari and Camille.

I hope you have someone other than yourself to confide in, Isabelle. I know you must think I've been quite forward in these letters that you told me not to write, designating us as friends without consulting you, but if you truly find my company distasteful, all you need to do is ignore these letters once you return to Paris. If you do respond, I will be thrilled. If ever you needed a confidante, I would be honored.

Let us return to what Ari and I surmised while we were lying together. It was an emotional conversation, as it began with us discussing our separation, and wondering if it could have been different. If we'd never been separated, or if I'd been free to search for him, and we'd found each other sooner... one can invent all sorts of endings to the story. After some time, this brought us to what did happen, and what we knew of it, and each of us had a piece the other was missing.

Namely, in early March, I entrusted you with Ari's compass and a mission to find him. You disappeared (and are still not returned from your mysterious travels). Unbeknownst to me, mere weeks later, Ari stumbled upon a magical coin in the shipyards of Toulon that facilitated his daring and improbable escape from prison.

To me, it seems possible that a person such as yourself, one with a collection of enchanted artifacts and a knowledge of Ari's predicament, might have contrived to place that coin in his path. It would be a simple, undetectable way to aid a prisoner. Whoever set those events in motion would receive neither credit nor blame. Nothing can be proven.

But I know it was you, Isabelle, and I love you for it.

·  ·  ·

Your friend,
    Delphine

CAMILLE DUPIN TO VICTOR
BEAUCHÊNE, MAY 28, 1825
WRITTEN ON ENCRYPTED PAPER

Dear Victor,

Here is an account of my conversation with Maximilien Taillefer that you may share with Isabelle de Tourzin. I don't fully comprehend this paper of yours that Julien provided—I suppose it's a fool's errand, applying reason to magic, but it's my nature to try—and while I feel that I know you well enough to think of you as I write these words, I've never met Mme de Tourzin, so I doubt my capacity to address anything to her. Will she be able to read this? I have written her name in the hope that it will help.

In honesty, I have also allowed Ari to read these pages, as he would not let me rest until he furrowed through every word, though I warned him against it. Delphine would have done the same were she here; I will relay all of this to her when I see her next.

Per request, this account is thorough. My very spirit recoils from the idea of including "every detail," as though I ought to describe the shape of Taillefer's fingernails and the precise curve of his forehead. My literary rivals engage in that sort of nonsense. I cannot bring myself to do it. Taillefer's fingernails are likely as repulsive as the rest of him, but I didn't have time to check. To be clear, it is his character that renders him repulsive. Physically he's a more or less symmetrical, pale Frenchman of unremarkable height and build, with wavy brown hair and thick sideburns, probably in his thirties. I hate him.

Let me begin.

I gave a reading at a salon at the home of the Comtesse de Davrance last night. I was accompanied by Julie Morère, henceforth Julien and "he," as that is how he has chosen to present himself in his association with Taillefer. As far as I know, Taillefer has no notion that Julien is anything other than the usual sort of man. He does, however, know that I am some distance from the usual sort of woman. I mention this because I believe it mattered for our rapport.

I dressed in a suit on the advice of my associate Delphine de Tousserat, née de Montfleury, dowager Marquise de Quennetière, which I am recording only for veracity, as she hates to be addressed that way. For reasons not germane to this report, I had disinvited Delphine from the reading; nevertheless I trusted her, her abundant experience socializing with the wealthy, and her perspicacity with people. Her sartorial advice proved sound.

Taillefer commissioned a portrait from Julien last year. Their relationship is not warm. I have met Taillefer before as he frequents some of the same salons I do, and I have no doubt that he remembers our last encounter. He assaulted me. At the time I was too stunned to retaliate, but I have refused to go near him ever since. Though it left a sour taste in my mouth, I smoothed over our past trouble, implying that I had been cold to him because of my mercurial writerly nature, and that I regretted my anger. Never have I felt I belonged on the stage of the Comédie-Française, but I must have done a passable job apologizing. Taillefer accepted it. He leered when I mentioned, as obliquely as possible, that I had heard he collected magical artifacts and was interested in starting a collection of my own.

The reading took place in a room decorated in a tedious neoclassical fashion, with fake frescoes framed by stylized white columns in bas relief. Between those, enormous mirrors surrounded us. Even in that cavernous room, Taillefer standing so close made me feel hemmed in and surveilled.

At first we talked of nothing relevant, and Julien stepped on my toe when I strayed too close to the truth, or politics, or anything else Taillefer would find objectionable. For someone who ostensibly enjoys salons, that man's ideas of power, class, and money are rigid and narrow. His lechery, however, knows no such limits. He has groped Delphine in addition to me, and you mentioned that he has also harassed you. We know from Ari Lazare's account that Taillefer has used magical artifacts to commit rape, thus justifying any seizure of dangerous items you or Mme de Tourzin might perform. I wish I had the skills. After what felt like hours of painstaking coaxing on my part—and a heroic, subtle effort by Julien to get me to restrain my disgust—Taillefer began to boast of his collection.

The comment that goaded him to do so at last was as follows:

"Perhaps you will not believe me, but I once witnessed

an item so powerful that it could completely capture a person's will," I said. "A man used it to make his wife more obedient. She was given to unseemly displays of rudeness and flights of folly, and he wanted a quiet, proper wife. He gifted her an emerald necklace, and after he'd clasped it around her neck, she could only move and speak in ways that he directed."

"No need to be so false and oblique about it. I know you don't care about what's proper and seemly, Dupin." He made a disrespectful gesture at my suit-clad body. Taillefer had been calling me by my surname all night. I haven't worked out whether he meant it as an insult, denying me "Mademoiselle," or an assumption of brotherly closeness, or some unpleasant combination of the two.

"Neither do you," I said baldly.

"So much the better. We can talk about what that emerald necklace is really good for." He leaned forward in his armchair, now eager to share what he knew. "There's only one like that in existence, and the Marquis was a rival collector. We were both after it. You must have been acquainted with him... or his wife, perhaps?"

"Widow," I corrected before I could stop myself. Julien gave me a look of despair.

It was foolish to display any interest in Delphine, but our connection wasn't a revelation to Taillefer. That isn't a surprise, considering that we met in public in October and my reaction to her was neither suave nor subtle.

"Gossip does say she has a fire up her ass for you, Dupin," he said. "You'd hardly need the necklace to get her on her knees or—whatever it is you do with a woman. Though it's the power that draws us, isn't it?"

I ignored that; no other response was wise. His desire

for the necklace struck me as an obvious avenue for manipulation. "What would you do with it, if you had it?"

"The same thing anyone else would—whatever I wanted," he said. "That kind of permanent, absolute control is a treasure."

"Is it?" I said, which he didn't seem to hear.

"Rumor has it the necklace disappeared when the Marquis died. A tragedy to lose something so precious. But you've been in the Marquise's company. Maybe you've been digging through her jewels." He leered.

I pretended not to see it.

"If you find it, Dupin, I'll make you an offer."

"Or kill me," I said, which made him bark with laughter.

"Indeed I might."

"What's in your collection that might tempt me, if I do lay hands on the necklace and decide to part with it?" I asked, hoping he'd continue to speak so freely.

He did. As you will see from the list I have included on the next page, Taillefer owns at least two dozen magical artifacts, and all can be put to evil use. He has a particular fascination for items that allow him to exert undue influence over the minds and bodies of others. I hope you rob him of every last one.

The only other discussion of importance is that while he was bragging about his hoard, I said, "You have enough to subdue an army. You hardly even need the necklace. I can't imagine you're missing anything."

"For a novelist, you have an impoverished imagination," he said, taking a sip of his brandy. "I could have so much more. I've lost things better than what I've told you about this evening."

"Like what?"

"The emerald necklace is gauche," he said. "Big and obvious, and you can't use it unless you clasp it around someone's neck, which no one will let you do unless they expect it. If I'd wanted to use it on you, for example, I would have had to trick you into it somehow. Make no mistake, I still want it. Its effect endures like no other. But the best thing I've ever found for inducing a docile, compliant condition was an unassuming little fire striker. Unremarkable and thus perfect. Anybody who breathed in the smoke from the fire would happily go along with whatever I said."

"Careless to lose something like that," I said.

"Oh, I'll get it back," he said. "I know who stole it."

"You know who the thief is and you haven't simply killed him?" I asked. My own knowledge that the thief was Ari Lazare—who I've been sheltering and protecting from Taillefer's wrath, who's reading these words even though there exists no magical artifact that can render an account of this conversation harmless—made a bead of sweat slide down my skin under my shirt. I don't think I betrayed myself.

I think Taillefer already knew.

Taillefer said, "The thief toyed with me by hiding it, so I've toyed with him in return by keeping him alive and tormented. It's a different, more distant kind of power than what I usually enjoy, but I have enjoyed it, so the theft wasn't entirely a loss. And soon enough he'll bring the striker back to me."

As Taillefer uttered this unmistakable threat, Julien shifted to press the side of his boot against mine. Whether he meant to prevent me from an angry retort or to stave off the chill running down my spine, I don't know. I couldn't stop myself from asking, "Why would a thief return what he stole?"

"Haven't you been paying attention, Dupin?" he asked. "I'll force him. That's what I do."

Julien and I left shortly after that. I spent the remainder of yesterday evening and some time this morning writing this report.


Camille

Dear Isabelle,

I thought you might like to know some of what occurred in my home today, or I suppose it was yesterday, since I'm writing after midnight. You are still out of town, so I have recorded it for you. Camille has provided me with this magic paper, via Julien, via Victor.

Camille encountered Taillefer the night of her reading at the Comtesse de Davrance's. It seems such a long time ago now, the lovely day we had, all three of us together and then Ari and I reminiscing and singing her praises while she was out. Anyway, naturally her encounter with Taillefer was horrible, as all encounters with him are, and he threatened her and implied that he knew about her connection with me and perhaps even her connection with Ari. She wrote it all down for you, hoping you might rob Taillefer, which you still could if you come back soon, but now her account serves the purpose of prefacing what happened this morning.

Ari and Camille came to my house. We'd been trying to avoid meeting here, as Taillefer had someone watching the house and because Octave is here and I don't want to expose him to danger. They deemed the matter urgent enough to come see me. When they arrived, I had Amélie and Marthe take Octave and Caro on a walk as a precaution, and I'm very glad I did that.

The three of us met in the parlor. Since I didn't know the motive of their visit, I had time and attention enough to admire the sight of them together in daylight. The two of them are so gorgeous, it's a wonder I stayed on my feet. I suppose if I had collapsed, the carpet is soft enough to save me from bruises.

Camille's success in making Ari look like his old self still leaves me breathless, mostly with heart-lifting wonder, but the sight has an edge, a little like a slap. We suffered and survived too much in our time apart. I missed him. I never want to be parted from him again. He was dressed in black and his frock coat fit him well. I could see her taste in the tailoring. His jaw was shadowed with stubble, but I didn't recognize it as a sign of hurry. He was always like that before. It suits him well. The fear and fatigue in his eyes suit him less well.

Don't think that Camille was any less striking to me. She is the most singularly alluring creature on this Earth— the way she cuts across a room, the way she lifts her chin. She had dark smudges under her eyes, just like Ari. I shouldn't have let them worry themselves into such a state. They think too hard, the both of them. Taillefer is frightening, but there are three of us and only one of him.

Since you entered my home through my bedroom window, Isabelle, you may not be familiar with the arrangement of the parlor: it is a long room wallpapered in blue, with windows that look out on the Rue du Bac, and it contains a pair of sofas and four armchairs. Should Camille and Ari have wished to sit any distance away from each other, they easily could have. They chose the same sofa, the one facing away from the window. I sat in an adjacent chair.

Ari fidgeted incessantly, sliding his hands in and out of his pockets.

With fond exasperation, Camille said, "Ari."

"What's wrong?" I asked.

"The coin," he said.

"The one you used to escape?" I asked.

He only nodded. It was Camille who explained to me how Ari had been touching it religiously and consulting it before he made any choices, even, for example, leaving his room in the earliest part of his stay with her.

"So this morning he flipped it, and it landed on its edge, and I said that wasn't conclusive proof that we shouldn't come here today," Camille continued. "Ari didn't accept that. He flipped it and flipped it the whole way over here, and the results were equal heads and tails, and finally, as we exited the coach, he flipped it and it rolled into the sewer, where we will never find it, which, as I said already, is a sign that it's finished with us and we should leave it be."

Ari curled and uncurled his fingers and wove his hands together. "I haven't been without it since—you know. I don't like it."

"You know many people simply walk out into the world with no prognostication at all?" Camille asked, which made him scowl, but she slung an arm around him and he relaxed into her touch. "You'll adjust. Let's live in the usual way, without knowing the future, and see how it goes."

After that, Camille recounted her reading and the subsequent conversation with Taillefer.

A round table stood between us. She extricated herself from Ari and dug in her pocket. Then she slid an object wrapped in chamois cloth into the center of the glossy, dark wood. Even before I unfolded the cloth, I knew it was the fire striker, the one Ari had stolen from Taillefer. Such a small and ordinary thing, that little curve of metal.

"I explained to Ari that the striker could be destroyed," Camille said. "Julien was able to destroy the emerald necklace, and I know he would do this for us. And Ari said—"

Ari swallowed, taking his time filling the silence she'd left. "I said we shouldn't destroy it until we're sure we don't need it."

It cost him a great deal to make such a suggestion. His voice was quiet and strained and his face had gone colorless. I wanted to leave my chair to give him a comforting touch, and I moved to, but Camille rendered it unnecessary. She put a hand on his knee and gave a gentle squeeze.

"We can destroy this and find another way," I offered, thinking of my pistol.

"Whatever gets it done," he said.

As the parlor faces the street and is near the front door of the house, sometimes noise from outside comes through the grand windows or the foyer. Chatter and footsteps, hoofbeats, carriage wheels, I hardly hear it anymore.

It was strange to hear someone playing a tune on a shepherd's pipe. Stranger still to realize the sound was so clear because a footman had opened the door.

Two soft thuds in the foyer, like bodies falling to the floor with no resistance.

"Shit," Camille said. Ari was already crouching by the foot of the sofa. I stood.

Taillefer came in through the double doors, his pipe dangling casually in one hand. My heart beat so loud in my ears—did he kill François and Louis, I remember thinking, François and Louis of course being my footmen, sweet youths who deserve better than to be summarily murdered by a monster like Taillefer— that I almost didn't hear what he said.

(The suspense nearly killed me, Isabelle, and while I know you cannot suffer such a fate, I don't wish to cause you distress: François and Louis are fine. The shepherd's pipe that Taillefer was playing turned out to be an artifact that induces an enchanted sleep.)

Taillefer raked his gaze over Camille and me, both standing in shock, and said, "I thought so. Where's Lazare? I'd like to chat."

Ari sprang over the back of the sofa. He vaulted across the room before I could cry out or slap my hand across my mouth. His fist hurtled into Taillefer's stomach. I've never seen him move like that—or commit any violence. Underneath the gentle and thoughtful man I know, there was rage. He was ruthless. Relentless. Taillefer was on the floor in seconds, and Ari reared back and punched him in the face.

It was bloody. It was awful. And there was something viciously satisfying in it. The pummeling didn't stop. Neither Camille nor I made any motion to intervene. In between thinking about how long it takes for a man to lose consciousness, and wondering if there had been a tooth in the mouthful of red that Taillefer had spit out, it occurred to me that he hadn't tried to put his hands in front of his face to protect himself.

He was worming his fingers into his trouser pocket.

Camille and I saw him grab something at the same time. I called out Ari's name as she darted around the sofa. Taillefer freed a small glass vial from his pocket and then twisted and kicked until he and Ari rolled across the floor in a tangle of limbs. Taillefer flailed until he could shove his arm into the air, fist clenched. I don't know what he intended—to unstopper the vial and hurl its contents at Ari's face, most likely. He never had the chance. Camille dove toward him.

Just as I'd never seen Ari do anything so remarkably athletic, decisive, and brutal, I had no idea Camille would jump into a fight like that. Ari had clearly been in many, many other fights. Camille had more courage than experience.

She wedged herself between them like an axe splitting wood. Either Ari hadn't seen that Taillefer was armed with something magical, or he simply didn't want Camille in the fight. He tried to yank her away, but she'd seized Taillefer by the wrist. His clenched fist rose above her.

Taillefer cracked the vial like an egg.

A clear, colorless liquid poured onto Camille's face.

All the windows shattered. The double door to the foyer slammed open from the force of the explosion. Camille, Ari, and Taillefer were thrown apart. I fell to my feet, all the armchairs and sofas tumbling with me as the room rocked like the deck of a storm-tossed ship.

All three of them lay unconscious among the glass shards.

The air hung heavy with the scent of roses, so thick it was sickening. I gagged. My head pounded.

Then I remembered Camille saying something about "a perfume that could make everyone like me" and lifted my skirt to cover my face, breathing in the scent of laundered silk. The pain in my head receded a little.

Camille and Ari had been too close to Taillefer when he'd broken the vial and caused the explosion. Magical artifacts were often volatile in their destruction—Taillefer himself had written that in one of his letters. Either the perfume itself or the force of the blast had knocked them out. The distance between us had been enough to save me from unconsciousness, but I was still breathing the same poisonous air. I didn't have much time.

At the hem of my petticoats was the striker, which had fallen to the floor in the chaos. I picked it up.

My ears were ringing. It felt like the sound was coming from within me, like the explosion had emanated from me, like I was living it. It propelled me forward. I knew exactly what to do.

From the age of eleven when I first grew tits and was pinched and groped and mocked by my older brother's friends, I have devised ways to protect myself, to offer just enough that I may keep some secret part of myself intact. Along with this body and this face, I developed an intimate understanding of what power is taken from me by being a woman in this world—and what power I can claw back. My late husband saw this, saw that his legal and material control over me would never be enough to crush me, so he resorted to magic.

It is a perverse kind of respect. His desire to possess me was inseparable from his fear that he never would. He died thinking he'd won, thinking he'd subdued me at last. I regret that.

I wish he could know that I am free now, and that like a wounded animal that still carries some splinter of spear in its heart, the cruelty I have experienced lives in me. I survived to wield it against a man like him, a man who has threatened, attacked, subjugated, and raped my loved ones, and who would do the same to me and to others if I allowed him to live.

I know you understand, Isabelle.

Glass crunched under my feet as I opened the double doors to the foyer, where the footmen were dazed but waking. What a relief to see them alive and unharmed. I instructed them to carry Ari and Camille's slack, unconscious bodies from the parlor to Camille's carriage and to tell her driver to take them home, to retrieve my correspondence, Octave's favorite toy (a stuffed parrot), anything of Amélie's and Marthe's and Caro's that they could find, and then to warn the rest of the staff to pack their valuables and leave.

I went back into the parlor and found a flint near the hearth.

I didn't know how long I had before Taillefer woke, so I worked quickly.

The spark was the easy part. Getting a large enough fire to fill the parlor with smoke was difficult. The broken windows saved us from the thrall of Taillefer's rose perfume, but they hindered my effort. There wasn't much wood for kindling in the hearth, not on such a mild spring day. I ripped strips of my skirt and petticoats and added them to the fire, all the while keeping one over my face. I took a painting of a naval battle from the wall and chucked it in. Cushions, footstools, the little round table, even one of the armchairs—I dragged everything into a pile and fanned the flames.

The smoke wafted through the room, escaping through the glassless windows. My fire grew. By the time Taillefer blinked and stirred, smoke had overtaken any trace of the scent of roses. It stung my eyes and made me cough.

"Delphine," he said.

I knelt by his prone body. He lifted a hand to my face and I let him. A cut on his palm bled from smashing the glass vial of perfume, but I could only smell smoke.

"You love me?" I asked.

"I do," he said. "I always have."

"And you'd do anything for me?"

"Anything," he confirmed. His eyes watered from the smoke, but he kept them open, huge and round, to gaze at me. Under the reddening bruises, there was something not quite right about his expression that had nothing to do with how many times Ari had hit him. The adoration, I think. It was too much, like a poorly done painting. Even when someone is truly in love, their face doesn't become an unchanging mask.

When I withdrew, he pushed himself into a seated position to close the distance between us. His nearness no longer made me recoil.

I pulled the pistol out of my skirt pocket. The crackling fire spilled out of the hearth, flames licking the air. I couldn't be satisfied with asking him to stay in the burning house for me. I needed to see it happen.

I could have shot him myself. I considered it. In truth, the simple violence of it appealed to me. But I didn't know what would be evident when the police came to investigate, and Octave had already lived through one of his parents being imprisoned for years.

Besides, I thought Maximilien Taillefer ought to do one good deed in his life.

"Put this in your mouth," I told him, "and pull the trigger."

He did it with no hesitation. I watched him splatter the walls and carpet with blood and brain and little bits of bone and I felt nothing. Not anger or the abatement of anger, not disgust, not relief. Even the sight of all that gore struck me as a meaningless mass of colors and shapes.

After the explosion that had knocked out the windows and the gunshot that had ended Taillefer's life, the fire didn't seem so loud. I only realized what a roar it was making, devouring the carpet and the brocade wallpaper, when I walked out of the house.

It was the middle of a beautiful spring day. That didn't seem possible. The air felt cool and clean in my throat. I crossed the street, sagged against a stone wall in my ruined dress, and cried.

It was a release. Of what, I'm not quite sure. Fear and anger. Regret, but not for what I'd done, only for the person I might have been in some other, kinder world. Perhaps I'm lying to myself, and my life could never have followed a smooth course that would have left me sweet and soft all the way through. Perhaps my temperament is such that I'd be capable of murder in even the most peaceful and ideal of worlds. I'll never know. The thought doesn't trouble me as much as it should.

Most of all, I cried for Ari.

I didn't do it for the scene it would make—if I had, I would have attempted to weep silently instead of in huge, shuddering, snotty sobs—but I don't mind that so many witnesses saw the widowed Marquise de Quennetière in frightful disarray after she was attacked and had her home set ablaze by Maximilien Taillefer. The story will be everywhere soon.

François and Louis came searching for me soon enough, and François gallantly offered me his frock coat to cover my shredded skirt. I sent Louis to tell the police and the fire brigade, and unfortunately, they did undo my efforts at arson. The parlor is wrecked, but I was hoping they'd arrive too late to save the house.

When Marthe and Amélie returned from their stroll with both children in tow, they were shocked at what had transpired in their absence. Octave was upset, but I soothed him by discussing the fire brigade and soon enough he was fascinated. All of us, including any of the rest of my staff who wished to come, went to stay at Camille's. I have more to tell you, but I have run out of this special paper, and once we arrived here, I found myself in charge of two households crammed into one house during a crisis, which is to say it has been rather a long day.


Your friend,
    Delphine

# ❧ V ❦
# MANUSCRIPT
## 1825

# THE LAI OF CAMILLE I

In days of yore gilded and fogged
with forgetting lived a brave knight
called Camille whose shield bore a quill.
Of knights she was neither tallest
nor strongest nor best in battle.
Neither the wisdom of ages
nor the grace of youth marked Camille.
Her heart, so noble and tender,
was loyal and unswervingly true.

In forests and fields, soft spring green
or brown and white with winter snow,
she rode, roaming rivers and roads,
doing kind deeds for all she met.
One day her path passed a tower,
a line of stone, black against blue,
cloudless sky, lonely and leaning,
its door locked. One little window
loomed at the top. A lovely girl
looked out and sighed in lost lament.

Camille's heart shuddered, struck with love.

"Who is that?" she asked and was told,
"That lady with the shining hair
and lush beauty is a princess
called Delphine. She is forbidden
from leaving by her cruel husband.
He wards her tower with magic."
Camille had no fear of magic
or cruel husbands, and broke the door
and the enchantment with courage.
She mounted the stairs two by two
to kneel before Delphine and say,
"My lady, I offer you my
loyalty. Come, let me free you."

Lovely Delphine said, "What is your
name, brave knight? Were you loyal to me,
I would have you bring to me my
long-lost love, who languishes in
a different form of prison.
He is a man trapped in the shape
of a wolf. A traitor tricked him
and now he must be tamed."

Camille's heart quailed at the mention
of another love. Quietly
and quickly she quelled this quiver.
"Kind lady, I am called Camille,
Knight of the Quill, and I accept
your quest. I swear to catch this wolf.
Caution and curiosity
compel me to ask how you came

to care for a creature while caged
in a castle? Tell me the tale.
How can a wolf be turned to a
man? I have traveled far but
never heard tell of a such a thing."

The Princess talked for such a time
that her words could have formed many
lais. Her werewolf was called Ari.
They met years ago in their youth.
She loved him so much that Camille
despaired deep in her secret heart,
but said nothing, for she was loyal
and longed to serve lovely Delphine.
"You must clothe the wolf," said Delphine,
"Then he will change into a man."

So Camille ventured deep into
forests and fields, far and frozen
mountains, and found the wolf forlorn
and famished. No fearsome wild beast,
but a man in fur. "Ari," she called,
and he paused to hear her voice, then
vanished. For days she approached and
for days he withdrew. Finally
she fed him and he accepted
her company. She coaxed him home
and clothed him. In time the wolf changed.
He lived as a man again. He was
gentle and handsome. Camille loved
him as much as she loved Delphine.
For his part, Ari loved Delphine
with his whole heart, and she with hers.

What place remained between them for
even the most faithful of knights?
Camille kept quiet her love and
fled once more into the forest.
Her heart, loyal and true, was broken.
Grief grabbed hold of her like madness.
She fell into an enchantment,
a long sleep between life and death.
So silent and still did she lie
that briars grew over her and
hid her from the eyes of the world.

# ARI TO CAMILLE, JUNE 8, 1825
## LEFT FOLDED ON THE BEDSIDE TABLE

Camille—

I don't think we ever established what we are to each other. Not enemies, not rivals, but we've never said friends. We're people who love Delphine. People who live together to make Delphine happy. People who share clothes. People who only use shaving razors and hair shears for their intended, peaceful purposes. People who go on midnight rides to dig up things buried in forests. People who drink ill-advised quantities of cognac in libraries. People who lie together in the dark and tell secrets. People who fuck to make Delphine happy.

That last one is a lie. I did it for myself and for you, too. But you know that.

This is all a clumsy way of telling you that I think—I know that I am in love with you. As much as I am with Delphine. Forgive me my faults of style. I would much rather tell you this to your face. My letters to Delphine aren't this messy, but the thought of you reading my writing makes me nervous. The only other time I wrote to you, I didn't know who you were.

I knew you only as a person who wrote me little notes of encouragement. So I am trying to be that for you.

Please wake up, Camille.

Delphine is beside herself and I hate to see her weep. Together we have gone through all your handkerchiefs. (In case it's not clear from the state of this paper, I have also been weeping. I don't look nearly as tragically beautiful as Delphine does, and Octave asked what was wrong with my face, so you would be doing the world a great service if you woke up and gave me reason to stop.)

Whatever you inhaled at Delphine's, the smoke or Taillefer's perfume or some combination of the two, it put you to sleep and you haven't twitched since. I woke up and you didn't. Nobody can figure out why.

I wish I'd heeded the coin and that we'd stayed in your house. Taillefer would be alive, but you'd be awake. I see now why the coin gave such variable responses that morning. I still reach into my pocket for it sometimes, though it's long gone now. You wanted me to learn to live without it, so I'm trying, but I'm still allowed to miss it, am I not?

What I miss most is you.

We asked your friend Julien and his lover Victor for help waking you and the two of them couldn't do much more than speculate and say things like "Magic is, unfortunately, neither systematic nor predictable," which I know from my own experiments, so it's embarrassing how much I wanted to hit Victor for saying it. Let's be grateful I didn't. You and Delphine would have been disappointed— and me too. People don't deserve to be punched for telling the truth. But I've been anguished, you know, having just realized that I'm in love with you and now you're not here to hear it and we don't know if you ever will be.

And if I wasn't such a brute, maybe things would have

gone differently with Taillefer. We probably should have just let Delphine execute her plan. She did it anyway, as you'll discover when you wake, cutting through our chaos and proving herself remarkably adaptable. Everything was tidied up in about a week. She saved her correspondence with Taillefer and her staff corroborated her version of events and the police haven't given her any trouble at all.

Still it's been a difficult time here. We're terrified for you. I'm out of my mind, but Delphine is worse. I had to beg her to leave your side for an hour or two a day just to care for herself. We take turns sitting with you now, and sometimes Julien comes by for a few hours. He's distressed, too. Everyone is, and we're a big crowd since Delphine brought so many of her people.

Repairs have begun on her house, and much of it suffered no damage, so a few of her staff have returned. Delphine won't hear of leaving your side. I also just learned she doesn't want to live in her house much longer, anyway. I was both shocked and charmed that she's been ridding herself of things her late husband owned. She's irritated that this spectacle has forced her to keep the house and slow the pace of her divestments for a time. When I asked her where she wanted to live, she said, "Here, assuming Camille will have us. Or at Verneuil, once she wakes. Octave loves it there and the best thing to do when two men have recently died mysterious and abrupt deaths in your home is to withdraw to the countryside."

I told her I was a little bit scared of her and that I hoped Taillefer wasn't the beginning of some larger plan to run around Paris dispensing vigilante justice, or conquer all of Europe. She said, "Ari, I can't even get our son to keep his shoes on his feet," which might have been a complaint that she lacks the time and energy for more complex schemes, or a simple comment on what was happening at the time (Octave taking his shoes off in your garden—apologies for all the holes he has dug, I didn't expect him to be so industrious with the trowel I gave him). Regardless, it is a great relief to me that she didn't confess a similar fear of me, since I beat a man bloody right in front of her—and you, too. I hate that I acted with so little intention. I don't remember anything but the overpowering fury of seeing Taillefer. My torn-up knuckles and aching ankle are all the memory I have. I told her as much, and that I felt sick to be capable of such violence, and she asked if I thought she was sick, too, and I said no.

"Perhaps not. But you're scared of me," she said.

"Maybe a better word is 'awe,'" I said.

"I'm not scared of you," she said, and wrapped an arm around my waist, and then Octave came over and dumped a trowel full of dirt on the hem of her dress and her dainty buttoned boots, and she laughed.

I went inside to relieve Julien, and later Delphine found me to say that not all violence is the same, and besides, we'd both lived through terrible things, and it was fine with her if we were terrible because of it, that she didn't care as long as we weren't terrible to each other or Octave, though she hoped we could give him the chance to grow up slightly less terrible than his parents, and I told her she was probably right, and she said "What do you mean, 'probably'?" and bent over my chair and kissed me. It would've been perfect except you were laid out in your bed next to us. Delphine's eyes welled up and she said, "I'd have everything I ever wanted if only Camille were awake."

It's good that we're everything she's ever wanted. If Delphine did harbor a secret ambition to take over the world, you and I would have to resign ourselves to sitting at the foot of her throne as decorative consorts because we'd both be powerless to stop her. I'd do anything to make her happy, and I know you would, too, because you took me in.

Luckily, what she wants isn't the world at her feet, but you, awake and alive and in her arms. I know we both hate to disappoint her, Camille, and we didn't fumble our way through these last few weeks to start now. You can find your way back to us. Open your eyes, Dupin.


Ari

Camille, my Sleeping Beauty,

Ari has persuaded me to channel my fretting into words, so I am writing even though you are right next to me. I am also narrating this letter aloud, so please forgive my long pauses while I scratch things out and rearrange them.

It's a glorious June day and I know you'd never spend it inside if you had a choice. I opened your bedroom windows just so we can taste summer unfurling in the air. Sunlight is pouring in. You look marvelous in the glow, like you're about to blink your eyes open and rise from a peaceful nap.

I, on the other hand, spilled ink on my hand and my cuff, and then rubbed at my tired, red eyes and got some on my face and probably in my hair, which isn't coiffed. Amélie is living here, and always offers her skills, but today I declined. Sometimes I want to look as bad as I feel. Perhaps I shall rend my garments. Nothing else has helped, but maybe that will do it.

I don't know why I'm telling you this. Your eyes are

closed. If you ever read this—please read this, Camille—picture me effortlessly dazzling, neither tear- nor ink-stained, but emanating a more refined sort of melancholy. Staring out a window with an unread book in my lap, not one bitten fingernail in sight.

I'm sitting in the armchair that's in your bedroom—you know the one—except I dragged it closer to you. I was going to use your bedside table to write but it's covered with the leavings of the meals I've taken in here, and the glass of water I keep trying to get you to drink, and a note Ari wrote you, and some half-drafted desperate pleas to Isabelle and Julien and Victor that I abandoned when the latter two explained to me in person that it would be unwise to try random magical artifacts from Isabelle's collection in the hope that they might cure you, and that they would not risk your death until and unless they had no alternative.

You don't seem to need to eat or drink. It's been more than a week and you're in perfect health—except that you sleep endlessly. You don't snore or twitch or roll, not ever, which I know because I've been sharing your bed at night. Ari tried to get me to rest elsewhere at first, but now he's given up and joined me here. If you do wake up one of these nights, you'll be surprised to find such a crowd. But you said you didn't want me to let go, and you must know by now, Camille, that is the one thing in this world I do best.

I kept my son safe in that accursed house no matter the cost to myself. I didn't let go of Ari when everyone—even me, some of the time—thought he was dead.

Was it wise? No. Was it reasonable? No. But I am who I am and cannot be otherwise.

I wrote to him, did you know? Letters I was half-sure

he'd never read. You'll be pleased that many of them were about you. I haven't let him read those yet; I ought to show them to you. The portrait they paint of us is too intimate to share without your permission, which I hope you'll grant some day.

Ari has asked me, very gently, what we'll do if this is it. If you never wake. I hate to contemplate it for even an instant, but I know the answer. We'll keep living. I'll keep your room comfortable. I'll still sit with you every day, but perhaps not for so many hours at a stretch. I'll let Amélie do my hair. I'll go on walks with Octave. I'll attend a salon every now and then. I'll love Ari.

I'll miss you all the time.

In great, crushing waves of sorrow at first, and then in little ripples and sprays of mist, but the grief will never go entirely. That's how it is when you love someone, and I love you a lot, Camille. I might not have your skill with metaphors, but I didn't choose the ocean by accident. We haven't known each other for as many years as I've known Ari, but my love for you is no less vast.

Still, I could do it. I could live. I could even be happy some of the time. I can do anything, Camille—I clenched my teeth and clawed my way through my marriage. I have, perhaps, an excess of determination. So I know I could do it. But it isn't what I want.

I want you. With me, with Ari, with Octave, making a funny little family, smashing snow down the collars of each others' coats in February and eating ripe tomatoes in August. I want to clink my glass against yours next time you finish a draft, and swoon theatrically in the front row of your next reading, and pretend to be very bad at shooting every kind of weapon, and kiss your face every night. I want to watch you and Ari chase Octave around the grounds at Verneuil. I want the two of you to exchange fond glances when I say outrageous things.

I'm not ready to accept any less than exactly what I want. I will keep searching. I will hound Victor and Isabelle and any passing acquaintance who knows anything about magic and I will try anything that might help. Taillefer already took so much from Ari and from me. He can't have you. He doesn't get to hurt us even in death.

Probably you would tell me to calm myself and be less concerned with vengeance, since it won't do us any good now that he's dead. If I though he could offer any kind of solution, I would plunge into Hell myself and drag it out of him. (I suspect Hell doesn't exist, and it's irrelevant anyway, as Taillefer would doubtless remain as worthless in death as he was in life.)

This is the sort of problem that's solved with—well, if I knew the rest of this sentence, I wouldn't be wasting time writing you letters. I'd wake you up and kiss you and promise to spend the rest of my life with you, if you'd have me, as violent and unreasonable as I am.


Yours,
Delphine

# PRIVATE DIARY OF ARI LAZARE, JUNE 15, 1825

It's difficult to write while Camille is in this uncanny sleep. I don't want to record all these unchanging days—not that there is time for that. When I'm not taking care of Camille or Delphine, I spend the rest of my time chasing Octave. I love it. I love him. But it's nice to sit.

I did want to record this: Delphine has been talking to Octave about me as "your Papa" for some time now, but today was the first day he called me "Papa" himself.

He didn't understand why I teared up, but he threw his arms around my neck anyway.

# THE LAI OF CAMILLE II

> In her bed of brambles she slept
> in the pink glow of sun-dappled
> roses, dreaming forgotten dreams.
> No one could find or speak to her.
> From time to time she heard voices.

"Delphine, she hasn't moved in days. It's not likely that anything will happen in the next few hours. You need to eat and sleep and spend some time with Octave. He won't stop asking me about you. You can't stay in this room indefinitely. You have to take care of yourself—Octave needs you. I need you."

"Camille needs me. What if she wakes up and I'm not here?"

"I'll stay. I'll tell her you waited.

I'll tell her you're coming back soon."

> The thicket lay hidden and heaped
> high with twining and tricky thorns,
> but the wolf's fur was thick. He twisted

> through and under the tangle to
> where the knight lay and said nothing,
> for as a wolf he had no words.

> Days passed and Camille did not wake.
> The breeze carried voices past her.

"Maman, why Cami still sleeping?"

"You remember the fire in our house, Octave? Camille got hurt that day, and now she's sleeping. Maman and Ari are keeping her safe and trying to wake her up. Let's not bounce on the bed. Be gentle. Oh—it's very sweet of you to kiss her cheek, darling, but I tried that already."

"Maman is sad?"

"Yes. I miss Camille very much. Are you sad? Come here. Sometimes it's better to be sad together."

> Sunsets and sunrises slipped through
> the shadowed forest. Camille slept.

"Victor says there's no way to tell exactly what the effect of Taillefer's perfume was, or how to reverse it, especially since Camille breathed the smoke from the fire—which is my fault. I did this to her."

"How can it be your fault when you couldn't have known, Delphine? After all, I breathed that same smoke and I woke up. And you were trying to save us—you did save us from Taillefer. Camille is still breathing. She's alive. We'll solve this."

"I can't help feeling that I failed her. That even if this isn't my fault, she never knew how much she meant to me. I didn't tell her enough."

"I didn't, either."

"Oh, Ari."

"It's late. Come here."

"What if we can't fix this? It's been weeks. What if there's nothing we can do?"

"Maybe there isn't. Would it change anything? Do you want to give up?"

"No."

> The wolf led the princess to her.
> With an ax she hacked the thicket.
> Sunlight sifted through the tall trees
> and touched the knight's wan face with
>     warmth.
> Still she did not stir from sound sleep.
> The princess kissed her silent lips.
> In the leaves next to the knight
> and across from the wolf she lay
> and said, "We love you, Camille.
> We will wait here until you wake."
> Washed wet in a flood of weeping,
> at last the knight opened her eyes.

Dear Julie,

Thank you for destroying the fire striker and thank you for your help with my household these past three weeks. Ari and Delphine tell me you were at my side nearly as much as they were, and given that both of them were in my bed when I opened my eyes, you must have been there quite a lot.

I woke to Delphine shrieking. That is my perception; hers is that my eyes opening caused her to scream with alarm and then a trembling, tearful kind of joy. Ari shouted my name and descended into sobs only an instant after she did. It was hard to breathe even before they both threw their arms around me and squeezed.

I didn't understand what was happening at all. I remembered a fight with Taillefer and a strange dream. Ari and Delphine's solicitousness, and both of them embracing me and Delphine stroking the pads of her fingers over my cheekbones and cooing my name, all of that made me say, in a tone as dry as I could manage given the environs, "I gather something befell me."

"Oh God, <u>Camille</u>," Delphine said, strangling her sob until it became a croak of laughter.

"Yes," Ari said.

The pillow was absolutely soaked with tears. I suspect that's what woke me, but Delphine and Ari aren't so certain—it wasn't the first or the only time they'd cried, they insist, not even the first or the only time they'd cried next to me, near me, on me, yes both of them at once, you begin to see how many times we've gone over these details. They credit me with waking myself. They think I simply needed time to heal from whatever harm was done to me, and that I slept until I was ready.

I don't know. I suppose we might never know the answer.

Their commotion brought the whole household—the whole of two households, since so many of Delphine's people are living here—to my door. With some help and many pillows, I sat up. Octave climbed into the bed and threw his little arms around my neck, and that, without even knowing what had happened, brought tears to my eyes.

Everyone crowded into the room for the tale. Delphine smoothly elided Taillefer's fate. The gap in her story confirmed my suspicions. (She told me the truth later, once Octave was in bed and we were alone with Ari.) Imagine my surprise when I learned that those events, which seemed like yesterday to me, were three weeks ago.

I don't feel as though I slept for such a long time. I didn't waste away without food or water, though I have been a little unsteady on my feet. Delphine and Ari won't let me walk anywhere alone, each of them leaping to slide under my arm and rest a hand on my hip whenever I go anywhere. This coddling is somewhere between endearing and tiresome, though every day the balance slides farther toward tiresome. Delphine would carry me like an infant if she had the arm strength. Ari could do it, and he considered it just before we descended the stairs yesterday, but thankfully he's responsive to a forbidding glower. Delphine would have disregarded it entirely and scooped me up, I'm sure.

I wasn't prepared for them to treat me this way.

If you'd asked me before I fell asleep, I would have said that Delphine would be sad without me, perhaps even wistful over my absence for years to come, but only on passing occasions, dwindling in frequency as time passed. She would make a home and a life with Ari and their child and know more joy than suffering. Ari would think of me even less, except perhaps as the author of a book he loved. From time to time, he might remember his fraught return to the world and the role I played as his host and the interloper in his lover's bed, stirring up no more than a touch of regret and an overwhelming relief that these things were now confined to memory.

I believed all that, Delphine's contrary claims aside. She wrote me an astonishing letter before my sleep in which she said she loved me and would always miss me if I were gone. I suppose a nobler and more gallant person would simply have taken her word for it, but I didn't. You know what passed between me and my former lovers, the source of all my skepticism. Her affection seemed ephemeral to me, but since I couldn't do without it, I thought to enjoy it while it lasted. A broken heart awaited me in some distant future, as it always does.

I did not imagine, could not imagine, that her heart could break. Not for me. She'd already demonstrated lavishly how it had broken for Ari. It made me by turns jealous, resentful, bored, and despondent—for me, for her, for him.

To see her so devastated by my condition reversed everything I thought I knew. It forced me to understand. She loved me. It was no passing amusement, nothing shallow or fleeting. It was real in a way that hurt. What could be worse for Delphine than the partial absence and lingering presence of someone she loved? To lose and not lose me was an unthinkable echo of what she'd already survived with Ari. Hope is a little splinter that she can never quite dig out.

"You would really have kept visiting me while I slept," I asked her while we were still lying in the tear-soaked bed, after the crowd had dispersed, "even if I never woke?"

"For the rest of our lives."

I glanced at Ari, seated to the other side of me, if lounging with an elbow propped against the headboard can really be described as "seated," who said, "Delphine and I waited for each other for almost three years. You thought we wouldn't wait three weeks for you?"

I had, in fact, thought exactly that. It is a stunning, dizzying pleasure to be wrong.

(It will not be a stunning, dizzying pleasure to hear from you that you knew all of this already and tried to tell me, so you can remain silent on that point, Julie.)

"Lucien and Félix wouldn't have waited for me," I said, and then had to explain to Delphine what had transpired with my former lovers. I'd already confessed it to Ari.

Afterward, she kissed my hair and let me keep speaking. "I didn't know it was three weeks. It felt like—three hundred years. Or no time. I don't know."

"You perceived the passage of time?" Ari asked as Delphine said, "You dreamed?"

A sort of delirium had taken hold of them by then, a mingling of relief and excitement and exhaustion that made them talk over each other and interrupt me at the least pause. Delphine had her head on my shoulder and the rest of her draped over me like a blanket. On such a warm day, the closeness made us both sweat, but I wouldn't have asked her to move for anything. Meanwhile, Ari slid his hand into mine as though if he interlaced our fingers with enough nonchalance, I might not notice or object. His half-shy, half-desperate attempt at sleight made me melt with tenderness.

I lifted our intertwined hands and brought them to rest on my heart.

I ought to have told them how much it meant to me that they had cared for me, that they did care for me, but I was overcome. Instead I struggled to explain what I had lived. Asleep, or enchanted, my mind invented a sort of medieval romance in which I was a knight errant. Naturally, Delphine was a princess. She smiled at that, delighted.

"I wasn't in it?" Ari asked when I didn't continue, an ebb of disappointment in his voice.

"No, you were." I squeezed his hand. "Delphine was in love with you."

"He was a rival knight," Delphine guessed.

"Is this some sort of Arthur and Guinièvre and Lancelot thing?" Ari asked.

"It's possible my mind was influenced by some of the texts I've been studying," I said. "Delphine, do you remember when we read <u>Bisclavret</u>? Ari, do you know it?"

"Which one was that?" she asked.

"Not only have I not read it, I don't even know what it is," Ari said.

"A medieval poem." Hesitant, I said, "It tells the story of a werewolf."

Ari burst out laughing and then, with mock outrage, said, "That's what you think of me?"

Delphine reached across me to flick him in the thigh. "You _are_ hairy."

"No, no," I said, "the wolf in <u>Bisclavret</u>, he's worthy and righteous, he's the hero, he's been a victim of a terrible betrayal that has left him unable to change back. And he just—he needs someone to give his clothes to him so he can be a man again."

"Hmm," Ari said, too loud and too long. "Hmm."

"My dream was sort of like that. I'll explain it better in writing." (This protest went largely ignored at the time, but I did write my version for them a few days later, and have included a copy for your amusement.) I let my head drop back on the pillows and waited until Delphine's fit of giggles subsided. When she quieted, I turned to Ari. "I promise I don't think of you as as a monster or an animal."

"I know," he said, too solemnly. "A werewolf is a man at least some of the time."

"That's not—I am _trying_ to tell you I love you," I said.

He cracked a grin, said "Do you know how long I've wanted to fluster you?" and kissed me before I could answer. (No. I had no notion.) It was a very flustering, animal sort of kiss, sudden and ferocious, subsiding quickly into playfulness. He nipped at my bottom lip and growled low in his throat.

I closed my eyes. Either the room had warmed or my cheeks had heated.

Delphine said, "This is the best thing I've ever seen."

"_You_ made her stumble over her words the first time you met," Ari told her. "I had to work for it."

"Please continue," she said, and he nuzzled my neck, causing her gales of laughter and me to grumble, "I hate you both."

"You do not," Delphine said and kissed me. As always, she was right.

Your friend,
Camille

# ARI LAZARE TO HASSAN EL BERBERI, AUGUST 2, 1825

## POSTMARKED VERNEUIL

Dear Hassan,

Years have passed since we last saw each other, and I don't know if you will remember me, or if you will wish to correspond. I did my best to find a current address for you, assuming you are still working in the King's menagerie. Delphine's sources for gossip—even if I have slipped from your memory, surely you remember Delphine —say that you are. As long as you have not returned to Alexandria to see your family or gone further into the wilderness to chase after some new discovery that will make you the world's foremost naturalist, this letter should find you.

I write with apologies for vanishing three years ago and abruptly ending our friendship. The circumstances of my disappearance are difficult to believe even for me, the one who lived them, and perhaps some day I'll tell you the whole story. For now I will simply say that I was unjustly imprisoned—no one in that place is <u>justly</u> imprisoned, no matter what crime they committed—and could not write. I returned to Paris this spring in equally unbelievable circumstances, and am now living in the countryside with Delphine, her son, and the writer Camille Dupin, at Camille's estate, which is called Verneuil.

Delphine withdrew from Parisian society under a bit of a storm cloud. If you're in the city, you might have caught wind of the rumors. She is much happier here in the rolling green hills. Octave (her son) is always chasing rabbits and stomping in puddles, and to see him howling and sprinting in circles and soaked with rain, you'd never know he was a future marquis.

Camille often invites other writers, artists, musicians, and actors to join her here for a stay, and she and Delphine have begun hosting a salon. It's an eccentric little community they've formed. People are always hauling instruments in and out of the house, or rearranging furniture to put on plays, and two or three times a week we have some kind of performance. The rest of the time, the house is simply chattering with the world's kindest, most unusual people, and all their lovers and friends and elderly uncles and little children. I like living here, and if I ever need quiet, it's easy to take Octave for a meandering walk in the woods. Camille is teaching all of us to ride, and every time I'm out in the fields with Arthur (my preferred horse), I think of you and your giraffe and the rest of the King's menagerie. How is it faring? Is that strange and beautiful animal still in good health?

If you are not gallivanting through the natural world, and if you can bear to leave the giraffe in someone else's care for a time, I invite you to join us here at Verneuil for as long as you wish. You could liven up the salon with some much needed scientific topics. The current guests, while all brilliant and excellent company, are too poetic for me. I'd rather discuss animal behavior or new paint pigments or steam locomotion. If you have any interest in assisting me with the first one, it would be my pleasure to see you again. If the salon sounds too poetic to appeal, please know I've reached out to some other old friends and am trying my best to recruit some chemists and astronomers to join us. And if you can't travel to Verneuil, perhaps you'd be interested in corresponding? It would give me great joy to resume our friendship.


Ari Lazare

Dear Isabelle, my most mysterious friend,

I do hope you're well, wherever you are. Please write when you can. Better yet, come to Verneuil.

My last letter to you was filled with alarming news, so I feel that it's my duty to offer you this one, which is so light it could float all the way to Paris by itself. Ari and Camille and I have been living at Verneuil, breathing in the honeyed summer air and watching Octave and the other children play hide-and-seek among the trees. It is wonderful here.

I thought I would miss the city, and was sad to have exiled myself, though I knew it was inevitable. But Camille saw that I was lonely, and yearning for a particular kind of society, so she has filled her house with exactly the sort of people I like to talk to, artists and thinkers and so on, and no one here is respectable, so they don't care that I am trailed by salacious gossip about sleeping with two people at once. It is, of course, all delightfully true. No one here finds it shocking. Indeed, many of them have liaisons whose complexities shift from week to week. Our arrangement has a pleasing stability to it. Sometimes we change who sleeps in the middle of the bed, because it is cozy in winter but less so right now.

Camille is so at home here. I've rarely seen her smile and laugh so often. She finished her latest novel recently, something set in the Middle Ages about separated lovers, and has promised to let us read it soon. That's not to say she never exits her study with a melancholy air, but I am adept at cheering her up.

Ari's melancholy is of a more profound sort, and I am still learning its contours. It sometimes manifests as long silences, sleepless nights, gloomy days, or fearful restlessness. These things happen less often now than they used to, and he told me that this gradual diminishment was better than what he'd dreamt of, and—how it horrifies me to write this—that he hoped I still loved him even though he suffers such episodes of spleen, and likely always will. I told him—rather tartly, I'm afraid—that I still loved him even when I thought he was bones in the ground, and that an occasional bout of melancholy would not be enough to stop me. He laughed at that, and so did Camille.

Then he said he had already experienced more happiness in our strange and wonderful little family than he'd ever thought possible, and he could hardly imagine what more might lie ahead. And I said, "What do you mean, you can't imagine it? Octave is going to grow up brilliant and compassionate and handsome, and the three of us are going to grow old and grey, and you will look very distinguished with your cane, and Camille in her spectacles, and I am going to become even more sublime and outrageous, and we will all live here happily until we die in our sleep at the age of a hundred. The people in the village will whisper scandalous stories about us long after we're gone."

Camille said, "See, Ari, this is why we need Delphine," and we laughed at that too. I will exclude what happened next from this letter; the future generations in the village can tell it however they wish.


Your friend,
    Delphine

# CAMILLE TO DELPHINE AND ARI, AUGUST 12, 1825

## LEFT ATOP A BUNDLE OF OTHER LETTERS BOUND IN STRING

My loves,

I've read all these letters, arranged them, and added a few missing scenes. Excuse the string. I am accustomed to having someone else bind my manuscripts, but didn't think it appropriate to send this to a bookbinder. Please also excuse me for leaving this packet on our bed; like everything else about you two, I judged it worth the risk. (Happily, Octave can't read yet, and I don't think today will be the day.)

Once you've read these, we should return them to their spot under the floorboards. I would do it myself, but I lack Delphine's facility with a crowbar.

Love,
   Camille

# THANK YOU FOR READING

I hope you enjoyed Delphine, Camille, and Ari's story. If you did, please consider posting a review or recommending it to friends who might like it. Word of mouth makes a huge difference for indie books like this one.

Turn the page for a sneak peek of the next book, which is the story of what Isabelle de Tourzin's been up to.

For more of my writing, you can find me online at FeliciaDavin.com.

# SNEAK PEEK

## PRIVATE DIARY OF ISABELLE DE TOURZIN, APRIL 11, 1825

### Written on encrypted paper

I have survived everyone who has ever loved me.

I have also survived Jean-Louis-Alphonse Malbosc, a man who pretended to love me and never did, but he will not survive me. I have never written that down before. What need is there for paper and ink when the vow is carved on my heart?

Granted, this paper is special. It reveals my words only to readers I permit. This magic encryption was devised by Sophie's ward Victor Beauchêne, a horrible child of twenty or thirty years of age, useful for their zeal in cataloging magical artifacts and for impersonating their dead brother, but otherwise a little blond pest. Like their aunt Sophie, they make tiresome daily attempts to befriend me. They share information with wild abandon. For the past year of our work together, I have been subjected to Victor's opinions on my home ("spooky, but I'm so concerned about the mess that I've stopped noticing") and my behavior ("it's very unsettling how little you sleep," "what if you went to the theater or for a walk in the park," "I've heard needlework can be soothing"). I have learned, against my will, their preferences regarding food, drink, clothing, literature, art, and whether their catalogue should be alphabetical, chronological, or by type. Worst of all, I have endured endless rhapsodizing about their lover, the young artist Morère, and how happy the two of them are.

I refuse to respond in kind. My preferences are of no importance and I have no happiness to speak of. They remain undeterred. Victor also explained how they like to be referred to as "they," in addition to "he," to reflect their status as something other than a man. I told them I didn't wish to be referred to by them or anyone else. They mistook it for humor. After much badgering, I relented and said if they must speak of me with Sophie or Morère, "she" is acceptable. They smiled. They have done that to me on several occasions. Unthinkable.

Enough of these annoyances. That is not why I am writing.

Victor is a gadfly, but there is a reason I tolerate them. This encrypted paper will be very useful to me. I have survived too long for memory—Victor's quest to catalogue all the artifacts in my home is often accompanied by exclamations over my stores of knowledge, but I can no longer picture my mother's face. There are things I need to remember.

Last night's events, for instance.

I was hunting Malbosc. I'd been on my feet for hours. Days, perhaps. The compass needle flicked wildly, following my discomposed thoughts as I trudged through

the darkened streets of an ostentatious Right Bank neighborhood. Finding and killing Malbosc is the sole purpose
of my interminable life, so my lack of focus was remark-
able. I know the problem was me; the compass had guided
me faultlessly on my long slog of a journey to Toulon and
back. Its magic requires nothing more than concentration.
I did not have enough.

It was likely a mistake to go in search of Malbosc as
soon as I'd returned to Paris, taking no rest after my weeks
of travel, but I had no chance of sitting still at home. Once
I'd secured the compass, its small brass case had a weight
in my pocket far beyond what it should. When I gripped it
in my palm, I swear my pulse made it vibrate. At last I had
a way to find Malbosc for certain.

In retrospect, that was a foolish hope, as hope often is.

I circled the house a time or two before determining
which one I sought. Renard Bertin's, I think, though I am
not as quick with the names and addresses of all of
Malbosc's disciples as young Victor, who spent so many
months hidden among them, and there were others in this
same neighborhood who might harboring him. Bertin, a
forty-something man of enormous wealth and the same
insatiable grasping as all the rest of them, had not, to my
knowledge, been one of Malbosc's intimates. But there
remains much I do not know.

A brief observation from the shadows was all I needed
to determine that a ground-floor window on the left side
of the front door would be the best entry. It was
unlatched.

Too easy, I thought, and had no idea how right I was.

I was armed, though only lightly. I did not intend to
engage Malbosc unless I was sure of my kill. He should
have died months ago when Victor cut his head off, but

through the intervention of some unknown person or artifact (likely both), his head had disappeared from the room by the time I arrived to burn his body. Ever since, I have fruitlessly observed everyone I knew to be acquainted with him. Has his head become a gruesome relic, or has he contrived some other embodiment? His cunning makes me suspect the latter. I cannot stop until I know for sure. What condition Malbosc is in, and how I might transmute it into death, remain mysteries.

First I have to find him.

If I could confirm that he was in Bertin's house, I could study its plan, watch his movements, and perfect my approach. Before his failed decapitation, Malbosc was in and out of Paris, hiding in the spare bedrooms—or sometimes the beds—of his most devoted followers, people who believe he'll deliver riches and magic and immortality.

Malbosc has clung to life for an extra century, but he possesses no immortality. Only a few secret caches of my blood, taken by force. Victor and I have discovered and retrieved all the ones we knew of. It gave me no peace.

The stone was rough under my fingers, the windowpane cool. The hinges swung silently. I dropped into a crouch inside what I suspect was a parlor. The room was dark and heavy drapes blocked most of my view. I pulled one over myself, crept to the side, and rose.

Someone slammed me against the wall.

The drape was between us, but I knew it could not be Malbosc. My assailant was too large in all dimensions, and Malbosc would never stoop to using his body if he could use a weapon instead.

I brought my knee up as hard as I could. My body is a perfectly serviceable weapon.

My assailant grunted. Hurt, but not debilitated. I'd

missed the point of greatest pain. Their forearm remained pinned across my collarbones, not quite pressing on my airway. Their whole weight pressed into me. We were so close that the heat of their body through the drape contrasted with the chill of the wall at my back.

My pulse ought to have been racing, but instead it was my mind. My knee to the groin had accomplished nothing. My assailant must be accustomed to violence. They'd taken me by surprise, moving noiselessly and effortlessly in the dark. They were likely the reason the window had been unlatched—not a member of the household, but an intruder.

I can hear Victor's voice in my head saying "a _fellow_ intruder"—what a curse, to hear them even when they are not present—but I feel no fellowship with anyone.

If my assailant intended to steal cursed artifacts from whichever of Malbosc's followers lived here, they were greedy, insatiably cruel, or both. If they'd come to find Malbosc, nothing good could result. Either way, we'd have to fight.

They ripped the drape away. It happened in the space of a second with no time for me to escape. They pushed me into the wall again, still not covering my mouth or cutting off my air, but trapping my arms. Without the curtain between us, my suspicion of their height was confirmed. My face was level with the top of their chest, or it would have been if their arm wasn't between us. When I inhaled, it was the mingled scents of sweat and some caustic laundry soap.

In the slant of light from the window, they squinted at me. I was in trousers with my hair braided and pinned up under a battered hat. It was how I'd dressed to ride into the city earlier in the day. I was still begrimed from my travels. Before breaking in, I'd tied a kerchief over my face.

They might as well have covered their face for all I could see of it.

They said, "Who are you and what are you doing here?"

Their voice was a low rumble. Based on that and the hard, flat plane of their chest, they might have been a man, but such things aren't always evident. I do hate to be wrong.

I hate to answer questions, too. Their forearm still barred my collarbones, and their other hand was on my shoulder. I brought my hands together, palms flat against each other, and speared them toward my assailant's chin. They jerked to avoid my sudden movement, allowing me to elbow them in the face instead. I wrapped my arms around theirs, twisted our position, and rammed them into the wall. They gasped.

I thought I'd won then. I should have climbed out the window and come back another night. The fight had roused something in me. My fatigue inverted into vigor.

I pulled a knife from my boot and brought it to their throat. "You first. Who are you and what are you doing here?"

In this position, with the advantage of the window, I could see the scruff of a beard on their face. The light was insufficient to determine whether it was brown or black. They were dressed in dark clothes, a shapeless coat and trousers.

"You're armed," said the stranger. The point of my knife might as well have been the tip of a feather for all they noticed it. "Maybe you have another little knife somewhere on you, but I'd guess not much else, so I don't think you came to do violence. No bag, so you can't be planning to steal more than what will fit in your pockets."

I had three other knives on my person, and I don't wear my sword when I plan to climb through a window. "'Little' doesn't preclude 'lethal.'"

They huffed through their nose. It must have been frustration; it couldn't possibly have been amusement. "You came here same as I did. You want a look around. I'd be happy to let you."

"Let me?" I dragged the point lightly over their skin.

"You're a criminal, I'm a criminal, no need for trouble unless we're after the same thing."

"We're not."

There is no one on Earth who needs to kill Malbosc as badly as I do, not even Victor, who nearly succeeded. I let Victor and their lover try, but I refuse to share my project with any strange interloper who comes along. I will find and end Malbosc alone.

"I don't think so either," they said. "Would be funny, though."

The alleged humor eluded me.

"Then you'll let me go? If Malbosc is here, I'd like a word with him," they said.

"You're... working with him?" The thought that I'd been touching someone who would willingly ally themself with Malbosc made me recoil.

An instant's error, but the instant sufficed.

They seized my wrist and wrenched the blade away from their neck. My reactions lagged with fatigue. Before I knew it, my knife was in their hand. I jumped back from a slash. Reaching for the knife in my other boot cost me precious seconds. Once it was in my grip, I lunged. They dodged. They were as agile as they were silent.

In the fight, I didn't have time for begrudging admiration, but now that I'm recording it and forced to reckon with my own defeat, I must acknowledge it. They bested me. I was exhausted and unprepared. Anyone else would be dead.

I don't think they meant their slash to cut my abdomen quite so deeply. My footing slipped and I fell toward the knife. There was the usual blaze of pain that accompanies a stab to the gut. I crumpled to my knees and then to my face. I wish I were not so well acquainted with the gore and humiliation of stabbings, but I prefer them to poisonings.

Pain always narrows my focus regrettably, but I do remember a detail from this portion of the night. The stranger muttered "fuck" after my collapse, and then several more times, quietly but with increasing panic, as they opened the window and slid over the ledge.

What they did after that, I don't know. I'll have to return to Bertin's house to determine if Malbosc is or was there, but all I could manage last night was to extract myself, bundle my coat over my abdomen to stanch the flow of blood, and drag myself home.

I lay down on the foyer carpet. It's ruined.

Victor found me this morning. They dropped to their knees. Their bag hit the floor and exploded into a flutter of loose papers. "Jesus fucking Christ, Isabelle."

They sounded distraught. They shouldn't have. I am, as always, unharmed.

Victor checked me for wounds, remembered that there wouldn't be any despite all the blood, and then went in search of a glass of water. I determined that prone on the carpet was an acceptable position and remained there.

Victor called me Isabelle. I can't remember when they

started using my first name. I shouldn't have let them. It breeds familiarity. Working together was unavoidable, but I've been lax. They should find me both disgusting and terrifying. That arrangement is safest for everyone.

It's hard to be afraid of the half-conscious, blood-soaked woman you're pulling into your lap and forcing to drink water. Of course I didn't plan to arrive home in such a condition, or be witnessed, but I will have to take more care in the future—and not encounter that stranger again.


## PRIVATE DIARY OF C. F., APRIL 11, 1825

### Written in an invented shorthand

Louise grabbed a fringed silk pillow from her enormous bed and chucked it at my head when I went to see her tonight. She meant to be playful, but I snatched it from the air and threw it back at her too hard. She still caught it —I didn't raise her to miss—but she was seated at her vanity and her elbow knocked over a vase of tulips and a bottle of perfume. Nothing broke, thank fuck. I would have bought her two new ones as replacements and still never heard the end of it.

"Oh, I see," she said. She righted the vase and the perfume and blotted the spilled water with a kerchief. "You only come see me when you've had a bad night. Is that how it is now?"

"I came to see you..." I tried to count the days, but my blood was still pounding from the fight—the kill. It didn't usually affect me so much, but I didn't usually do it by accident. "Last week."

"Two weeks ago, you ne'er-do-well," she said. She clasped her peignoir closed with a little brass filigree clip and gestured at her round, absurdly luxurious bed. "People pay handsomely to arrive there and I let you sit on it for free, yet here you are, looming in your greatcoat and glowering at me. I have an appointment in an hour, so you'd better get to your point quickly. Sit down. Take your hat off. What I have I done to merit such a visit, since you never come see me anymore?"

I shouldn't have gone tonight, but the thought of tossing and turning in my boarding house room until dawn made me want to tear my hair out. I was angry at the stranger and angry at myself. That fight had annihilated my chance to search Bertin's house. Robbery takes careful preparation. There's not much else to do in the small hours now that I've given up sex. Louise was a better choice than drinking. I don't have to be careful around her. And my visit was, as she never fails to remind me, overdue.

I shouldn't piss her off. She's the only person in the world I give a damn about.

"You know I hate to come here like this," I said.

"What, like a cop?" she asked. "You look far too disreputable for anyone to recognize you, and if you think you're the only cop who frequents Florine's, then you don't know nearly as much as you pretend to."

"You <u>know</u> what I meant," I said. I tossed my hat and greatcoat on the floor and sat on the edge of her bed. I put my elbows on my spread knees. I managed not to put my face in my hands, but only just.

Louise said, "It's been four years of this, Cheat. Are you going to be angry about it forever?"

"Yes," I said.

"You always liked it before," she said. "Why don't you like it now? And even if you don't like it, it's your life.

You're alive to live it. Half of what you want is better than nothing."

I couldn't explain it to her so I didn't try.

"If posing as a cop makes you miserable, quit," she said, though that wasn't the problem and she knew it. "Go back to your roots."

"I've lost my talent for crime."

"Ha," she said. "Can a fish lose her talent for swimming?"

I didn't tell her about the house I'd broken into, or the fight I'd won, or the bloody scene I'd fled. I just slumped backward onto her bed and stared up at her sky-painted ceiling. When the gilt-framed mirror hung over her bed showed me my stubbled, scowling face, I turned my head to look instead at Louise, twenty-four years old and resplendently fat, happy, and beautiful in her printed silk robe with chestnut curls cascading down her back. That Louise survived our childhood in the orphanage is the only good thing I've ever done in my life, and I like to see her thriving.

"Ah, Cheat," she said on a sigh.

"Nobody calls me that but you."

"Cheat, darling, _everybody_ calls you that. Cheats Death, master of disguise, legend of the underworld, undetectable thief. The cops couldn't catch you or kill you. Nobody's seen you in four years and people still talk about you. Besides, everybody calls me Butterball and that's not _my_ name."

"Do you like it?" I wasn't sure how I'd get all of Paris to stop saying it, but that didn't matter. If Louise didn't like it, I would make it go away.

"I love it," she said. "Fame requires a memorable nickname. You taught me that. We were born starving and now

I've made these"—she pushed her breasts together—"entirely out of pastry, which I can afford to eat whenever I want. What could be better than that?"

"Fame for you," I corrected. "Infamy for me."

Louise swept a fan-shaped brush through a pot of powder, then tapped the handle, clouding the air with a shimmer of excess. She flicked the brush expertly, letting the bristles kiss her pale cheeks. "You and your words."

A memory intruded from earlier in the night: the stranger saying "'little' doesn't preclude 'lethal'" in that low, serious voice. Enunciation like the tip of their knife against my throat.

Not quite their last words, but close enough.

My head swam. The sweet, perfumed air of Louise's room turned sickly.

It had been a long time since I'd killed anybody, and I didn't like to kill a thief if I didn't have to. It hadn't even really been self-defense. The stranger had moved in a way I hadn't expected, and the blade had gone deep.

I wondered who they were, what their corpse would look like when the morning light came through the drapes. If they were a man or a woman or something else.

My money was on "woman," though they'd been dressed in trousers. Then again, people thought I was a man and half the time they were wrong.

I didn't want to think about that. To Louise, I said, "We could work on your letters while I'm here."

"You're having a bad night so you want to ruin mine?" she asked. She was pulling one eyelid closed to draw a line of black along her lashes. "I told you I have an appointment. And reading makes me feel worthless. I don't understand how it's so easy for you. I can never keep all those little marks straight. One of my clients tried to help me with my letters last year, you know."

"Oh?" I said. I propped myself up on my elbows.

"Stop that," she said, lining her other lashes. "You always want me to snitch. I won't do it."

"Not on the ones you like, anyway," I said. Florine was pretty good about kicking out men who misbehaved, but for Louise, I was always ready to step in.

"I did like that one," she said. "As peculiar as he was, I liked him a lot. He stopped coming. He sent me flowers and a very flattering sum about a month ago and that was goodbye forever, I suppose. I heard he sold his house and gave away his fortune and retired to the countryside. Can't imagine. Not even if my whole family died, which is what happened to him. Of course, you're my whole family, and I don't have a house to sell. I've never been to the country-side. Is it nice?"

"Louise," I said, sitting up fully. A rich man giving away a fortune was a rare and notable thing. "Are you talking about Horace Faucheux?"

"Oh, here we go," she said. "I shouldn't have told you that."

Louise wouldn't talk to me if she thought I wanted information about Horace Faucheux as a collector of magical artifacts, as an associate of the man I was looking for, even though Faucheux's connection to Malbosc was all I could think about. My approach had to be more noncha-lant. So I said, "I'm surprised you liked him. Faucheux had a reputation as a cruel and thoughtless man—that is to say, before his change of heart and move to the countryside. You know if you ever have a concern, even the slightest worry..."

"I didn't. He wasn't anything like his reputation."

And wasn't that interesting? I prompted, "He sent you farewell flowers and tried to teach you to read."

"Get over here and do my hair."

I washed my hands with the ewer of water she had at her washbasin before I touched the silk of her brown hair or any of her delicate hairpins. Already set in pristine ringlets by nature and devoted care, her curls needed nothing. I gathered a mass of them to twist into a bun at the crown of her head. Each of her pins was tipped with a little paste gem, worth no more than its sparkle. I slid them in without jabbing her scalp, more gentle than I would have been with myself. Here and there, I let one tendril escape to loll against her neck.

I worked in pleasant, silent concentration for a time— I've always liked using my hands, long-fingered and dextrous in all my forms, good for arranging hair or picking locks—until I judged it safe to say, "You were telling me about Horace Faucheux."

"And you care too much about him," she said with finality. "It must have something to do with your obsession. I don't want to tell you any more and I don't know anything, anyway. What you need is to go home and rest and maybe go for a walk in the sunshine tomorrow. Stop working yourself to the bone chasing a ghost."

"Louise," I said, not quite a plea.

"What you need is to fuck somebody new," she opined. "You need to find somebody to fall in love with so you can forget all this."

I grunted in response. There was no chance of that. But if I argued, she'd really get going. I finished her hair and retreated to the bed.

She continued, "And before you say anything about how I have a lot of opinions for somebody who doesn't fall in love, we're not the same. I'm not made for love, but you are. That man broke your heart."

"My heart?" I said incredulously. "Louise, he ruined my life."

"No, you did that," she said. She's brutal when she wants to be. "Plenty of people suffer a heartbreak and pick themselves back up. You didn't. You can't stand that you're Cheats Death, legendary thief, and he stole from you. Who are you if some halfway handsome stranger can sweet talk his way into your bed and steal your most precious possession? It's like he stole your whole self."

Malbosc had been more than halfway handsome, and I don't care much for sweetness, but she'd grasped the betrayal and the loss. My heart wasn't broken. It was the theft that hurt. "Now you understand."

"I don't, really. Why have you been living like this for years?"

"You know what he stole from me."

"You made yourself. Just do it again." Louise pulled an enameled metal comb out of the top drawer of her vanity and tossed it at me.

I caught it out of the air. I ran the pad of my index finger along the edge. "The teeth on this are too fine. They'll break your curls."

"Do you give your cop friends hair advice?"

There was a note of genuine curiosity in her voice. I rolled my eyes. "I don't have friends."

"That's not a good thing, Cheat. And I see you trying to change the subject. I'm serious. Stop living like this. Make a new comb—or whatever. Fuck a new man—or whoever."

"You think I haven't tried?"

"The combs, sure. I saw you eyeing mine every time

you came over here. I bet every surface in your little rat-infested boarding house cell was littered with combs. I bet you spent every spare centime on new ones. I bet you fell asleep with your sweaty hands clenched around a different comb every night and woke up with teeth marks in your palms."

The only thing worse than having a sister—somebody who knows me well enough to be fucking mean about it—is not having a sister. I raised Louise to observe people and go for the throat in a fight, but Jesus.

She was also right. I couldn't let her know that, though.

"I can't just make another one," I said. "Magic isn't bound by rules. Doing it once doesn't mean you can do it again. Maybe you can, maybe you can't. What I did to that comb, how I made it, I'll never know exactly. It was just the right moment."

Every other moment had been the wrong one. I tried enough times to know. I might get lucky if I spent the rest of my life working on it, but it's a surer bet to steal back the one I already made. It's mine by rights.

And if I have to kill Malbosc to get my life back, that's fine by me.

# ACKNOWLEDGMENTS

Dear Readers Who Made It This Far,

I am so grateful to you for reading *The Mischievous Letters of the Marquise de Q,* or even just for skipping right to the acknowledgments, if that's what you did. Either way, thank you.

Some of this text appears in the acknowledgments of *The Scandalous Letters of V and J*, but it also applies to this book. I am reprising it here with apologies to those who have already read it. This series owes a lot to the years I devoted to my doctorate in French literature, and what follows is an incomplete list of influences and thanks.

To Honoré de Balzac, I owe many, many character and place names in shuffled variations. (This includes my pen name, which is a variation on a pen name Balzac once used himself, borrowed from his friend journalist Félix Davin.) He's got a Delphine of his own, a Camille, a Taillefer, a Verneuil... the list is long.

More than that, this whole project started as something I was calling "Balzac, but horny and queer and magic," which I had to amend to "Balzac, but with explicit sex and a happy ending," because original-flavor Balzac is, in fact, already horny and queer and magic. You can hardly turn a page in Balzac's sprawling, interconnected world of novels and short stories, *La Comédie humaine* (The Human Comedy), without coming across a young man who is beautiful because of his feminine hips or his smooth young girl's face, or a woman with masculine strength and dark hair on her upper lip. I love *La Comédie humaine*, but it's steeped in nineteenth-century prejudice and doesn't always treat my favorite characters right, so I took a few elements and did whatever I wanted. My result bears little resemblance to Balzac's work, but he still belongs first in my ingredients list.

To George Sand, I owe both gratitude and an apology. In my defense, Balzac wrote real-person fiction about George Sand while she was alive and they were friends—she inspired his character Camille Maupin. So mine is the copy of the copy, a shadow on the cave wall, and not meant to resemble the historical George Sand. She *was* a cool, suit-wearing nineteenth-century literary superstar, though.

This book in particular contains an homage to two of the most famous French novels of the nineteenth century —*Les Misérables* and *Le Comte de Monte Cristo*—and as such is another (lesser!) variation on an unjustly imprisoned man escaping and returning to what's left of his life.

And thank you to the real historical Hassan el Berberi, whose portrait hangs in the Louvre and who really did transport and care for a giraffe in the King's Menagerie in 1820s Paris, for lending his name to a minor fictional character here.

Moving from the nineteenth century to the twenty-first, I owe a huge debt to my fellow author Skye Kilaen, whose insightful beta reading improved this novel immeasurably. Thank you also to my fellow author Chace Verity, who provided a valuable tutorial on designing a print cover.

Thank you to my mom, image librarian and art historian, who helped me figure out how to license a high-resolution digital image for the cover. It's a detail from *Portrait of Marie Antoinette* (1785) by the workshop of Élisabeth Vigée Le Brun.

Thank you to my beloved, without whom nothing is possible.

And thank you to every single reader who read *The Scandalous Letters of V and J*, whether in book form or in daily email form—your posts and replies and general enthusiasm were such a gift. In return, I hope I can give you more books to love.

Please accept, dear Readers, my most respectful sentiments,

Felicia Davin

# ABOUT THE AUTHOR

Felicia Davin (she/they) is the author of the queer fantasy trilogy *The Gardener's Hand* and the sci-fi romance *Nowhere* series. Her novel *The Scandalous Letters of V and J* was described as "a string of natural pearls, each a luminous gem on its own but even more exquisite in sequence" by *The New York Times*.

She lives in Massachusetts with her family. When not writing and reading fiction, she teaches and translates French. She loves linguistics, singing, and baking. She is bisexual, but not ambidextrous.

She writes a biweekly email newsletter about words and books called *Word Suitcase*, which is available at feliciadavin.com.

# ALSO BY FELICIA DAVIN

## FRENCH LETTERS

*The Scandalous Letters of V and J*

## THE GARDENER'S HAND

*Thornfruit*

*Nightvine*

*Shadebloom*

## THE NOWHERE

*Edge of Nowhere*

*Out of Nowhere*

*Nowhere Else*

## CO-AUTHORED AS L.K. FLEET

Errant, Volume One

Errant, Volume Two

Errant, Volume Three

Errant: The Compendium